The Boy who Climbed Mountains with Me

Dani K. West

Contents

Plalylist

Songs are an important part of this book. If you would like to listen to songs mentioned in this book and others that fit it, check out the spotify playlist here: https://open.spotify.com/playlist/6Hxfl0DIM mDXApmXeatwzo?si=e054b8dc38834c85

Chapter One: A Hundred Mountains

The black leather, chaotic hair, wild eyes, and revving motorcycle belonged about anywhere else but the church parking lot. But Conor Henderson had my heart, or at least my belly flops. His younger brother, Ezra, stood beside me with a tight mouth as he stared at his brother.

Conor had his helmet tucked under his arm. He shook his dark hair free and ran his fingers through it for extra effect. "You're the preacher's daughter, right?" He nodded toward the two-story brick building behind us.

Tiny bugs zipped around in my stomach. Oh, my word. Conor was talking to me. I nodded slowly.

Ezra had stopped staring at his brother and turned his attention to me. He had a strange look on his face that I shrugged off.

Conor stepped closer. "Have you ever been on a motorcycle before?"

I shook my head and widened my eyes at his proximity. I could smell his aftershave, which was intense, and if I stretched the description, lovely. "N-no, I never have."

"Want to ride one?"

"Me?" I glanced around and caught for a brief second Ezra's scowl.

Conor threw in a lopsided grin that made me ponder our future marriage. "Would you like to ride my motorcycle now?"

"Yeah." I looked up at the church steps, thinking my parents would be occupied with ministry for a little longer. They'd never know. Most likely, they wouldn't. If they did, it would be trouble, but Conor's mischievous eyes were too blue and gorgeous to resist. He threw his thumb behind him. "Why don't we go for a ride?"

"Sure," I squeaked.

He instructed me how to hang on and what to do while we were in motion. I climbed on and clung to his jacket. I leaned against him, closing my eyes to breathe in the mix of leather and woodsy cologne. We could have traveled across the country, and I wouldn't have minded. We went around the block, and I floated as he dropped me in the parking lot and drove off into the night.

I sighed and watched the dust kick up behind the now-distant motorcycle. "Your brother is awesome, Ezra. Maybe we could hang out before he goes back."

His lips pressed as he met my eyes. The way he always thought through his words. "He's nineteen, Mila, and in the army."

I smiled and thought about how nice it would be to hold on to Conor's leather jacket again. "I know! It's exciting."

"You're sixteen."

"Yeah, and so are you."

"So, I'm not wanting to date a nineteen-year-old."

My eyes widened for a second, and I shook my head. "That's not... I don't... No, Ezra, come on."

"You were practically drooling."

I gaped. "I don't drool."

"You came pretty close. Look, my brother is... He's not someone you should want to hang out with, and he'll be gone in a week, anyway."

"We could have a great week together."

His shoulders dropped. "You could always have a great week with me."

"We do things every week. We'll continue doing things after your brother returns to the base he's on. Do you think he'd give me his email address? Maybe you could ask him?"

"No."

"Come on, Ez! Please."

"No!"

The church doors opened, and people rushed outside. I put on the smile my parents would want me to have and shook hands with everyone who asked me questions. It exhausted me, but show was everything. How I appeared in front of all these people was one of the most important things.

My dad walked up with his black suit and blue dress tie on. You wore your best to church, three times on Sunday and once on Wednesday night. He stood taller than most people around him and had a receding hairline. His blue eyes and what was left of his dark hair matched mine. A lanky man with a mustache stood next to him.

My dad pointed at me. "This is my daughter. She's around the same age as a few of your girls. Mila, this is Mr. Thompson. The Thompsons are moving here from Durango along with their thirteen children, and

Mr. Thompson will be our new youth pastor. We'll get to finally start a youth group."

I smiled warmly the way I'd been taught. "It's nice to meet you. A youth group would be great."

The man smiled and shook my hand when I extended it. "We'll have to have you guys over when we get settled, and our girls can meet."

"That would be great. I look forward to it," I said.

My father and the man started chatting, and I slipped away.

Amber ran up and hugged me. "Hey, girlie! Can you give Ezra and me a ride home? Our parents want to stay late and discuss the new Bible study."

"Yeah, that's fine. Let me just ask my mom."

"You can stay the night if you want. That's the nice thing about summer."

"Okay, yeah, I'll have to run home and feed my children first."

She laughed. "Sure thing."

I found my mom talking to some other women, and she okayed the sleepover. Alamosa, Colorado wasn't a big town. It took maybe fifteen minutes to drive across it. We lived on the outskirts in a double-wide trailer. Ezra and Amber helped me feed all my ducks, chickens, and geese.

Ezra brought the last water dish over and set it down in the chicken coop. "Tell me their names again."

"The ducks are Tobias, Tillie, Tanner, Thomas, Terrance, Tessa, and Theresa." I pointed at each bird as I rambled off their names. "The chickens are Cole, Carissa, Camy, Connie, Cate, and Cara. The Geese are Alfred and Julia."

His face scrunched as he turned it sideways. "Why don't the geese get matching names?"

I shrugged. "They looked like an Alfred and Julia."

"Fair."

I checked on my dog, KiKi, and then we set off to Ezra and Amber's house. They lived out of town on the opposite end of my house. We lived in the San Luis Valley, and it cut us off from all major cities. Mountains towered on three sides, and mesas rose on the last one.

Ezra reached over from his spot in the back seat. "Turn the song up! I love this one."

"Crazy for This Girl" by Evan and Jaron poured from the speaker.

Amber turned it down. "We need to be careful, you guys! This is very close to Devil music."

I turned up the dial and grinned at her. "We'll ask forgiveness later."

Ezra and I belted out the song, and the one after, followed by the one after that. Our lyrics rumbled as we rolled down the dirt road. Ezra and I brought our heads together as we yelled, "Kryptonite!" into the car. We pulled in front of their trailer. Most people in the country lived in these trailers that were surrounded by many outbuildings where they kept animals.

Amber took my hand and then Ezra's. "We should pray, guys. That God will help us make good choices."

I took Ezra's hand to complete our prayer circle. Amber's hand was icy against mine, while Ezra's was large and warm. Amber started praying a prayer I knew would take a while. About a minute into her prayer, I opened my eyes a slit to find Ezra staring at me.

I held back a laugh as I opened mine wider when he stuck out his tongue. We proceeded to see who could make the most ridiculous face. Amber said Amen, and we straightened our faces and clenched our eyes shut.

We all went inside and popped in the DVDs we'd picked up at the video store. By the end of the movie, tears were rolling down my cheeks.

Amber, who sat between Ezra and me, shook her head and handed us both tissues. "I'll get us more popcorn while you two process things."

Ezra turned to me with tears streaming down his face. "Did you know she was sick?"

"I had no idea." I sniffled.

"That was so beautiful and sad."

"It was. Look at how much he loved her."

"He stuck with her through all of it." He blew his nose.

"If only we could all be so lucky."

He threw his hand out. "I know, right? You find that perfect one for you, and they stay with you forever."

We both stared off, pondering it.

Amber returned and plopped between us. "God will bring the right person for all of us. We pray, and it will happen."

"Yeah." I nodded

Ezra did the same. "We know. That's what we'll do. Pray for love like that."

We started another movie, and Amber stretched and yawned. "I'm too tired for the last one. Are you two going to stay up and watch it?"

"Yeah," Ezra and I said at the same time.

We waited ten minutes after she left, and Ezra went to the back of their trailer, only to return about a minute later. "She's out."

"Roof?"

"Roof."

We hurried out into the breezy June night. The best thing about Colorado was that the evening cooled the air, even on the hottest summer day. Most people didn't own air conditioning of any kind in the valley. We went out to the third outbuilding. It was an unpainted brown with a flat roof, and we used a ladder to climb on top. We tucked our legs under us and stared at Mount Blanca, like every time we did this. It was the highest and prettiest mountain in the area, and it contained one of our favorite spots.

He nudged me with his elbow. "What are you thinking about?"

"How everyone stays stuck in this valley. You never get out once you decide to move here."

He nodded toward the enormous blue mountain where snow covered the top. "Who wants to leave this view?"

"Someone who wants to see a hundred mountains."

"Are there a hundred mountains in the world?"

I laid back, rolling my hoodie under my head. "There has to be. At least the stars are nice. When I go to Denver to visit my grandparents, we can't see them."

He laid back next to me, using his hands to prop up his head. "You say that every time we do this."

"It's worth repeating." I glanced over at him. "Why do you never bring a hoodie for your head?" I scooted closer so he could have half of mine. It made mine too flat, and I used my hands to support it.

He pulled out his disc player and popped in a mix CD that he must have burned on his computer. He gave me one headphone, and we listened to the very close to Devil music again while we stared at the stars.

He wrapped up the headphone cord around the disc player and sat up. "Tell me why you want to leave the valley again?"

I sat next to him, and our shoulders brushed as I got comfortable. "To see a hundred other mountains."

"Maybe we'll do that together someday."

"Maybe." I studied the shingles on the roof.

"What is it?"

"What's what?"

"That sadness or doubt in your voice."

I stared at the big mountain, thinking about everything beyond it. "I'm not sure I'll ever get to travel. If I leave here, it'll be to go to Bible college. There's no other choice I'm allowed to make. It's either marriage at eighteen or Bible college."

"You should tell your stories. The ones you tell me."

"No one would want to hear them."

"Write them down so they can read them."

I snickered, and my grin matched the level of his. "No one would ever read them either."

"I would. I'd love to know all the things going on in your head."

"You don't like horror."

"Neither do you, so I think I'm safe."

I tucked my knees to my chin, wrapping my arms around them. "Someday, maybe we will see a hundred mountains together."

"I'd leave the valley for that."

"Who wouldn't want to travel all over?"

"It wouldn't be the travel that would get me out of here," he said.

I furrowed my brow and met his deep hazel eyes. "What would it be, then?"

His lips parted a slight bit, and then he pressed them. "Something much better than that."

My brows knitted further, and I returned my gaze to the sky.

Chapter Two: Hidden Things

♥

I held up the paper like gold that could shatter and dissolve. "What am I going to say to him, Riley?" I'd victoriously achieved Conor's email address.

"Let's write it down in a notebook, and then you can type it up when you get back to your computer."

"If he writes me back, it'll be this all over again. It's too much pressure!"

Riley rolled her eyes and pulled out a notebook. She tucked her extremely short blonde hair behind her ears. She had a pixie cut with an edge. "What would you like to say to him?" Her greenish - yellow eyes, which were the most unusual shade I'd ever seen, stared at me intently, waiting for an answer.

"What's it like being in the army?"

"Okay and?"

"Do you ever think you'll make it back to Alamosa? If so, we could go to Pizza Den."

"Pizza Den? Why wouldn't you guys go to Trujillo's?" She tapped the pen to her teeth. "You should say Trujillo's. He has to have lots of money because he's in the army."

"Trujillo's is expensive. The most expensive in town. I've never been there. There's no way I should expect him to pay $15 for me. That's a lot."

Riley shook her head. "You only think that because you work at KFC, and that's three hours' pay for you."

"You make the same at Subway."

"Yeah, that's why I'd let a grown man take me to Trujillo's. If Lonzo asked me out and asked me where I wanted to go, I'd have no problem picking there."

A sharp pain shot through my stomach at the mention of Lonzo. "I really think you should forget about him. He's twenty-five."

"Yeah, and? He likes me and asked me to hang out at his house the other day."

"He lives on his own, and that could put you in a vulnerable position."

She snorted and let out her unusual laugh, sounding like the girl Jody from the movie Gold Diggers. That's what we always talked about. She was Jody, and I was Beth, and we would be best friends forever like they were.

When her laughter died, she shook her head. "Who says vulnerable position, Mila?"

That's right. That was dumb to say. I was dumb. That's why I didn't usually say things like that to her.

She held up the piece of paper. "Besides, you're wanting to email a nineteen-year-old."

"That's only three years between us, and I'm not going to his house."

"You go over to his house all the time."

"He's not there, and he's grown up, which means it's not really his house anymore. I go to see Amber."

"And Ezra."

"And Ezra."

She smirked. "More so Ezra."

"Yeah, and? We get each other. All I'm saying is to be careful. He's almost ten years older than you."

"He's too hot, though, with his spiky hair. He looks like Keanu Reeves."

Riley loved Keanu Reeves. She'd made me sit through every movie he'd ever been in, and we would go to the video store and try to find at least one movie with him in it every Friday night. We'd pile junk food around us on her bed and binge.

"He doesn't look that much like Keanu Reeves. Their hair is the same hair is about it."

She hopped off her bed and pulled the box out from under her bed, handing me a picture of Lonzo. "How does that not look like Keanu Reeves?"

I stared at the picture, wanting to tell her Lonzo looked nothing like the actor, but I just nodded. "I can kind of see it. Don't let the resemblance lure you to his house to do things that make you uncomfortable."

"Lure? I swear you're a walking thesaurus with all the books you read."

"Books help me escape."

"Escape what?"

"Life. Pressures. Not being who I'm supposed to be." I grabbed one of her pillows and leaned back, looking out her window to see the cows grazing in the large open field.

"What does that even mean?"

"How can I be what my parents want me to be? I don't want to go to Bible college. My mother gave me a list of appropriate schools to pick from. I don't want to go."

She gawked at me like nonsense had come out of my mouth. "College is two years away. I don't know how you deal with it, honestly."

"I'm scared that I'll never do anything or go anywhere. I'll be lost in what is expected of me."

"So don't do what is expected of you."

The thought paralyzed me. "How do people do that?"

She put her arm around me and pulled me close. "They write emails to nineteen-year-old men, asking them to take you to Trujillo's next time they're in town."

I set my journal down and hurried to find an approved show on the TV. My parents walked in the front door from visitation. It was where my parents and other church members shared the gospel door to door or visited people who had attended the church. I shut off the TV, hoping I hadn't stopped it on a sinful channel.

My dad loosened his tie. "Great night. Three souls won for heaven today."

"That's great, daddy!"

My brother, James, barreled from the back. "Mila was watching MTV."

My eyes almost fell out of my head. "Did not!"

"She did. I didn't say anything because I wanted to see how long you'd listen to it."

My heart pounded. "It was a Christian special. They talked about the cross."

My mother froze. "Was it contemporary Christian? Did it have drums in it?"

"No, no drums. I promise."

"It had drums! I heard them," my brother said.

I closed my eyes to hold back the tears. "I'm going to go to bed."

"You know we don't listen to music with drums in it." My mother sent me a worried look. She was afraid for my soul. I knew that was it, so how could I be upset with her? She wanted to make sure I had a good eternity. It was the same reason I needed to go to Bible college.

"I know. It won't happen again." I hurried to my room and hid my journal inside the vent, where I hoped my brother wouldn't find it.

I hid so many things. Proof could be found in every corner of my room. My beanbag chair used to hide my books until my dad found them one day and threw them away. He said if I hadn't known they were wrong to read, I wouldn't have hidden them. I wanted to tell him I hid them because I knew he thought they were wrong, but I didn't.

I never told people what I really thought. It might start a fight, and that was something that put my stomach in knots. No one knew what I really thought. No one except maybe Riley, Erin, and Ezra. They were the only people it was safe to say what I thought to.

**

Erin burst out of the office, grabbing me into a hug. Her wild brown curly hair flung all around in its usual fashion. It was beautiful, but she always lamented about its maintenance. "You've made my day, Mila! This is like the best thing ever when you do this."

"It's almost summer vacation for you. We won't get to do this too many more times, but then I guess we get the entire summer to do things."

"You're soooooooooo lucky you're homeschooled and are already on break."

I glanced over her shoulder. "Is Melissa coming?"

"No, she's sick today. Can we go to Arby's?"

"Yeah, where else would we go?"

She squeezed me. "Absolute best you are!"

Erin loved Arby's the way Riley loved Keanu Reeves. I picked her up about once a week from school and drove her there for lunch. She was two years younger than me, and it wasn't something she could do herself. Arby's was too far to walk to and make it back to class in time.

She bounced around in the passenger seat next to me. "Is there any way at all you could go to the Linkin Park concert with us in the Springs?"

My chest sank into my stomach. "Not unless I lie to my parents."

"Do that."

"I think it's going to be a no. Sucks."

She flopped down in woe. "Majorly. My dad says when you get out on your own, you're going to rebel. He says all good preacher's daughters do. He's talking drugs, alcohol, and men. Lots of men."

"I've heard that before. Many times, actually. From too many people. That and preacher's kids have no manners from people who have never interacted with me. Everyone assumes I'm going to go insane the moment I break free of my parents. I'll suddenly find wild parties fun and not exhausting and drink myself to blacking out."

"Your parents should let you go to the Linkin Park concert, so that doesn't happen. Maybe I should come over and explain that to them."

My head whipped to her. "No! No, that's the last thing you should do. I can't even tell them I want to go to the Linkin Park concert."

"Your parents suffocate you. You know I love Jesus, but I think he wants us to enjoy life too, not be so terrified of the next one."

"Yeah, you're probably right." I turned up the music that had lots of drums in it, realizing I was already rebelling by listening to the music that reached me on a soul level that would, perhaps, condemn my soul to a dark afterlife. There seemed too much irony in that.

We ate lunch while Erin did most of the talking about any topic that popped into her head. I nodded and listened, taking all of it in to keep forever. If I was good at anything, it was listening to people and remembering their words. Once I dropped her back at school, I stared at the building, wondering what it was like to go to high school in a building where you got to interact with people all day. Jealousy twinged as it always did every time I watched Erin go back into school.

I drove to Monte Vista, about twenty minutes from Alamosa, where my online school was based. I did school mainly at home on the computer but could go into the building for events or to talk to teachers. My English teacher had said he wanted to talk to me if I got the chance, and I needed to pick up some final projects. The building was four stories and old. There seemed to be endless curves and surprise rooms. It had an ancient smell. Mustiness might have been the right word for it, but it was unique and old.

I knocked on Mr. Draper's office and stepped in when he acknowledged me. "You wanted to see me?"

"Yeah, yeah, come in. Have a seat."

I avoided looking at the small trash can next to his cluttered desks as it might encourage my nerves to throw up into it. "Is my grade okay?"

"Yes, excellent. High as it could be."

That was good. College wasn't threatened. "What is it?"

He got up and went to his file cabinet. It looked about the only organized thing in the room. He had shelves of books that had no order. Some lay on their sides, while others stood like proper library books.

He pulled out a file and opened it, sliding a paper my way. "Your last creative writing assignment."

I studied it and noticed the "A" at the top. "Was something wrong with it?" My mind always assumed the worst. It zeroed in on nuclear war when all that was happening was a fire drill.

"No, it's well done. I want you to know all your pieces are. If you ever write that book you mentioned, I'll help you get published."

I looked away and blinked a few times. "It's not written, so you haven't read it. It could be terrible."

It probably will be terrible.

"I don't need to read it to know I'd help you get published. Also, your breakdown of *Macbeth* was great. It was insightful and not something I see a lot. Can I use it as an example for future students?"

"Sure. Are you sure you want to?"

He leaned back in his chair and smiled. "Yeah, I'm sure."

I got up to leave after he handed me several of my papers from the semester. "Thank you." I stepped to the door.

"Mila?"

I turned back halfway out the door. "Yeah?"

"Write that book. Okay?"

I nodded and rushed to my car. Who would ever want to publish anything I wrote? That seemed crazy. I went home and turned on my computer, waiting for the internet to load. I searched for writing colleges and stared at the screen, wanting that so badly.

My mother popped her head into the room. "What are you doing?"

"Umm... Just looking at writing colleges." I flinched.

"I'm sure there will be lots of writing for you to do at Bible college."

I lowered my gaze to my lap. "Right. I'm sure there will be."

"You still have the list I gave you?"

"Yeah, I pinned it to my board to help me decide." I saw the paper in my head and compared it to the screen in front of me. Two very different yet similar paths I could pick. Why did it feel I had no real choice in the matter?

"Good. Supper is almost ready."

"Okay. I'm going to go check on my birds."

"Okay. Don't be out there too long."

I went out to my little barn. That's what I called it, but it was an extremely long, durable shed I'd insulated and made pens for. I'd also created outdoor pens with fencing, so the birds could be inside or out. I loved them, and as long as I lived, none of them would be a food source. I sat on the dirt floor, facing my animals, and told my birds several stories. They were a captive audience, after all.

Chapter Three: Dangerous Naivety

❤

Erin straightened the little figurines on her dresser. Everything had a place in her room. Sometimes I messed with her and moved something, only to have her step into the room and frown. She always knew I'd done something but didn't know what for a few minutes. Sometimes she'd glare and demand to know what I did. Her room was bursting with sunflowers. The flowers made up her bedding, artwork, and several pieces of her clothing.

"What would be the worst thing that could happen if your parents found out you went to the Linkin Park concert with us? You could tell them we're going shopping up there and staying overnight."

I squeezed her sunflower pillow, breathing in its unique flowery scent that Erin carried with her wherever she went. "The belt."

She froze and spun around. "They'd beat you?"

"No, not beat. I'd deserve a severe whipping for rebelling. Spare the rod, spoil the child. Then they would remind me I was lucky we're under grace and not law anymore."

"What would happen if we were under the law?" She climbed onto her bed, making us dip up and down as her waterbed settled. It'd sprung a leak once, and we'd both woken up soaked.

"I'd have been stoned. Rebellious teenagers were stoned."

"Like lined up and pelted with rocks?"

I nodded. "Stoned until dead. It kept them from rebelling. The belt isn't that bad."

"I don't know what to say, Mila."

"I'm fine. It's really fine. If I make bad choices, they want to make sure I don't continue to make them. It deters a lot of things."

"Yeah, I've noticed. We should watch *Interview with a Vampire*. Have you seen it?" She looked through her DVD collection and put the disc in when I shook my head.

We sat and watched the movie. Erin was a cuddler, so by the end of the film, she was holding me tightly. There was a knock on her door, and she opened it.

Her dad stuck his head in. "Pizza has arrived!"

We went out into the kitchen and grabbed plates. Everywhere we walked, some type of animal could be seen. The Malone's had four cats, three dogs, a snake, a turtle, a cockatiel, and several fish. It seemed like something was constantly being added to their menagerie, which was a big reason I loved spending time at their house.

Mr. Malone hugged me as I went out into the kitchen. "How is my favorite Erin friend?"

"I'm good."

He handed me a plate. "Erin tells me you get to keep some of the food if you close at KFC."

"Yeah, anyone closing gets to pick leftover food to take home."

He opened the pizza box. "Help yourself. I keep telling Erin when she turns sixteen, she needs to get a job there so we can have the leftovers."

"She should. We'd have so much fun."

"Any luck getting your parents to agree to the concert?"

"No, sir, I don't think it's going to work out."

"Call me, Ron. Not sir or Mr. Malone. You know that." He shook his head. "That's a shame. When you get out on your own, I'm sure it'll be so freeing. You'll probably party nonstop. That's what happens when parents are too strict. Their kids go crazy when they are on their own."

"I've heard that."

"It's true. They won't be able to say anything if you get into trouble with drinking or worse. They'll have no one to blame but themselves."

"Yeah." I grabbed a pizza slice and sat at their table that had fifty houseplants covering it. There was a little space on the ends to eat.

The Malone house was one of the larger houses in Alamosa. Mr. Malone was in charge of all the IT for the local hospitals, so he made good money. Mrs. Malone loved to collect unusual art that I loved staring at every time I came over. They had four children, and each had their own large room. Their parenting style was the exact opposite of my parents'. Even though they went to church, it was a different sort, and they believed their children needed to find what was right and wrong for themselves. I often envied that about Erin. I envied Erin for many things, which I knew was wrong.

We ate pizza, and it came time for me to leave for work. I put on my blue uniform with red stripes running vertically across it. I pinned on my name tag and hugged Erin goodbye. Mr. Malone and Erin's three younger siblings also hugged me, and I drove to work.

"I apologize for the dry bun," I told the customer as I took her sandwich.

"Don't I get to keep that one, too, since it's not my fault? You guys made the bun too dry. It's the least you could do for compensation."

I stared at the sandwich that looked like all the others we served. "Oh, I thought since it was dry, you wouldn't want it."

She rolled her eyes. "Can I get someone smarter to deal with?"

"Yeah, I can do that." I placed the sandwich on the counter and went to the back to grab Carylon. "The customer at the front wants someone smarter to deal with than me."

Carylon finished washing her hands and leaned around to see the front counter. "She said that?"

"Yeah, I figured that was you."

She sighed. "Mila, Mila, what am I going to do with you?"

"Hopefully, not fire me. She said the bun is too dry, but I put it through the machine and took it out right away. I'm not sure why it's dry. She wants it and a new one."

"Of course she does." She scowled. "Trust me, you're not going anywhere. Go make her a new sandwich, and I'll deal with his."

"How do I toast it less?"

"You don't. The sandwich isn't too dry. She wants two." She went to the front.

I made the sandwich and hurried it off the toaster as it burned my fingers through my gloves. After bagging it, I took it to the front and held it out toward the woman.

She was in a staring showdown with Carylon. "You're not going to let me keep the bad sandwich? You're just going to throw it away, right? It's a waste."

"If it's a bad sandwich, I'm sure you don't want it." Carylon sent her a too-sweet smile.

"Is there a manager I can speak with?"

Carylon pointed at her badge. "That would be me."

The woman's face stiffened even more as she jerked the bag from me and stormed out of the restaurant. A few more people came in, and I took their orders. Jack came in the side door and waved. He'd worked as lead cook for over twenty-five years. He was a kind man in his sixties who was always happy. Even on our most chaotic days, he seemed joyful and calm.

His smile showed through his eyes. "How's your day, Mila?"

"Great. Only one complaint, so overall good."

He gave me a thumbs-up. "That's the spirit." He went to the back to start more chicken.

Ted, a tall man with a curly mullet, walked in. He was a regular and always asked for me when I wasn't in the front. I knew his order by heart, and had it put into the register before he even got to the front. I smiled warmly at him and handed him his cup.

He put his hand over my hand and kept it there as he looked me over. "Did I ever tell you, you have the body of a Texan woman?"

"Oh." I blinked several times and pulled my hand back as much as he allowed. "Is that a good thing?"

"Yes, it means you have curves in all the right places."

My smile returned. "Thank you."

Carylon shoved his change to him. "You have to be what, forty?"

Ted nodded. "Close. Forty-five."

"She's sixteen. I suggest you get your order to go."

"He always eats here," I said.

Ted smiled. "The pretty girl is right."

"Today. He's getting it to go." Carylon grabbed his sandwich that the back had already sent up and opened the hot wells to grab his sides. She placed them in a bag and handed them to him. "Have a good day somewhere else."

He gave a nod and left with his bag.

She turned to me. "Mila, you realize he's a pervert?"

"What do you mean?"

"The way he was looking at you and touching you." She rubbed her forehead. "Honey, if he comes back in, let me take his order. Okay?"

"Okay."

"Why don't you take over drive-thru?"

"Okay."

She put her arm around me. "If anyone ever makes you feel unsafe, let me know. And have Gary walk you to your car from now on."

"Are you sure he'd want to do that?"

"After I talk to him, he definitely will."

The rest of the day went by uneventfully, and closing time drew near.

I pushed down on the black receiver button. "Welcome to KFC. This is Mila. May I take your order?"

"Yeah, I'd like a chocolate pie and to ask you a question."

"Okay. Feel free to ask whenever you're ready."

They didn't say anything, and I looked over to see they'd already pulled forward to the window.

I ran to the window as excitement bubbled in my chest. "Ezra!"

"Yeah, what do you think of my new wheels?"

I gaped and beamed at him. "You got a very rusty, dented truck."

"Beautiful, isn't it?"

We both burst into laughter.

"I love it and am happy for you. No more rides from me, I guess."

He shrugged. "We can take turns giving each other rides."

"I'd like that."

"Me too."

Someone poked me in the back, and I whirled around to see Gary holding a bag.

He wiggled it. "Your order. The pie."

"Right." I handed the bag to Ezra. "A dollar six."

He gave me the money but didn't roll up his window. "You want to go to Sonic after you get off?"

"It's going to be another hour, and I was going to take the Malone's my share of the leftovers. Mr. Malone thinks it's neat I get those."

"I can wait."

I glanced at the clock. "Alright. I'll meet you there at about ten? Does that work?"

"Yeah, I've been needing to go to the skate park, anyway."

"You can do that more now with your truck."

"One of the reasons I'm excited. One of a few."

"What are the others?"

He smiled and rolled up his window, driving off. He was a such a strange boy sometimes. I helped close everything up, and Gary walked me to my car.

He waved goodbye. "You stay safe, chica."

I thanked him and drove to the Malone's, where I dropped off all the chicken and sides I'd gotten for the night. Ezra was sitting on a Sonic table with his skateboard leaning against the red bench. He had his blue ball cap turned backward, hiding his dark hair. A few strands poked out the front.

He set his drink beside him. "Hey."

"Hey."

"How was work?"

"Good, it was good. Gary has to walk me to my car now."

"Why?"

I told him about Carolyn's odd reaction to the guy.

Ezra's face grew tense. "That guy said that to you?"

"Yeah, he's a regular. He always says things like that to me."

"Like what else?"

"He really likes my uniform. Talks about how it fits me nicely a lot. They are nice uniforms."

His fists curled. "If Gary isn't around some night, call me. I can walk you to your car."

"Okay. Did you hear we're going to the sand dunes for youth group. Two weeks after the purity party?"

"Yeah, not like we haven't been there a hundred times before."

"It'll be fun." I pressed the red button and ordered a drink.

Ezra and I tucked our legs under us on top of the table, facing each other as we sipped our drinks. We talked and laughed as we enjoyed the cool summer evening.

Chapter Four: Purity Party

I pressed my pen to the lined paper of my leather dragon journal. Riley had given it to me for my sixteenth birthday last November. I'd filled it more than halfway already with my ramblings. My door opened, and I threw my journal under the comforter. Dragons were evil, and it'd get thrown away if my parents found it.

My mom popped her head in and pressed her lips in a way that always made them disappear. They were on the thinner side, and I sometimes envied them because I thought mine looked overly large. I also often envied her wavy hair to my straight and her less curvy body. Envy was clearly a sin I needed to work on. I'd gained her petite size, but the curves made me have to wear baggier clothes to not be a temptation, and I wished I didn't have to do that.

She sat on the end of my bed, holding a small pink book. "As you know, the youth group is starting, and we're going to the Thompson's tonight for the purity party. I wanted you to make their girls feel welcomed. They're around your age and in a new place. They could use some friends."

"Yeah, of course. I can introduce them to Erin, Riley, and Melissa, too."

"Maybe wait on that. I thought maybe you could hang out with the Thompson girls a little more. They're the same denomination as us, so they align with our belief system."

My smile dropped, and I nodded. "Okay."

She handed me the book. "There's going to be a discussion on purity as clear by the name. They're going to split the boys from the girls, so it's appropriate to talk about. It made me realize I've never discussed purity with you."

I coughed and tried to regain control of my lungs. "It's okay! Mom, really. We can just let all that be a surprise, like my period was."

"You're sixteen now, which means boys could be a temptation. You could be a temptation to them, which is why we stress the importance of how you dress. You don't want to be led astray or lead anyone astray. This book has everything in it you need to remain pure. Sex is shameful outside marriage. Showing your body is shameful to anyone but your husband. You are never to be alone with a boy. Not even in public. It's too much temptation."

I nodded, hoping she would stop. "Yes, I know. I don't even notice boys. They walk into the room, and I feel nothing. You don't have to worry."

She smiled and handed me the book. "That's good to hear but read this to guard your heart against wicked things."

My eyes shifted around the room. "Okay. I will read it. Thank you."

She finally left after an awkward hug, and I opened the booklet, afraid she might quiz me on it. I scratched Kiki's ear. His real name was Akela, but I called him Kiki for short. He was a miniature American Eskimo and border collie mix. He looked like a mini black wolf with his facial markings, fluffiness, and tail that wrapped around his back.

"Okay. Kiki, let's see what this is about."

Riley looked over the book and laughed. "This was your sex talk with your mother?"

I'd driven to her house, hoping she could clear some of my new-found confusion.

"Yeah, I'm more confused now than before I read it."

She flipped through the pages. "What's confusing about it?"

"It says if I sleep with a man before marriage, my husband will never trust me to be faithful."

Her eye twitched as she looked up at me. "What?"

"Yeah, it says that if he realizes I gave into temptation with him or someone else, he'll think I could give into temptation with someone else after we say vows. Our marriage will be tainted from the start."

"It doesn't say that."

"It does." I grabbed the book, turned to the right page, and handed it back to her. "Here."

"Oh, wow. It does say that. Okay. You know that's not true. If your husband doesn't trust you because you were with someone before him, then you shouldn't be with him."

"I don't even know what it means." I chewed on my lip as my cheeks heated.

"What?"

My eyes shifted to the floor, and my cheeks grew hotter. "To be with a boy. What does it mean?"

Her eyes jerked up, and she stared at me. "You're serious? You can't be. We've watched movies."

"Yeah, but it's not super clear. It's just kissing and being close. I think."

She gawked at me in a way that made me squirm. "No, Mila, there's more involved than that."

"What then?"

She leaned forward and whispered details in my ear.

My eyes grew to the size of the CDs sitting on her lap. "Why would anyone do that? That's terrifying and gross?"

She laughed. "No, it's fun. Lots of fun."

"How can that even be a temptation?"

"Oh, sweetheart, it is."

I stood up and grabbed my keys as a new terror for boys and men set in. "I need to pick up Ezra and Amber for the youth group thing tonight."

"Mila, don't look so scared. It's really not as scary as your face says it is."

"Yeah, no, I mean. I'm fine. It's just a lot to process." I hurried from the room and drove to the Henderson's house.

Ezra and Amber bounded out of the house and fought over who would get the front seat next to me. Amber won like always after reminding Ezra it was inappropriate for him to be that close to me. After my day, I didn't want to think about the why, and the pending youth group purity talk had me on edge.

I turned on the radio and let Amber do most of the talking, as my mind was even more confused and embarrassed than before the booklet and my talk with Riley. My body felt shameful, and I adjusted my shirt as Ezra got into the car.

We drove to the other side of town, where the Thompsons had the typical setup of a large trailer and outbuildings for animals. While it was larger than most trailers, I wondered how they fit thirteen kids inside.

They had an enormous garage that we were led to. It was made of blue-painted metal and had concrete flooring. The ceiling rose a couple stories high, and Ezra helped the boys and men set folding chairs into rows while Amber and I helped the girls and women with the refreshments. My dad and Mr. Thompson walked up with four girls who looked close to my age. Amber and I stopped our tasks to shake their hands.

Mr. Thompson pointed to the girls. "These are my daughters. Ruby is fourteen, Kyra fifteen, Hannah sixteen, and Jennifer seventeen."

We all waved and smiled at each other, and the adults left us to get to know each other.

Kyra seemed the most outgoing and did most of the talking. "My cousin said she knows you. Valery Thompson."

"Yeah, we both went to the Christian school throughout elementary and middle school. She's a good friend," I said.

"That's what she told us."

The silence grew between us, and Amber stepped forward. "We should have an icebreaker. What's everyone's favorite Bible verse?"

We all rattled off our favorite, and then Amber asked for our testimonies, which we all knew by heart. We talked a little longer until the meeting started, and we were divided into two groups. Boys stayed in the garage, and girls went into the trailer. We sat in the large living room on several couches and chairs.

Mrs. Thompson took the chair and opened up the Bible. She warmed us up with a Bible drill, which I'd always excelled at. I could find any book of the Bible and verse faster than almost anyone, and I oddly prided myself on it.

Mrs. Thompson read several scriptures that had to do with purity. When she got to the end, she said similar things to what I'd always heard about our bodies being a temptation to men and how we could easily lead boys and men astray if we didn't dress conservatively. It was why long dresses were essential to wear. We shouldn't show any skin that wasn't from above our elbows, upper neck, face, and feet.

"It's important to remain pure until marriage. One reason is that birth control is sinful. It kills babies, and you shouldn't use it. If you fall into sin with a boy, you could get pregnant, and you will disgrace yourself and your family. It's safe and right within marriage to get pregnant and have as many children as God wills you to have. You can trust God to support your family within marriage. You don't have that outside the safety of marriage."

We had an open discussion about what purity meant and why being alone with a boy in any capacity was wrong. To feel anything toward a boy or man we weren't married to was shameful and wrong. When it was over, my parents encouraged me to get to know the Thompson girls more. We all took a walk on their property. Ezra and several of the other boys came with.

Kyra and her sister started talking about which country music songs they liked, and I told them the songs I liked.

Amber stared at us and looked back toward the house where all the adults were talking. "I don't think we should talk about worldly music at a church event."

Kyra crinkled her nose. "Yeah, maybe. But we've talked about church things enough for one night." She turned to Ezra. "Why don't you tell us about yourself?"

I watched the way she looked him over. Something weird flopped in my stomach.

"Ummm... Like, what do you want to know?" He glanced at me and back at Kyra.

"Anything you want to tell us?" She batted her eyelashes.

He gave some facts about himself that I already knew, and I grew uncomfortable as she stepped closer to him. Their back and forth went on for probably about twenty minutes. I didn't understand why it upset me to watch them interact.

I cleared my throat. "Ezra and Amber, I'm going to head back if you guys want a ride home." I rushed to my car.

Ezra hurried to catch up with me after talking to them for a few more minutes. "You alright?"

"Fine. I'm fine. Why wouldn't I be fine? I always am."

He grinned. "Mila?"

"Yeah, they offered to take Amber and me home."

My lips went tight. "Oh, okay. I guess they can give you rides now when you don't have your truck."

He let a laugh escape him before he straightened his face. "I told them I wanted to go with you."

I got in my car and stared out the windshield, and he climbed into the passenger seat.

"You want me to go with you, right?" He waited for me to respond.

I kept my face forward, not wanting him to see my ridiculous watery eyes that made no sense. "You can do whatever you want. If you'd rather go with them, I get it."

He bumped his shoulder gently into mine. "I'm in the car I want to be in."

"Okay."

He bumped me again. "Mila?"

I finally turned to look at him. "Yeah."

His smile grew warm and familiar. It became contagious, and I smiled back as we shared another moment of staring at each other.

Amber opened my passenger door. "Seriously, Ezra! We just had an entire night on purity, and you get into her front seat alone where the entire church can see you and spread rumors. Get in the back."

He climbed in the back seat, and Amber got in. We drove toward their house, where I used their phone to ask my mom if I could spend the night. She okayed it, and we watched movies. After Amber went to sleep, Ezra and I went to our roof to talk under the stars. I didn't know entirely why Ezra and I had such a pull to sit on the roof together and stare at the sky. He was a boy, and according to everything I'd learned that day, he should have terrified me. But he didn't. His smile and eyes felt safe and sitting with him brought peace. I wasn't supposed to be so close to him, alone. Why did it feel right to do?

He put his arm around me, and I leaned my head on his shoulder. We didn't say anything for a long time as we both absorbed the view of our mountain.

Chapter Five: Sand Dunes

♥

The trip to the sand dunes arrived on a near-perfect day. Mid-June had remained mild in the upper seventies and low humidity. The valley stayed dry and was similar to a desert in many places, with shrubs and dirt. Grass usually stayed limited to yards but often remained yellow most of the year, except in the richer neighborhoods. The beautiful mountains made up for the dull landscape surrounding the forest terrain. The San Luis Valley had two unexpected things that shocked tourists.

The first was the largest sand dunes in North America that sat directly north of Mount Blanca and rested against another mountain. The second was an alligator farm that had several exotic reptiles. Along with two ski trips, it had made up one of three field trips every year when I attended the Christian school that only allowed students up to eighth grade.

I put on my swimsuit with short sleeves that stopped at my upper arms. It had a flowing skirt and shorts that ended below my knees. It was the riskiest thing my parents let me wear. My mother handed me sunscreen and a white cover that would go over my swimsuit. It was a short-sleeved jacket that would hide my backside to right below my knees.

I looped my ponytail through the back of my white ball cap and waited on my steps for Ezra to pull up in his truck with Amber. My parents and brother left to the church for another event. My friends pulled up, and I bolted to the passenger side of his truck. Amber scooted over to give me room.

Ezra had his blue cap on backward again and messed with the radio dial. "Crash and Burn" by Savage Garden played from his speakers. I watched out the window as the tumbleweeds changed into grassland on one side and mountains on the other. Buffalo grazed in a field, and I watched them as Amber talked about the Bible study she'd had last week with her mom and some neighbor ladies. Ezra and I didn't mind sitting in silence, listening to music, but Amber liked to talk.

Most of the youth group had accumulated by the river in front of the sand dunes. It was shallow with a mild current, which made crossing it to climb the dunes easy. Mr. Thompson prayed and set some ground rules. We could venture within the boundaries he set as long as we stayed in groups and returned by noon.

Kyra walked up with her three sisters and her cousin Valery. I hadn't seen Valery in a while, but we used to see each other all the time at school. We hugged and caught up a little. The distraction made me miss Kyra pulling Ezra away from me. The sharp twinge from a couple weeks ago returned, and I had to fight thoughts of shoving my way between them. He was my best friend, and she wanted to take him.

Valery asked me a question I had to have her repeat. I answered it as I stared at her cousin taking Ezra somewhere. The twinge had grown into anger and disappointment. I'd looked forward to this day for weeks and had fully expected to spend the entire day with him.

A massive beach bag plopped on the sand, and Valery removed shovels and buckets. "I know it's kiddish, but I thought it would be fun to build a massive sandcastle." She adjusted her giant blue sunhat as the wind picked up a slight bit.

I glanced around to see if any adults were close and removed my cover. Valery and I spent the next hour building a castle. We added a moat and thumbprint windows. Rocks made a bridge, and we created tiny stick people to set in various places around the structure. I enjoyed catching up with my old friend, but in the background, my irritation with Kyra grew. Cold wetness struck my back, and I jumped up to see Ezra holding a large super soaker squirt gun.

He tossed me a smaller water weapon. "You have ten seconds to find cover."

I stared at the midsize soaker he'd given me. "How come you get the bigger gun?"

"10... 9... 8..."

"That doesn't seem fair."

"7... 6... 5."

I screeched as he kept counting and dove for the lone bush off to the side. He took chase, and I bolted out into the open to make my stand on a large boulder. I flung my flip-flops to an unknown location when they slowed me down. My feet and knees scraped against the rock, but I kept going.

I pointed my soaker at him as he jogged closer. "I have the high ground. You might as well surrender."

"Why would I do that when I can climb?"

I fired repeated attacks, and he cried out as I got him right in the eye. He made it in front of me, and we both drenched each other. He removed his canister and poured it on my head.

"Cheater!" I hurried to unscrew mine, and he grabbed at it. We tugged it back and forth until most of it spilled on both of us.

I grabbed the large gun he'd set down to steal my canister and leaped off the boulder to fill it.

"Hey! You think you can just steal and get away with it?"

I screwed it back in and got him right in the face. "Already have!" I screamed as he leaped after me.

He gained on me as his longer legs covered the ground much faster. I tore for the sand dunes. The closest one seemed an eternity away when my feet kept sinking into the almost too-hot sand. I made it to the base, rushed to the top, and slid down the other side. Ezra grabbed me before I made it to the second one. He tickled me, and I squirmed, laughing against his chest.

We plopped to the ground, hidden by the first dune. We caught our breath and sat up. No one could see us, and we propped our backs against the gritty hill. It reclined, and once my skin adapted to the temperature, it grew pretty comfortable. It was like we'd found a little haven to be alone, like on the roof. Our mountain looked much larger, making me realize we'd never climbed it.

"Where did Kyra take you?"

He took his gaze off the sky. "What?"

"When you left with Kyra, where did you go for so long?"

"She said they needed help with some coolers. Mr. Thompson had me help set up the lunch area. Then he said we could use any of the squirt guns. I knew right away we needed to battle."

"I'm glad you came back."

The right side of his mouth tipped up, and his hazel eyes lightened to an almost green. "Yeah?"

"Yeah."

"It looked like you and Val made quite the castle."

"We did. Could have used your help."

He returned to looking at the sky. "We can make it bigger later. This is nice. Just sitting here together."

"We do that a lot."

"Because it's nice."

I laughed and watched lazy, wispy clouds drift by. "Why in all our staring at Mount Blanca have we never climbed it?"

"You want to climb that?" He pointed at the enormous blue peak.

"Don't you? I bet the valley is pretty from all the way up there."

"Okay. Let's do that then."

"When?"

He shrugged his left shoulder, which made it rub against mine. "Sometime next week. We could have a picnic and sit there and do nothing."

"Finally, go to the place we stare at."

"Sounds perfect." He slid down, so his back rested flat, and he tipped his head at an odd angle.

I scrunched my nose. "What are you doing?"

"Just hanging by a moment here with you. There's nothing else to lose. There's nothing else to find. There's nothing in the world. That can change my mind. There is nothing else," he sang out.

"You and your lyrics."

"They're life."

"I thought skateboarding was life."

He straightened his head but remained flat. "Why can't both be?"

I slid down next to him. "Is the view better down here?"

He turned his head and locked his eyes with mine for a few seconds. "A lot better."

My chest fluttered at his smile and the slight bend in his nose, and the way the right side of his mouth tipped up a little. I whipped my head to the sky to stop the increased bubbles in my stomach.

"Favorite cloud?"

I forced my eyes to stay fixed on the above. "Right now? I have to pick one of these?"

"Yes, are they not good enough for you?"

"They're a little pathetic. Like, do they even qualify as clouds?"

"What else would they be?"

"Fluffy wisps," I said.

"Fluffy wisps? What the heck is that?"

I pointed at the sky. "Those white blobs that are so weak you can see all the way through them."

"Okay. Which is your favorite fluffy wisp?"

"The one that is an almost bird."

"You and your birds."

"Birds are life," I said.

"I thought writing was life."

"Why can't both be?"

"We both have our things, I guess." He relaxed his head, resting it against mine.

His hand tingled next to mine, and it took all my restraint not to intertwine our fingers. I wondered if it would have been wrong to start a prayer circle just to hold his hand. He slowly rested his pinky over mine, and I liked the small connection. It was like we couldn't give in to holding hands, but we still had something.

I yawned and realized we needed to move before we took a nap together. "Do you think they miss us yet?"

"Who cares?"

"We might when they go looking for us and find us lying on the ground together."

He sat up. "Good point. My reputation is one thing, but yours is entirely different."

He stood up and helped me to my feet. We grabbed our squirt guns and walked back to the river.

Valery was still working on the castle. She glanced up. "You two want to help me expand this?"

We both agreed, and Ezra gathered sticks and stones to help stabilize the towers. He shaped some turrets, and we created an elaborate medieval castle before Mr. Thompson called everyone to lunch. He gave a message while we ate and sent us back out.

Kyra walked up to where I sat alone, waiting for Ezra to get out of the bathroom. "Where did Ezra go?"

"Up the sand dunes, maybe."

"Which way?"

I pointed in a random direction and cringed as she went where I'd indicated. Lying was very bad, but I wanted so badly to have her search for him in vain.

I sighed at my guilt and ran after her. "He's in the bathroom, actually."

"Oh. Okay." She narrowed her eyes like she couldn't figure me out.

She waited outside the bathroom for him, and I jumped up to help Valery carry the leftover cups to be packed up in the Thompson's van. I kept glancing back to watch Kyra talking to Ezra.

Val touched my arm. "Do you want to climb to the very top? There's a rumor that if you make it to the highest dune peak, there's a time capsule. You can open it and fill out a paper to say you made it and make a wish."

I followed her gaze to the tallest dune. "That sounds fun. I've been here probably a hundred times, but only made it to the top once. Never knew about the time capsule."

We headed back to cross the river, and I made sure to pass by Ezra and Kyra, sending Ezra a look as I went by. I mentally smacked myself. What was wrong with me? What did it matter if Ezra talked to a girl who clearly liked him? Anxiety zinged my stomach the more I thought about it. What if Kyra stole my best friend and he looked at Mount Blanca with her instead?

Val turned her head to look at me. "Are you alright?"

"Yeah, I'm fine."

"You're crying."

I flung my hand up to act like I was scratching my cheek. "My eyes are dry."

Dang, it! Second lie in one day.

"I have some unopened contact solution. Would you like some?" She rifled through her purse and pulled out a white bottle with a green label.

"No, I'm okay, but thank you."

Ezra jogged up next to me. "I thought you were waiting for me."

I looked over my shoulder to see Kyra grabbing a backpack from a table. "You looked busy with Kyra."

His eyes looked down and to the right, like my words made no sense. "You're that much in a hurry to get back to the castle?"

"No, Val and I are going to climb to the top and find the time capsule."

"They say it brings good luck," Val added.

"She didn't tell me that part, so now I'm even more sold."

"Let's spend two hours trudging through hot sand for a little good fortune, then." Ezra glanced at his watch. "That will leaves us an hour and a half to get back down here and to the bonfire."

We waded through the river, and I tried not to groan when Kyra and her sister caught up to us. I chided myself that I was supposed to help them feel welcomed to the area. I was failing at my assigned job, but the fear of losing Ezra remained strong.

Chapter Six: Bears and People

I t took approximately two hours to climb the sand dunes to the highest peak. I'd done it once before with my uncle and cousins. During a thunderstorm, it became a dangerous place with frequent lightning strikes. Black melted sand appeared every so often, showing where each strike had occurred.

Val led the way up each dune, humming as she went. She froze when she reached the top of a large one before us. "Guys! Look! Guys!" She waved us up the dune.

My calf muscles ached from the ten hills we'd already climbed, but I hurried to see the source of her excitement.

I made it next to her first and gaped at the tiny blue bird with the faded red chest. "It's beautiful! It is so sweet, and it's just hanging out here."

"It's adventurous. Maybe it wanted to find the time capsule too." She chuckled and grabbed a yellow disposal camera from her bag. She flipped down the little black flap in the front to turn off the flash. It clicked as she took several pictures.

Ezra trudged up, panting from running to catch us. "What's all the excitement about?"

I pointed. "A mountain bluebird. It's the prettiest thing."

"Makes complete sense it's a bird."

"What are you trying to say?"

"You could see a sparrow and be like, oh my word, Ezra! Look at the little bird we see every morning outside our windows," Ezra said.

"Are you mocking my fascination with winged species?"

"Maybe a little." He smirked.

"I'll have you know Val is just as excited. She used five of her pictures on it."

Disposable cameras usually only had about twenty-four pictures that could be taken with them. You had no idea how your photos turned out until you got them developed at Walmart.

Val rapidly nodded. "How can you not be excited? It's so cute, and it's ticking its little head around. The coloring is perfect. Couldn't have chosen the hues better myself."

Kyra and her sister Hannah finally joined us, and Kyra rolled her eyes. "Seriously, you all are carrying on about a stupid little bird." She rushed down the hill, scaring our little friend off. "It's not like we have all day to stand around and stare at birds."

Ezra slid down the hill after her. "We had to wait for you to catch up."

Val snickered, and the rest of us followed them down. We all looked ready to collapse in the sand by the time we made it to the tallest dune. I crawled to the top, and Ezra grabbed my hand to help me up. Kyra held her hand out toward him like she'd die without his assistance. He helped her and Hannah up, and Val made it to the top before us.

Ezra and I both looked out at the view at the same time and mutually gasped. The river snaked like a blue thread connecting life from the evergreen trees to flocks of birds that were dipping low to take drinks and grab fish. Campgrounds with colorful tents backed up to the blue mountains. Herds of buffalo grazed in tall grass fields, looking no bigger than the people splashing in the water directly below. Everywhere we turned sat a magnificent new surprise. The varying colors of sand, from white to yellow to almost orange, looked so much clearer and prettier when looking at it from above.

Val got right to work throwing sand around. We all got on our knees, searching for the time capsule. She triumphantly yelled when she found the metal cylinder. She unscrewed the lid and pulled out the paper. It had lines to put your name and a wish. She wrote her name and wished to go to Ireland and Japan. She handed it to Kyra, who passed it to me.

I scowled at Kyra's wish for Ezra to kiss her and resisted the urge to cross it out as I wrote that I wanted to leave the valley for the world. Ezra wrote his wish next and hurried it to Hannah. Hannah stopped for a moment and glanced at me and then Ezra before writing her wish down and handing it to Val to return to the time capsule.

"Who's ready to roll?" Ezra rolled down the hill.

I went right after him and crashed directly into his chest. "What did you wish for?"

His eyes shifted. "Nothing important."

"Why wouldn't you wish for something important after all that work?"

"Okay. It was super important, but I can't tell you, or it won't come true. I really want it to."

"But everyone who looks at it afterward, including Hannah, will know what it was."

"Yeah, don't ask Hannah what it was, okay?"

I stuck my lower lip out. "How come Hannah gets to know and I don't?"

Val smashed into me, and Ezra jumped up, hurrying up the next hill. I was glad Hannah knew the wish, not Kyra. The two sisters slid down rather than rolled and whispered to each other. It made me realize Kyra probably did know now, and it made me irritated at Ezra for having a secret with them. It wasn't like he'd told them, but it was still a secret.

The sisters kept sending me looks, and I wondered about the weird shift in attention. Going down the sand dunes was much easier since the peaks got lower and lower. It was still a fair amount of work as you had to climb some before rolling down. We made it a race to see who could get to the bottom fastest. Val, Ezra, and I kept up the races until we reached the river.

The sisters didn't roll as they didn't like the idea of sand in their hair. We washed off as much as we could in the river but decided to reach the showers before the bonfire that seemed close with the dipping sun. I grabbed my bag from Ezra's truck and pulled out my black skirt and blue shirt. The shower spouts were thin rods that poured out one large stream of water rather than the many tiny streams of a standard shower.

I cleaned the sand off, dressed in the fresh outfit, and braided my hair into two French braids. I rounded the corner to put my bag back in Ezra's truck and bumped into Hannah.

She crossed her arms and pressed her lips together. When she relaxed them, tension remained on her face. "Look, my sister, Kyra, really likes Ezra."

"I've noticed."

"Why don't you let them have some time together tonight?" Her tone sounded forceful, like she was demanding it.

"Why don't you let Ezra decide who he wants to spend time with? If it's her, then he can decide that."

"You see, the problem is you're what he's used to, so he doesn't realize he likes her yet. Once he gets to know her, I'm sure she's where he'll spend his time."

Sharp pains rolled under my ribcage because a big part of me believed her. "We'll see."

She stepped closer. "We will. Tonight, you let my sister have a chance."

When my sweet Erin got angry at her siblings for messing with her things, she'd scream at them to go to Hades. I so wanted to scream that at Hannah. I wanted to so badly, but no matter how much I hated her, I didn't wish eternal damnation on her.

I took a deep breath, and somewhere from the pit of my stomach, words miraculously formed. "If Ezra is going to clearly choose your sister, why do I have to do anything to give her a chance?"

Her jaw dropped, and I shoved around her. It felt like a victory, but my nerves didn't get the message. Conflict made me shake and cry in a way I couldn't control, no matter how hard I tried to make it stop. We were supposed to go to the bonfire, but I went into the forest instead, where I cried against an enormous spruce tree. I sank to the ground, cried into my knees, and cried harder because I felt stupid for crying. I sat there for a long-time watching chipmunks and deer. Even when the hymns started, I rested against the tree and didn't move when they ceased.

"Are you alright?"

I looked up to see Val standing above me. "Yeah, why?"

"Everyone is looking for you."

"Me?"

"Yeah, are you okay?" She sat down next to me and studied my face.

"I'm fine. Just needed a minute."

"You took lots of minutes. Ezra was looking for you before the bonfire happened. Now I think he's going to blow a gasket."

"I'm sure it gave him some time with Kyra." I smacked my forehead as I realized that's exactly what I'd let happen.

"She sat beside him, but he kept nervous glancing everywhere. His thoughts were on where you were. Do you want to talk about what you're upset about before we tell everyone you're okay?"

I wanted to suffocate in all the sand more than I wanted to face everyone. "I needed to be alone for a little while. Time got away from me."

"Your wish to leave the valley. That was pretty much my wish, too."

"You want to see Ireland and Japan."

She nodded. "And so many other places. We will. You know, someday we'll both get out of here."

"I hope so."

She gave me a side hug. "Have some faith."

"That's all I seem to be allowed to have."

She touched her chest. "My soul feels that."

We both laughed, and I hugged her back. She helped me up, and we headed back into the camp, where Mr. and Mrs. Thompson rushed toward me and lectured me about wandering off.

"Sorry. It's easy to lose track in the forest." My cheeks were hot as I hated all the stares from others.

Mrs. Thompson grabbed my hand and thanked God for my safe return. "That's very understandable. We're just glad you're safe. Do you have a ride home?"

"Yeah." I helped them finish packing and waited by Ezra's truck.

It was odd he wasn't helping with clean up. Kyra and Hannah sent me glares as they climbed into their older sister's jeep. They had probably hoped I'd met my demise in the forest. I waited by Ezra's truck after pretty much everyone left.

Val's voice appeared before she did. "I promise she's fine and with everyone."

Ezra ran around the side of the shower house. When he spotted me, he shot forward and pulled me into a hug. "Where were you? We looked everywhere."

I hugged him back, taking a moment to appreciate his scent. It was one I could never really describe. It was unique to him and nice. "I lost track of time in the woods."

"Don't scare me like that again. There are bears in these woods."

I laughed. "Bears?"

"Yeah, it's on the info board."

Amber cleared her throat. "Yes, we are glad to see her, but you need to stop hugging her, Ezra. It's not appropriate."

He squeezed me tighter for a couple of seconds before letting go. "Don't do that again, okay?"

"Get lost in the woods?"

"Going off alone without a word. Anything can happen to you here. Did you read the board at all?"

"I didn't but will next time." I hugged Val goodbye. "We should hang out more often."

"We should. It's been too long," she said.

"Thanks for finding me."

"Someone had to. You're too good of a friend to lose."

I smiled and got into Ezra's truck, leaning against the glass while Amber talked about the Bible verses I'd missed from the bonfire. We went to their house and watched a movie. Like always, Amber grew tired early and went to bed. Ezra and I went outside but didn't go to the roof. My legs burned from the day's activity, but I wanted to walk with him.

He climbed onto the brown fence. It consisted of two wooden beams that ran parallel, with a large space in between. Vertical posts every few feet held the horizontal beams up. He sat on the top beam and rested his feet on the bottom. I climbed up next to him and stared at the brush and mountain.

He put his arm around me and pulled me close. "You really scared me tonight."

"You know bear attacks are rare."

"That wasn't the only concern. People are a lot worse than bears."

I rested my head on his shoulder and watched the black and white cattle munching in the field. "How was the bonfire?"

"Missed most of it, wondering where you were."

"We'll have to have another one sometime."

He unraveled the cord from his disc player, and we shared the headphones. Life House, Three Doors Down, and Nelly Furtado sounded into our ears.

"I'm like a bird. I'll only fly away!" we sang out into the summer night.

When the song ended, Ezra wrapped up the disc player. He turned a slight bit to catch my eyes. "Some day when you fly away, Mila, don't fly too far."

I glanced at our mountain. "The pull of Mount Blanca is too strong to escape. When I'm out there running from all the bears, it'll eventually bring me home."

"I'm counting on it."

Contentment filled me. Kyra might have gotten the bonfire, but I had this with Ezra, and no one could erase the memories. No one ever could, and as I stared at the mountain, I realized the blue snowy peak meant home like nothing ever had or ever would again.

Chapter Seven: Fear of Small Children

A delmo, Chano, and Elina crouched down, staring at my duck, Toby.

Chano turned his head to the right. "Can we pets him?"

"Yeah, he's a nice duck." I demonstrated how to be gentle.

Each of the children took a turn petting the duck, and they laughed as he waddled back inside his house.

Elina tugged on my skirt. "Ms. Mila, can we go to Mcdonalds after church Sunday?"

"If your mam says yes, that will be fine."

They jumped up and down, cheering.

I pointed at their small adobe house that sat one lot over from my trailer. "You better get ready for tonight."

They hurried home, and I finished my bird tasks before going inside to shower and get ready. Adelmo, Chano, and Elina were three of seven children in their family. Their mother, Mrs. Barrios, was an immigrant from Guatemala and spoke only Spanish. My parents had planned on being missionaries to Mexico at one point, and both spoke Spanish well. It was a big reason we had moved to the valley, so my parents could minister to the Hispanic population.

Mrs. Barrios's husband had been deported a short time ago, and she was pregnant with her eighth child. Before they lived next to us, they lived in a section of town that consisted of one-bedroom homes that were about 500 square feet each. Their new home had a second bedroom and was about twice as big. I often picked up the three smaller children and took them to church for children's activities. My parents communicated with their mother, and she always gave them permission to go.

Our town favorite was my church's vacation Bible school, where an outside church group would come from Wyoming and help. It was five nights of games, Bible lessons, and fun prizes. It all led to a Friday night carnival that our church collected prizes for all year. Kids from all over the valley would attend.

I'd loved it every year as a kid, and for the last three years, I'd taught the three, four, and five-year-olds. After I finished changing, I grabbed the three kids and made sure they were all buckled in my car. We drove to church, which was already abuzz with more activity than it had seen most of the year. Kids were lined up at the registration table in the front of the church.

Children were exchanging money for coins because in a battle of boys vs. girls, whoever had the heaviest offering bucket won points for prizes at the end of the week. I dropped the kids off in line and went inside to get my classroom ready in the church nursery.

I stacked all the toys in the crib and put blankets over it to keep the kids from playing and not listening. The felt board came out of the closet, and I cut out my felt people to demonstrate the day's Bible story. The nursery door squeaked as it opened.

Ezra stepped into the room, holding a little red piece of paper. "I've been assigned to the preschoolers."

"You're in the right place. Have you done this before?"

"I have no prior experience of working with four-year-olds."

"You get to add three and five-year-olds to your resume too."

"Yay!"

I laughed. "You'll do fine. You treat them like people and tell them Jesus loves them. That's about it."

He stepped into the room, looking around like the baby swing and changing table might grow teeth and bite him. "This is my fault."

"What?"

"They asked me where I'd like to volunteer, and I peeked at the sheet and saw your name."

"You're facing your fear of small children to spend time with me?" I touched my chest in exaggeration.

"Yeah, I didn't know what room 140 was until I got down here."

I pressed my lips together, trying to taper a giggle. "You can always back out. There are plenty of other jobs."

He shrugged. "I could, but I kind of like the teacher more than the children scare me."

"You may change your mind by the end of the night."

"Not likely."

The first child ran into the room.

Ezra waved and plastered on a stiff smile. "Welcome! Jesus loves you!"

I suppressed more giggles at him running with my instructions. Little by little, children trickled into the room. Ezra made the mistake of sitting on the ground. Five toddlers piled onto his lap, and three tried to climb on his back. His eyes begged me for help, but I found it too amusing to rescue him.

I gave the Bible lesson while Ezra refereed arguments over apple juice and toppled block towers. I packed up the lesson to start song time when Ezra walked over.

He rubbed the back of his neck. "One of them is crying."

I turned around and looked over each child. My eyes landed on Chano, curled in a little ball with tears streaking his chubby little baby cheeks. "Did you ask him what was wrong?"

"He didn't answer."

"Okay. I got this. Sing some Bible songs."

His nose twitched. "Like what?"

"Surprise me." I walked over to Chano and sat in front of him. "What's the matter, buddy?"

Ezra belted out Jesus loves me, and several children attempted somersaults but only got one leg in the air. They wobbled on one leg with their heads on the carpet.

Chano sniffled and hid his picture in his lap. "I can't colors nice."

"What do you mean? Can I see it?"

The nursery door opened, and another teacher gathered the rest of the children. It became background noise as I waited for Chano to show me his coloring sheet.

Once the room was empty, he turned the sheet over. "It's bad."

Purple scribbles covered the hands and face of the man, and blue ones decorated everything else.

"I love purple and blue together. They match. Like peanut butter and jelly."

A tiny sob escaped him. "But the kids say people don't have purple skin, and it's bad."

"How can purple be bad? It's my favorite color."

His eyes lit up. "It is?"

"Yeah, I think it's the best color ever, and I love that you picked it."

"Really?"

"Yeah, if you want me to, I'll put it on the board as the drawing of the night. It comes with a prize."

He wiped his tears. "A prize!"

"Yep, let's go see. Can I hang your picture here?"

He grinned and handed it to me. "Yeah!"

I took him over to the board, let him tell me where he wanted it, and allowed him to pick a small trinket from our toy box. Chano ran off to play with the other kids. I picked up discarded papers and turned around to see Ezra leaning in the doorway, smiling.

My eyes shifted to the side and back to him. "What?"

He shook his head a little. "Nothing."

"You're smiling like a crazy person for nothing?" There was nothing crazy about his warm smile that lit up his hazel eye, or maybe the way it made me feel bordered insanity. I wasn't sure, but I liked how my question made his grin grow.

"You're good at this." He glanced around the room.

"I guess I better be. It's what I'm destined to do."

"Mila is destined for other things."

"How do you know?"

He shrugged, and the right side of his mouth rose. "Just a hunch I get when you tell me all your stories."

"Your hunches might need more practice."

"Never failed me yet."

One of the Deacons, Mr. Gonzoles, paused in the doorway. "Hello, Molly and Elijah, it's time to go to the auditorium."

"We'll be right there, sir." Ezra watched Mr. Gonzoles disappear down the hall. "You think he'll ever get our names right?"

"Eight years after I met him, it's not looking good. He's a kind man, though."

"Yeah, just terrible with names."

"He always gets the first letter right. That's something."

Ezra and I helped with cleanup and then went to Sonic after I took the three kids I'd brought home. We sat on top of the table, like always. We ignored the existing benches. A man with spiked black hair came out from the restaurant, wearing his red Sonic shirt and black pants. He leaned against the building and puffed his cigarette. I tried my best to not glare at him.

Ezra nudged me. "What is it?"

"What?"

"You look like you want to punch someone. That's tough to imagine with you."

I shook my head. "It's nothing."

The man blew smoke out and walked over. "It's Mila, right?"

Ezra stiffened as I felt him move closer to me.

"Yeah, you're Lonzo. Riley introduced us that one time."

Lonzo grinned. "You remembered."

"It's difficult not to." I wanted to say a lot more to him, but nothing right surfaced in my mind.

"She's fun to hang out with. You can join us sometime."

Ezra scooted even closer to me. "How old are you?"

Lonzo puffed smoke in our direction. "Old enough."

"I'm sure." Ezra gritted his teeth.

Car doors and voices broke the tension. Other teens from our youth group joined us at the table. It was where most teens in Alamosa went to hang out. Kyra and Hannah sat on the bench Ezra and I sat on top of. I hopped down to hug Valerie. We'd hung out a few more times since the sand dunes. When I turned around, Ezra plopped on the bench to talk to Kyra.

I sat with Val, and she told me about her new job for a party planning company outside town close to the animal shelter I volunteered at. It hadn't occurred to me that enough happened in our town to justify a party planning company, but there were a lot of towns around the valley. Alamosa, as small as it was, had the largest population in the valley—that wasn't saying much.

I tried to focus my attention on Val and not Kyra making Ezra laugh about something. It was tough, but Val deserved my undivided attention. My head jerked up when Riley's tiny turquoise Geo pulled in, and she got out. Riley wasn't part of my church world. She was about as separate from it as possible. Disorientation played with my head at my two worlds mixing. She hopped out and walked over to Lonzo.

He stomped out his cigarette and nodded toward me. Riley looked up, and her eyes widened. She waved, and I waved back. She spoke with him for a few more minutes before they got into his car and drove away together. My stomach rolled with a sharp twinge of unease. I worried for her, but nothing I said kept her away from Lonzo. If anything, it made her spend less time with me and more with him. I talked with Val for a while, and we set up a time to have lunch together. Spending more time with Val lately kept my mind off slowly losing Riley to a guy so much older than her.

Ezra, Kyra, and Hannah were still talking, and it worried me I'd have no friends left in the end. At least I had a growing friendship with Val, and I'd always have Erin. That made me miss her, so after Val left, I waved goodbye to Ezra. Kyra was still talking to him, but his attention went to me as I got into my car. I drove away before he could get up and ask me more about it.

Erin's little sister let me inside and hugged me. I knocked on her door, and she threw it open with a glare. "Jenna! I told you not...." Her face lit up, and she threw her arms around me. "It's you! I'm so happy it's you." She squeezed me. "It's been too long! Way too long!" She dragged me into her room.

"We saw each other yesterday."

"Yeah, but I needed Mila time so badly! My siblings are driving me insane. Up the wall, insane!" She picked up her snake from her dresser and put him back in his terrarium.

I walked over and stroked his head. "He's such a pretty snake."

"I know. Best snake ever."

We plopped on her bed and put our heads together. I closed my eyes, letting the lull of her water bed soothe my anxiety.

She squeezed my hand. "Mila, what's wrong?"

"Nothing. I'm fine. Why wouldn't I be fine?"

She smiled. "Every time you say you're fine. I know you're the exact opposite."

Erin seemed to be the only person to see through my fine mask. I loved and hated it.

"You can't take what I say for it being true?"

"Not when you say you're fine."

I sighed and hesitated. "It's about Riley. You probably don't want to hear about it."

"I generally don't like hearing about Riley, but if she did something to upset you, I will listen."

Riley and Erin used to be friends, but they'd had a falling out. I'd stayed in the middle, trying to keep the peace between all of us. In the end, I couldn't, but I had to keep them both in my life. Someday maybe they'd be friends again. I told her all about Lonzo and Riley.

"Riley knows better. If she gets herself into trouble, she has no one to blame but herself."

"Yeah, I guess." I sat up and rested against her headboard. "She's going to the youth group all week. I wanted to invite you but figured you probably don't want to come if she is."

Erin sat up, causing her brown curly hair flew in every direction. "Why would you invite her before me?"

"I saw her first."

"Well, I'm going to go then."

"Okay. I'm glad."

She jerked me back down to the bed, and her bright blue eyes met mine. "Why do we have to get older, Mila? Why?"

"I don't know."

"We're going to be adults, and it's the worst thing ever."

I hugged her and nodded. "Yeah, maybe it will be."

I'd never met someone as young as Erin, who hated getting older. She cried at every birthday and insisted she'd die by thirty. I always wanted to tell her she'd probably live to ninety because life would find a way to spite her drama.

Chapter Eight: Marriage Pact

E very afternoon during VBS week was a youth group event. The first one of the week was Bible drills, a message from the visiting preacher, and then a water balloon fight to end the day. It probably wasn't the best idea to invite my two feuding best friends to the same event, but a deep part of me wanted to play peacemaker. I dreamed we would all get along again, like when we were kids. It was probably a foolish hope.

Erin and I arrived together because I'd stayed at her house for the night after I'd left Sonic. Ezra, Kyra, Hannah, and Val were already there, and I didn't want to think about how much time Kyra had gotten with Ezra. It would be a fun day, and Ezra and I would teach the preschoolers. Riley arrived, and she sat on the other side of me. Neither Erin nor Riley said anything to each other, but I became delusional as I imagined we lived in old times.

I won the Bible drill and got a yo-lloon as a prize. It was a made-up toy that was a water balloon tied to a rubber band, making it a Yo-Yo mixed with a water balloon, giving it its name. The preacher gave the message, and prayer time started, where the pastor would pray for a really long time for our souls. Prickles ran down my neck, and I looked around Riley to see Ezra staring at me. He mouthed something I didn't catch, and I hurried to close my eyes when I spotted the preacher sending me a stern look.

The water war started, and Erin sent the first balloon flying at Riley. That prompted an onslaught of balloons flying in both directions. Their fight distracted me from Ezra sneaking up behind me and smashing me in the back with a balloon. I launched three more at him and ran around the back of the building. He ran after me, and I hurried down the concrete steps that led to the large basement door. The white chipping paint showed its neglect, and I hesitated. Basements spooked me. Ezra's footsteps gave me bravery, and I slipped inside.

He flung the door open and flung three balloons at me. I threw the one I'd hung onto and sacrificed my yo-lloon on his head.

I ducked around some boxes. "We shouldn't throw balloons inside."

"The floor is concrete. You only say that because I have an entire bag full."

"You can't waste them all on me."

"We could team up and throw them at Kyra."

I popped my head out of hiding. "Really?"

He launched one that got me in the shoulder while laughing. "Yeah."

"Cheater! You lure me out and then pounce."

"It's a good war strategy." He moved around the boxes with his hands up. "We'll go throw balloons at Kyra if you tell me why you left in such a hurry last night."

"I needed to see Erin."

"Did she have an emergency?"

"No, I missed her."

He stepped closer. "I missed you after you left."

"Well, here we are now."

The whistle blew, calling us all back to the front of the church. I stepped around him, and he took my hand to lead me up the narrow basement steps and back outside. We both released hands as soon as we came into view of the street. We found everyone at the front waiting, and Riley grinned when she saw me walk around with Ezra.

Erin had her arms crossed, glaring at Riley. She leaned over to me. "You shouldn't have left me with her," she whispered.

"I got caught up in the battle." I smiled at Ezra.

The preacher prayed one more time and dismissed us. We all decided to walk to the park at the elementary school. Riley pulled me back with her, and that left Erin and Ezra ahead to talk.

"Why haven't you asked that boy out yet?" Riley stared at the back of Ezra's head.

"Ezra?"

"No, that man picking up pop cans over there. Of course, I mean Ezra."

"I don't know. He's my best friend. That's all."

She snickered and shook her head. "Sure, Mila, keep telling yourself that."

"You remember when we were little, and we'd cross our arms and spin with our hands holding tightly together? We'd spin so fast and pretend it made us go other worlds."

"Yes, nice subject change. Your point?"

"Sometimes I wish it really worked. We could spin into another life." My eyes stayed focused on the boy several feet in front of me.

"A life where you didn't have strict parents and could be with Ezra."

"That's not what... It's not."

"Sure, Mila, everyone believes that." She elbowed me.

"I think he likes Kyra. He talked with her for a long time at the Sonic last night."

"Kyra?"

My eyes shifted to where Kyra walked on the grass with her sister and Val. "The one in the middle."

"You have nothing to worry about there, Mila."

"You can't tell that."

She looked me up and down and then looked at Kyra. "Yeah, I can. You realize you're a carbon copy of a young Kate Beckinsale."

"Who?"

She rolled her eyes. "The Pearl Harbor actress."

"I have no idea who that is."

"Of course, you don't. My point is you always sell yourself short. You want me to assassinate Kyra for you?"

"Don't tempt me."

She put her arm around me. "I got your back always."

"Same. That's why Lonzo worries me."

Her arm dropped. "Not again, Mila. Come on. I support you in who you like; you support me."

"He's twenty-five, Riley."

"Age doesn't matter."

"It does when you're sixteen."

She shook her head. "Whatever. I was going to tell you what we did last night but never mind."

I stopped walking, feeling dread creep into my feet. "What happened?"

"Never mind."

"You're going to end up like Rachel."

"I'm not that stupid. I'd never marry a guy because he knocked me up and my church leaders said I had to. I don't subscribe to that kind of crazy."

We arrived at the park and sat down on the swings, racing to see who could get the highest like we had as kids. It was like all the drama flew away as we fought to reach the sky. Metal chains fastening to the wooden seats kept dragging us back to the ground. Flying would always be an illusion. We leaped to the ground, and gravel flew at our landing. Riley brushed off her knees and groaned at Erin running toward us.

Erin threw her arms around me. "I'm getting married!"

"What?"

She pointed at Ezra. "Ezra and I made a sacred pact. If neither of us gets married by the time I'm thirty, we're going to marry each other."

"You just met him." I hugged her back. "You can't get engaged to a boy you just met!"

"We're not engaged. Only if we don't find our people by the time I'm thirty."

"You like him?"

"No, he's a nice guy, but neither of us wants to end up alone."

"Well, that's just great! Do I get to be the maid of honor and best man in this wedding because which best friend do I choose to be there for?"

"Why are you mad? We have a lot of years before I'm thirty, so it's not like I'd marry someone I don't know. I'll get to know him better," she said.

"I hope you live happily ever after."

Erin frowned. "You don't sound like you wish that."

Riley rolled her eyes. "You're pretty dense, Erin. You should realize why Mila is upset."

Erin looked at me. "Why?"

"I'm not mad. I'm fine."

"Oh, you are mad."

Ezra jogged over. "What's up, everyone?"

I pursed my lips. "You're engaged now."

"Oh." His eyes shifted around like his engagement was a crime against me.

"Congratulations!" I stormed back toward the church.

Riley caught up with me and waited until we got a bit away from the others. "Yeah, you don't like Ezra at all. You realize Erin is just dramatic. She always said she'll be dead by thirty."

"I have to dread her turning thirty years in advance. She will either die or marry Ezra."

Riley put her arm around me as though she'd forgotten everything I'd said about Lonzo. "Neither thing is going to happen. You're as dramatic as her sometimes."

"You're right. I'm being dumb about it." I didn't understand why I reacted so strongly to Erin getting fake engaged to Ezra. Both were hopeless romantics, and it shouldn't have been a giant surprise they'd want to secure not being alone in the future.

"I don't think it's that you're dumb. It's that you wish Ezra had made a marriage pact with you."

I opened my mouth to refute her comment but realized she was right. "Why wouldn't Ezra make that agreement with me? We actually know each other."

"Because I think he's hoping he'll end up with you long before he has to follow through with Erin."

I lowered my eyes to the sidewalk in defeat. "Ezra doesn't feel that way about me."

"Whatever you say."

Riley and I shifted the conversation to our jobs. When we got back to the church, I got my classroom ready. Ezra and I taught the little kids but didn't speak much. He kept glancing at me like he'd done something wrong I should be mad at him for. When VBS ended for the night, Amber invited me over to her house. I agreed, and after taking care of my birds, I drove to her house, where we watched one movie before Amber went to bed.

Ezra and I took a walk and stopped in the middle of a field. A tumbleweed rolled by as we sat with our legs tucked under us.

"I don't want to end up alone," he said.

I jerked my gaze from the stars to his face. The moon lit up his squared jawline with a tiny bit of stubble that showed the boy I loved deeply was growing up, and I didn't know when that had happened. The years slipped away, never to be seen again, and Erin's dread for fleeting youth burrowed inside me as I stared at Ezra. It made me push back tears.

"There's no way that will ever happen." I put my hand on his knee like that sealed some kind of promise I was giving him.

"How do you know?" He placed his hand over mine.

"Because there's no way you won't ever be wanted by someone."

He chuckled. "Sure."

I know because I will always want you. I bit my lip to keep from saying it. "If nothing else, you and Erin will have each other."

He took out his music player and handed me one earbud. "Well, maybe if your wings weren't so itchy, I wouldn't have to make life-changing promises with Erin."

"My wings itchy?"

He turned his head to face Mt. Blanca. "They like the idea of flying over the mountain too much."

"So fly away with me."

"Maybe someday I will." He turned on the music.

I closed my eyes to take the moment into my soul, wishing that someday Ezra would fly away with me.

Chapter Nine: Mr. Rogers Bites

♥

I kept glancing at the clock, eager for Ezra to pick me up, so we could climb our mountain for the first time. He'd be picking me up at 2:00, and the last hour crawled with the pace of a snail stuck in a blizzard, trying to make his way home. I loved it at the animal shelter, but hiking with Ezra had me too excited to focus entirely on the animals for the day. With a ton more effort than usual, I gave them my best. It wasn't unusual for Ezra to visit me at the shelter or even pick me up, but today held even more excitement.

The half-wolf dog howled in grief at what he had just lost. He intimidated many of my fellow volunteers due to his wild half, so I'd accepted responsibility for him. His eyes had shown, despite sharp fangs, he had a gentle soul, and he'd proven me right.

It didn't mean I didn't respect he was inherently untamed. Wild animals needed to be seen as such. They couldn't be expected to behave the way humans called civilized. Chico and I got along with mutual respect, my knowledge of wolf packs, and a kindness we both valued.

He plopped his head in my lap and gazed up at me with sad yellow eyes, whimpering.

I scratched behind his ear. "It couldn't be helped, buddy."

He howled in disagreement and seemed to feel deeper than the other dogs I'd cared for over the last two years I'd volunteered at the humane society. We were the only no-kill shelter in the Valley. The alternative was the pound that euthanized after only 72 hours. I believed strongly in the humane society's mission, so week after week, I spent hours helping them out. I had two primary jobs there, and a bunch of smaller ones.

The first was taking care of any wild birds that came into the shelter. The more delicate ones I took home to care for more frequently. My second job was to run the recovery room at the spay and neuter clinics. The shelter director, Mrs. Malone, had promoted me pretty quickly.

Chico's owner arrived, and I went over discharge instructions. The wolf-dog howled all the way out of the building.

"Mila!" Carter shouted from the hallway.

I groaned at not having made it through my entire shift without interacting with him. He tormented me endlessly, and Riley told me it was because he liked me. That seemed a backward approach to it. If a boy wanted me to like him, he should be kind.

I turned to Laura, who was helping me in the recovery room. "Are you okay if I go see what Carter needs?"

"Yeah, we only have two dogs left. I can handle it."

"Mila!" Carter shouted louder.

I hurried into the hall, where he stood in front of a large kennel. "What is it?"

He lifted his hand, and blood dripped to the floor. "It bites!"

I walked around the front and peeked in at the black and tan, snarling Rottweiler mix. "What are we so angry about, Mister..." I glanced closer at his tag. "Rogers. Oh, that's an ironic name for an angry animal."

"He doesn't seem the type to be friendly to his neighbors."

"Maybe he's misunderstood. "

Carter gritted his teeth. His bleached blonde hair flopped in front of his green eyes. "My hand disagrees. "

"Okay. What did you try?"

"I tried to stick the leash on him, and he bolted. The back door started to open, and he went right for it. I tackled him. "

"You tackled him?"

"That's what I said. "

"Well, that's why you got bit, but at least we don't have a loose dog on our hands."

"No kidding, Sherlock. I took one for the team." He stuck his lip out as he frowned at his wound before he stuck the injury in my face. "Do you think it needs stitches? If Doc okays it, we can go in the back, and I'll let you stitch me up."

I inspected his wound. "You can go to the ER for that. It doesn't look super deep, but I'd at least call your doctor and hear their recommendations. You have to report this too."

"Can you at least help me out with some first aid?" He stuck his lip out more.

I rolled my eyes. "Go have Carla help you."

"Carla works the front desk. She doesn't have your touch." He placed his hand on mine.

I jerked away. "Hands to yourself."

"Come on. Please! I don't want an old lady fixing my ouchie up."

"Ouchie? What does it matter? "

"You have a steadier hand. I've seen you work surgeries. "

I squinted. "You act like I'm the vet. Just because he let me assist with surgeries a few times doesn't mean I can stitch you up."

"You stitched up that cat."

"With his guidance. I will get you a Bandaid, but that's where it ends."

"I'll take it to get you alone in the supply closet. Seven minutes in heaven, anyone?"

"Seven minutes in heaven? Is that where you hyperventilate and then hold your breath until you pass out? I had a friend do that once and..." My voice trailed off as he roared in laughter.

He caught his breath but let out small gasps. "Why don't you let me show you exactly what it is?"

"I do not want to resuscitate you."

"If you have to resuscitate me after what we're about to do, I will marry you."

I scrunched my nose. "No, thank you!"

He grabbed my hand with his non-bloody one and yanked me toward the front. We made it close to the exit where the supply closet sat next to. Ezra was standing at the front desk talking to Carla. The elderly woman walked to the back office, leaving me alone with the two boys.

He turned and stared at my hand in Carter's. "Umm... Are we still hiking?"

Carter jerked me forward. "You can have her as soon as I show her what seven minutes in heaven is."

Ezra coughed a little. "What?"

"A dog bit him, and he's about to do something stupid, I think."

Ezra gaped slightly and moved closer to me, pointing at the clock. "It's two."

Carter tugged me closer to the closet. "All I need is seven minutes."

Ezra took a step toward the closet. "With yourself. "

Screams came from behind us, and I jerked my hand away from Carter, bolting toward the back. Laura was gawking at the door that gave a nice view of tumbleweeds and dry shrubs. Mr. Rogers's cage door was wide open, and he appeared nowhere around.

I ran toward the exit to see a brown and black streak tearing off toward the mesas. "You let a dog out while the back door was open?" I turned to face Laura for an explanation.

Her shoulders raised, and she lowered her head. "Doc said he needed the dog that was in the hall. I thought I would put its leash on like normal, and it would be fine. He tried to bite me, and I got scared."

I relaxed some tension on my face. "It's okay. This is Carter's fault, anyway."

Carter gasped. "My fault! How do you figure that one?"

"If you hadn't been trying to pass out in the closet, you would have told Doc what happened before Laura was told to get Mr. Rogers."

"Everyone knows I don't have an ounce of responsibility in me, and you are the epitome of responsibility. That makes this your fault."

"Okay. You're kind of right on that."

Ezra leaned on the doorjamb. "We all know it was his stupid fault."

Carter sized Ezra up. "What do you know?"

"A lot more than you."

"Really?"

Ezra pushed off the door. "Yeah."

I put my hand up. "At this point, it doesn't matter whose fault it is. We have to report this and get Mr. Rogers back. We need to tell Doc."

Carter threw his hand in the air. "One-two-three! Not it!"

"I'll do it."

Laura shook her head. "It's really my fault. I'll tell him."

"Okay. I'm going to go look for him then."

Ezra pulled his keys from his pocket. "My truck can go over rough terrain."

I grabbed a few treats, a special harness, and a leash. "Okay. Let's go."

Ezra and I rushed to his truck, and he sped in the direction I'd seen the dog bound. We drove for a while, not spotting anything promising.

"Seven minutes in heaven, huh?" Ezra fiddled with his radio until he found "Kryptonite" by Three Doors Down.

"Yeah, he wanted to show me what it was."

"Of course he did. He's such an idiot."

I leaned forward and pointed. "There! I think that's him."

Ezra shot the truck forward until it became clear Mr. Rogers was ahead. He stopped the car, and I threw my door open.

He touched my arm. "You're just going to run after a dog that bit someone and almost bit another?"

"Yeah, that's my job."

"It could attack you."

"Yes, it's about respecting that."

"What?"

I jumped out of the car. "I know what I'm doing."

Ezra got out on his side and grabbed his skateboard. "I got your back."

"You're going to hit him with a skateboard?"

"If he attacks you, yeah."

Mr. Rogers stopped running in circles and snarled. I tossed a treat at him, and he gobbled it up. After a few more treats, he cautiously approached. He growled, keeping his tail down and ears back. He gave fair warnings that people seemed to have missed.

"It's okay, buddy." I held the back of my hand out to him and tossed another treat.

He stretched his head toward me without taking a step forward, sniffing my hand. I turned my hand over with a bunch of treats in it, and while he gobbled them, I eased the harness around him. He jerked back and growled, snapping at me. Ezra stiffened and lifted his skateboard. I held my hand up to stop him and tossed more treats on the ground. Mr. Rogers gobbled them down, and I made a trail to the truck until he hopped into it. Ezra got in the other side, and we drove back to the shelter.

I got Mr. Rogers out of the truck and walked him inside, where his owner stood with his arms crossed, glaring at a sheepish-looking Carter. Mr. Rogers's butt wagged, and he leaped at his owner. The crisis had been averted, but it meant I had extra paperwork. After all the time we'd spent searching for the dog and filling out reports, it had grown dark.

Ezra walked me to the parking lot. "I guess we better take on the mountain another day."

"Maybe next Saturday. There's no clinic, so we could go in the morning."

"Sounds perfect. How about Pizza Den instead, then?"

I nearly jumped up and down. "Best pizza ever!"

"Yes, my brother told me you thought that."

My cheeks burned. "He told you about the email?"

"Yeah."

I shifted my eyes. "Pizza Den, then?"

Carter walked out of the building and snapped his fingers into a point my direction. "You, me, the closet next time?"

"Go suffocate yourself on your own time," I said

Ezra burst into laughter. "Brilliant suggestion."

I covered my mouth. "Don't actually do that. I didn't mean it the way it came out. Ignore that. But I'm not getting into a closet with you next time."

Carter shook his head. "Your innocence is hot sometimes. I'd like to help you lose that."

Ezra's jaw twitched as he glared at Carter. "I could help you lose something."

Carter waved his fingers toward himself. "Go ahead."

Ezra stared at him, and Carter stared back as some sort of challenge passed between them.

I stepped between them and waved my hands. "Boys to their own cars."

As soon as Carter retreated to his car, Ezra got in his truck. He rolled down his window. "Meet you there?"

"Yeah," I said.

Ezra drove off, and I waved at Doc, who was walking out with a couple of techs. I climbed into my car and studied the mountain as I drove. One day, Ezra and I would finally make it to the mountain. He had a table waiting for us when I arrived, and we spent the evening eating pizza and chatting. Although it wasn't what we'd planned, I still loved any time I got with him.

Chapter Ten: Finally There

♥

I threaded my hair through the back of my ball cap and ran to the kitchen at the sound of Ezra's truck pulling into my driveway.

"Where are you going?" My brother blocked my way to the front door.

"I'm going out with friends." I grabbed the small cooler that held the sandwiches I'd made and tried to step around him.

"Did you tell Mom and Dad?"

"Yeah, move!"

"So, you won't mind if I tell them then," he said.

"Go right ahead."

On more than one occasion, I'd wished that our trailer had more than one exit, and that desire was strong at that moment. My bedroom window became an alternative route, and I rushed to climb out of it. I slid the blue cooler to the ground, hopped down, and ran around to the driveway.

My brother popped his head out the front door. "I'm telling Mom and Dad you went out your window because you were going somewhere you shouldn't."

I leaped into Ezra's truck. "Go!"

He stared at me for a second. "Nice hat."

"Thanks. Go!"

He stared at my brother. "Am I your getaway driver?"

"You're supposed to be, but you're doing a terrible job at it right now."

He grinned and put his truck in reverse, finally driving us toward our mountain. It was a breezy summer day, which caused tumbleweeds to dart out into traffic. My stomach bubbled the closer we got to our destination, even though I'd probably driven by Mount Blanca a hundred times or more.

Usually, when we turned north toward the dunes, we didn't stop until we reached them. This time, Ezra traveled about halfway down the road until we turned at the sign that announced the Zapata Falls entrance. I bounced around in my seat and leaned against the window to watch the desert terrain morph into pine trees and yellow grass. We pulled into the parking lot, and I jumped out, flying to a large boulder.

I flung my arms into the air. "We made it to our mountain!"

Ezra leaned against a tree and laughed. "We haven't made it far enough yet."

"Yes, but this still counts. The soil is Mount Blanca soil!"

"You're technically on a rock."

I hopped to the ground and charged toward the trail. "The waterfall is going to be pretty amazing."

"Yeah, pretty much anything is when you get this excited."

I stopped, causing Ezra to nearly slam into my back. "The picnic!"

He pointed to the chipping benches that were probably a bright red at one point. "I thought we'd eat there after we worked up an appetite on our hike."

"We should eat under the waterfall. That would be amazing."

"Soggy bread is the lunch I've dreamed about."

I started back up our hike like I had ten minutes to halt an explosion. "It's in plastic, but you have a point that it's probably not ideal to have a picnic there. It would be a lot of work to haul it all the way up."

"Exactly."

"For the sake of your laziness, we'll eat at the end."

He jogged to catch up to me. "Appreciate it. It's tough enough on my lungs to keep up with your enthusiasm. I thought you'd want to soak in every moment of this."

I picked up my pace to a near jog. Even with the path steepening, I had no choice but to go full speed toward something I'd dreamed about every time I'd gazed at the sign announcing the entrance to Zapata. "We can enjoy it on the way down or the million other times we'll have to go here. Now that we know what we've missed, staring at it from the distance of your house will leave us only wanting to be here."

"Yeah, but staring at the mountain also involves the stars."

I pointed to the narrow dirt trail to our right that wound up a higher part of the mountain. "Imagine what the stars would look like from the top of that."

"We'll have to find out at some point when we have flashlights. Wouldn't be ideal for navigating that through the dark."

"One misstep and the rocks spell doom."

Our path tilted at a slight angle, and a sharp ache settled into my calves as I forced them up the brutal incline. The ground leveled out into slimy brown rocks. Ezra took my hand as he helped me over the terrain that grew slippery the closer we got to the tranquil stream that led to the waterfall. Extensive rock walls closed in to create an almost cave, and we carefully hopped onto stones protruding from the chilled water that nipped at my ankles.

My jaw dropped as we reached our goal. A rush of white water cascaded down the coppery rocks that green moss covered in patches. We leaned against the naturally formed wall and dangled our legs inches above the stream. No words passed between us as we absorbed the moment. We'd found the stillness Ezra had thought I'd find on the journey up, but it was the roar and frothy white bubbling with a beautiful background that called for me to take inside my soul to keep forever.

That moment would wrap around me until Zapata became something in my blood. It would circulate into nostalgia any time I recalled the memories made there. A ghost of myself would always remain in the mountains long after I left. Part of me sensed it even then, sitting next to Ezra, and it seemed the experience was the same for him.

We crept along the edge until we made it to the wider opening. My fingers wiggled in the water as it fell over my arm. It sent shivers through me. Ezra stood close to me with his arm hovering around my waist as though he worried I might fall. I leaned back into his touch, enjoying how it sent flutters through my stomach. There in an isolated world, we could pretend stringent rules didn't apply to us.

I didn't want to analyze what it meant to feel this way about a boy because forced principles might ruin it, and I wanted nothing terrible to touch the way Ezra held me. The sweetness of it didn't feel like temptation; it felt like home. Maybe that had always been the point of the mountain. We stared at it, knowing it was a place that belonged to us, where everything that burdened us couldn't reach.

He rested his head on my shoulder and wrapped his arms around me. "This is the best."

"It is. Can we move here?"

"Sure. I'll build us a log cabin at the top of the mountain."

"The very top, top of the tallest place on Mount Blanca?"

His laughter moved against my back. "Would there be anywhere else to put it?"

I shook my head and smiled at the idea of it. "No, nowhere else."

A group of tourists with cameras around their necks interrupted our dreaming, and we headed back toward the trail. We took our time on the way down to soak in the landscape. Ezra sat on the table rather than the bench like he always did at Sonic, and I grabbed the picnic from his truck. We sat cross-legged in front of each other and munched on our sandwiches.

He finished one and grabbed another. "You make the best sandwiches. Seriously, have I ever told you that? Your pies are the best too. It may be why I'm in..." He stopped talking and rushed a bite.

"Why you're what?"

He shrugged. "It's getting late, or I'd suggest we try the trail to go higher."

"That would be an adventure. Imagine if we could do this on a hundred mountains. We could get a list and check them all off."

"That works for me." Our conversation lulled as Ezra finished two more sandwiches. He seemed a bottomless pit when it came to food; that's why I'd packed him so much to eat.

I was more of a snacker. Small amounts, more often, and everyone said I ate like a bird. I didn't mind the comparison.

The sky had dimmed into the purple of almost night when we packed everything up and got back into Ezra's truck. On the way home, Ezra turned on the radio and took my hand. I leaned against the window and let the warmth of his hand and the truck's sway lead me to sleep.

I woke up to Ezra nudging me and blinked my eyes open. "Back already?"

"Time flies when you're sleeping."

"Time flies when you're having the best time." I hopped out of his truck and stopped to smile at him. "That was the best ever."

"Yeah, it was."

My parents' car still wasn't in the driveway, which brought relief. I went inside and put the leftover items from the picnic into the fridge.

"You were out with Ezra. Mom and Dad are going to love that."

I jumped as a sharp twinge shot through my chest at my brother's voice sounding behind me. "Were you staring out the window, waiting for the second I came back?"

"His truck is noisy, and I saw you leave with him. As soon as they get back, they're going to know about this."

Nausea tried to break through the blissful warmth of a perfect day with Ezra. "Why are you so against me? Everyone talks about how an older brother is supposed to protect their little sister. All you do is try to sabotage me."

"I am protecting you from your flesh."

"Yeah, that's why you smile while I get punished."

"If you sin, you deserve what you get."

I blinked away tears as I headed to my room to await my fate. When the knock hit my door a couple of hours later, I was nearing hysteria. No one would notice the storm making anxious holes in my stomach. I did all I could to make sure my outside only looked calm and came nowhere close to matching the inside.

Faking calm and downplaying my emotions would help me survive this. Invalidating how I felt was a survival mechanism that had served me well through childhood. I unlocked my door and retreated to the safety of my bed. My parents entered, and my mom had her overly concerned eyes that watered and made her brows knit together. My dad's tight mouth made me want to shrink under my covers and never leave.

My dad crossed his arms, and his mustache twitched a little. "James says you were out with the Henderson boy."

I glanced at his belt and gripped my blanket until my knuckles shot pain through my wrist. It grounded me, and I did a terrible thing. "Erin and Riley went with us, and we just had a picnic and looked at the waterfall." It would have made sense to use Amber's name, but she wouldn't have covered for me if my parents asked her.

"They were there the whole time?"

"Yes, Ezra's has tinted windows on his truck, so James probably didn't see them."

"Okay. You know the rules. You're not to be alone with a boy, not even in public. If you ever want to court, we would need a sit down with the boy and his family to come up with guidelines that would involve a chaperone schedule and a pathway toward marriage. This is for your protection."

My eyes stayed fastened to my pink quilt that had colorful silhouettes of fancy ladies holding umbrellas. The little threads that purposefully stuck out between squares calmed me when I picked at them. "I know, Daddy. Can I go to Riley's?"

"Yes, call us from her house when you get there."

They left, and I hurried to pack my bag. I'd lied to my parents, and it was unraveling me. I had to be more careful in the future. Ezra and I would have to be sneakier. I drove the thirty minutes to Riley's house in tears. Her mom called her when she opened the door to see me.

Riley looked me over and stepped outside, closing the door behind her. "What's wrong?"

I told her the entire thing and sunk in shame onto her porch swing. "I lied to them!"

She put her arm around me as she sat down. "Good."

"What?"

"I'm not normally for lying, but I'm for my best friend not getting beat. Good for you for going out with a boy and having a great afternoon."

"Everyone is right about me. I'm going to grow up to be a terrible person. I sit in church, staring at my Bible, feeling this terrible pull to other things. All I can think is someday I'm going to disappoint my mother exactly as she expects me to." I shoved the tears off my cheeks.

"She expects you to?"

"Why else would they feel they have to restrict me so much for my protection? I have an evil heart, and they know that. My lying proves it."

She used her feet to start the swing up. "You know what strict parents create more often than alcoholics, drug addicts, and sluts?"

I gaped at her word choices. "W-what?"

"Liars. Their kids become natural liars because they have to avoid things that come naturally to them. When the kids inevitably do things they shouldn't, they have to lie to protect themselves. All it does is make the parents not know anything about their kids' lives."

"Their strategy works on my brother. He's perfect. That's why they love him more. Especially my mom. My dad might like me slightly better than James."

"That's sad you think all that, Mila. James is far from perfect. He lives to see you punished, and he throws chairs at you. That's about as far from perfect as you can get."

"He only hit me once. I get out of the way fast now."

She sighed and rubbed her forehead. "There's so much wrong with all of that, Mila. You need to learn to not make excuses for people who hurt you. You're not to blame because your brother gets violent."

On the surface, I acknowledged her words, but what I saw as my depravity made it seem like my fault. Lying protected me from judgment and consequences. That was the terrible truth I realized that day. The Bible said lying was an abomination, and I often felt that's what I was by all the urges and feelings that wanted to pour out of me. They would disappoint my mother, exactly how I feared. What would that mean then?

Riley gently elbowed me. "Tell me all about this hike with Ezra."

Guilt played in the background to become louder later. "It was the best day ever. It really was."

"Then don't let anyone ever punish you for it or any other day like it."

My anxiety took a break, and warmth flooded me as I remembered what it felt like to have Ezra's arms around me and his wonderful scent lingering with his cheek next to mine. I stored the memory in a place where it felt safe from my parents' sharp gazes.

Chapter Eleven: Grief and Sin

The internal walls to my trailer were comprised of thin wooden panels. The one subject notebook that rested on my end table was several times thicker than the boards dividing up the rooms in my house. Additionally, our phones were all connected, which meant if you made a phone call, another person in the house could listen in without you being aware. They could simply place their hand over the receiver to block out their breathing and background noise.

My brother's favorite pastime was listening to my phone conversations. Luckily, he was at college most of the year, but in the summer, nothing was safe, and I had to take extra measures to hide everything. Nothing thrilled him more than to tell my parents the latest way I was slipping spiritually. Between the walls, the phone system, and my brother, nothing was private.

This also meant I heard every phone call made to my parents in the middle of the night about everything terrible happening with church members. Not from listening in on the phone but from their voices flowing clearly through the walls. When the phone next to me woke me at one in the morning, I knew things were bad. They were always bad when that happened.

My dad's voice leaked through the walls. "She had the baby already? Okay. We'll be right there."

My mother had a quiet voice. Even when she was upset with me, her volume stayed soft. It was in her eyes and mouth I could tell her emotions. She said something I couldn't make out.

"That's what happens when people allow sin to grow in their lives. There are consequences. Sometimes very difficult ones," my dad said.

A few minutes later, my door opened, and my mom popped her head in. "Kendra Gonzales had a baby. It's too little to make it, and Dad and I have to go to the hospital to be with the family."

I sat up, sucking in a harsh breath dealt from shock. "Okay. Can I do anything?"

"Pray. This is an example of the pain sin brings."

The door shut, leaving me in the darkness that spread the heaviness faster. Kendra Gonzales used to be a close friend of mine. We'd run away together when we were eight for about fifteen minutes until we got scared and returned home. For a long time we were inseparable. It was before Riley, Erin, and Ezra became my everything, and Kendra found her own set of friends.

My heart ached for her, and it didn't feel like sin was causing her pain. I wanted to run all the way to the hospital and tell her that, but most of me hoped no one would tell her sin caused this. It would be bad to dispel something no one had said to her, so I stayed fastened to my bed, praying no one would say that to her until sunlight dawned a morning that arrived grey.

The funeral happened five days later, after Kendra's one pound son had held onto life for three. I helped set everything up and waited for her to arrive. I sat on a pew in the nearly empty auditorium, hearing things I didn't want to hear. The black dress I wore expressed my support the best I knew how, because I thought that was what you wore to a funeral. I'd only been to one before; that was my dad's dad when I was eight.

My grandma had called while my parents were out and, in one sentence, told me my grandpa had died. She had schizophrenia and bipolar disorder, so the abruptness was something I was used to. When I'd told my brother what she said, he screamed at me for ten minutes that I was a liar. It seemed all he saw was my sin every day since. That was what people saw so clearly about everyone in this place. Sin was on display, and the somber occasion of burying a baby was no different. Our church had held many funerals, but I was never allowed to go. My parents wanted me to see this one. My dad and the deacons stood at the front of the church with a few women, including my mother, as we waited for the casket to arrive.

"Obviously, the way to fix this in God's eyes is for her to marry him. That's how her sin will be forgiven," someone said.

They all agreed my sixteen-year-old friend needed to marry the twenty-five-year-old man who had gotten her pregnant. That would bring them forgiveness. A plan was made then for arrangements that included counseling sessions on how marriage should work. When I took my seat to wait for things to start, Vallery sat on one side and Ezra on the other.

Vallery pointed to the window where a little blue bird sat. "Look, it's like the sand dunes."

Ezra snickered. "You two and birds."

I squeezed Vallery's hand. "It's something we bond over."

She smiled back at me. "True. The bluebird represents all of us."

Ezra narrowed his eyes at the window. "How so?"

"It represents our friendship. Bright color in an otherwise dull world."

I nodded, watching the little bird peck on the glass. "And how someday we'll soar away to bigger things."

The casket arrived, maybe the size of a ruler, and a doll dressed in white rested in it. It was the smallest person I'd ever seen while I arranged bouquets around it as I'd been asked to do. Flowers to decorate what many saw as evil's consequence. The service started, and Kendra sat at the front with Daniel, the man she was supposed to marry. She had no apparent bones as she wilted and wailed.

Silent tears flowed down my cheeks. Ezra handed me a tissue, but I used it to twist and rip in my icy hands. He sat next to me, but we kept a hymnal between us when I needed to remove it. When I saw Kendra, I saw Riley; when I saw Daniel, I saw Lonzo. Fear for one friend consumed grief for the other until they blurred into unrecognizable things.

I needed to stop because none of this was about me or what I felt. It was all about Kendra, but that was precisely it. My body took her blatant pain inside until I couldn't breathe. When they took the casket to the graveside, I ran into the small church bathroom and threw up my breakfast. I collapsed on the tiny floor, not understanding why my spirit had become tumultuous.

I grabbed a small waxy paper cup from the dispenser and drank some water, wiping my mouth with a paper towel and making use of the gum in my pocket. After a few more minutes, my face had calmed enough to look fine. I plastered a stoic expression and went to the parking lot where Ezra was waiting. He opened his truck door for me and got in the other side.

He said nothing but reached over and took my hand, running his thumb over it. The heavy air sat between us, but he made it breathable.

We watched the tiny casket drop into the ground and went home. Ezra came out to my barn shed and helped me feed my birds.

I made it through the chickens before my shoulders shook, and a cry fell from me that I muffled with control. Ezra grabbed me and turned me to face him. I sobbed against his chest, keeping as quiet as possible. He let me cry and handed me another tissue from a pack in his pocket.

I met his eyes and realized he was crying too. I wiped one of his tears away, threw my arms around him, and we wept together. This had to be the worst grief I'd ever feel, and it wasn't even my own. Many times, since I wished it had been the worst. Not because I wished this had happened, but because one day, it would be sorrow that wholly belonged to me that would fracture my heart. That moment with Ezra in the barn was a preview of things to come. I walked Ezra to his car and went inside.

My mother was in the kitchen, stirring the crock-pot. Chicken and cream soup had a garlic scent that filled the air. It was what she made nearly every Sunday and on funeral days. "Can you set the table?"

I washed my hands well at the sink and got down the plates and cups. "Only four places?"

"Yes, I wanted to talk to you."

My entire body flinched, and I rushed to the table to avoid my mom noticing. "About what?"

"I know you think we're tough on you."

"I-I don't think that."

"Certain friends you have might make it seem like we're too strict, but today should be a clear picture as to why. What happened to Kendra is what happens when parents don't enforce proper conduct. Like your cousin. Her parents were loose on their standards and look at what happened there. I hope you understand now why your dad and I have the rules we do. We care about your soul and the battle of the flesh."

I grabbed the silverware and placed it on the blue plastic tablecloth. "I know. You only want to keep me safe."

"We've done a good job because you stay out of trouble."

"Right."

My mom called my brother and father, and we started the meal. My father reinforced my mother's words, and my brother agreed. They all agreed this was a good lesson for me not to learn the hard way. All I saw replaying over and over was Kendra's pain, and while I couldn't relate, I knew it would stay with her for the rest of her life. This lesson I was supposed to learn was too high a price for me to make it a cautionary tale for myself. It deserved more thought and meaning than that. That was all I knew as everyone but me sat there agreeing this would help me think twice before sinning.

I glanced at the clock for the fiftieth time. Where was Riley, was the question for the hour. We'd decided to sign up for a membership at the rec center together. I'd confirmed the time with her three times, but she was nowhere in sight. Normally, panic would have been reigning the situation as I cycled through horrific things that could have happened to her. Instead, a sinking disappointment had taken over because I knew where she was.

She'd stood me up three times in the last couple of months, and it was always for the same reason. When the clock on my dash glowed an hour beyond our meeting time, I started back up my car and drove to where I knew I'd find her. Sure enough, her turquoise Geo with the purple mirror dice sat in the parking lot of the pool hall, which was Lonzo's favorite place to hang out.

I waited hours for her to come out because I was never one for public confrontation. She talked to Lonzo at the exit, and he left. She headed to her car, and I jumped out. The time waiting had left me enraged, and I was going to yell at her until she felt guilty for not showing up for our plans.

Her eyebrows popped up. "Mila?"

I crossed my arms tightly and did nothing to hide my emotions. She was clearly wrong, would see that, and feel bad. "Did you forget we were meeting about the gym today?"

She glanced at her watch. "No, I remembered, but Lonzo invited me to play pool. You know I couldn't pass that up."

"You could have called my emergency phone."

"And hear you complain that it's a dollar a minute?"

"You could have come out to the gym and told me we needed to reschedule."

She crinkled her nose, and her upper lip twitched. "Why? You should know I can't pass an opportunity like this up. Clearly, you figured out where I was, so it wasn't like it was a big mystery. You could have come in and joined us."

"That wasn't the point! You shrugged me off for a guy almost ten years older than you! We're best friends! Best friends don't do that to each other. Beth and Jody wouldn't have done that to each other!"

She rolled her eyes. "Yes, because we're still kids. They wouldn't have done that to each other because they are fictional characters with excellent screenwriters. You're so naïve it makes you delusional. An innocent little church girl has no idea how the world works. I have to guide you through all of it. Well, it's exhausting."

"I'm sorry I'm such a burden to have as a friend!"

"Times like this you are! Trying to shove your morals on me when I don't want them!"

"I'm not trying to shove my morals on you. You stood me up! Left me waiting for an hour."

She shook her head and opened her car door. "That's what I'm talking about, Mila. No one else would have sat in a parking lot for over an hour, believing the person might be running late. You see life through an ignorant lens; that's why Lonzo and I make little sense to you."

"But Kendra—"

"Wasn't the brightest. That's not going to be me. Stop bringing her up."

"I'm scared for you! Terrified."

She bit out a sharp laugh. "You're always scared of everything. A coward, too terrified to stand up for yourself and face reality. You hide away and let everyone take advantage of you! You're scared for me?" She snorted. "You should be scared for yourself when the world eats you. You should be scared for the day you will help someone, and they hurt you because you believed too much in people. Because you excused their wrong actions too often! You wonder why I didn't show up? Because you drag me down when all I want is to have fun. Good luck figuring the world out, Mila! You're going to need it." She slammed her car door after getting inside. Her tires squealed as she flew out of the parking lot.

Chapter Twelve:
Period

♥

I stared at Erin's brown ceiling fan swishing and sighed. "Riley isn't wrong. Everything she said about me is true."

Erin looked up from where she was sorting her CDs. Her brown curls were pulled into a ponytail. "You can't be serious, Mila. You should be furious at her. Not just for the horrible things she said, but for not showing up. That should still make you mad for a long time."

"I get her perspective, is all. I pushed her too much on the Lonzo issue, and now I've paid the price. Everything she said about me was true. The world is going to eat me because I don't understand it, and I rely on her too much to tell me how it is. I'm too much."

Erin pressed her lips together in an exasperated scowl. "The only thing she was right about is that you excuse people's actions too much, and you forgive them too easily while you continually think you're the problem and the bad one in the situation."

"It's easy for me to see why people think the things they do."

"And even easier for you not to see why you think the things you do."

I shifted my gaze to the left. "Yeah, something like that. I don't understand myself or anything I feel. I feel everything and nothing all at once, which makes no sense half the time. Everyone's opinions make sense except my own until my feelings burst out of me like the pipes under my trailer did last winter."

"You gotta wrap them and let the faucet drip a little."

"Yes, we know that now. But when it gets forty below, and your house isn't well insulated, stuff happens."

"True." She climbed onto her bed and put her arms around me. "I love you exactly the way you are, my friend. I wouldn't change a thing about you. Don't let anyone ever convince you that you need to be anyone different."

I squeezed her, and our heads touched. "Same, Erin. I mean it. Your joy is going to change the world."

"Your mercy is. I mean that. You have a huge chance of being hurt by it, but it's one of the best things about you. Even animals sense it."

"Animals are easy to show mercy to."

"Why don't I retrieve my hidden stash of chocolate, and we'll put in *Galaxy Quest* and laugh the evening away? You know which character reminds me of you in that movie?"

I crinkled my nose. "In *Galaxy Quest*?"

"Yeah, the characters remind me of each of us."

"Okay. Who am I?"

She unzipped her black binder that held all her DVDs in transparent sleeves. "Alan Rickman's character, Alexander Dane."

"I remind you of a man playing an alien on TV inside a movie?"

She laughed and pushed the button that ejected the disc tray. "No, his attitude. You know when they all think they're going to die? He's all in a super calm voice, hey, guys, I thought you should know we're all about to be toast. That's exactly what you would do if we were all doomed and could do nothing about it. Cool as a cucumber in a walk-in freezer."

"Frozen sounds about right. I sound so calm on the outside because I've already exploded with anxiety and mentally checked out."

"No one would ever know it." She put in the disc and sat next to me on her waterbed.

"True. My anxiety is extremely high functioning to everyone but me."

"The rules you live with would give anyone anxiety," she said.

"That's why I come to your house."

We watched the movie and talked about life, the universe, and all the deep topics we loved. It was like I did with Ezra, but it was different. I could have heavy, complex conversations with both, and they got me. I understood them, but at the same time, it wasn't the same. With Erin, this bond we built flowed naturally and seemed like an everyday normal thing that I loved.

With Ezra, it felt natural too, but the level that we reached together felt intense. Almost like we were looking for reasons to give into a tide we'd both struggled against. Like if we let the ocean take us, we feared we would drown, but really, we'd find an oasis where we could exist away from everyone else. Being ourselves together wasn't the terrible end everyone warned us about. It was peace and home and everything worth fighting for.

The next day, he proved all that again when I called him to tell me I couldn't hang out because I wasn't feeling well.

He said nothing for a few seconds. "You're sick?"

"No, not exactly."

"It's back?"

"Yeah," I groaned.

"I'll be over in an hour."

"No, you go on without me. There's no reason for you not to enjoy your day." I put little effort into the argument because a big part of me wanted his comfort, and my parents were gone for a week to take my brother back to college in Florida. Twice a year, I got seven days of freedom.

"One hour." He hung up, so I couldn't protest further.

By the time he arrived, the pain meds had worn off. They weren't the kind I usually used, but they would have to do. I curled into a little ball, clutching my stomach.

When I didn't answer the door, he came around to my window. "Is it alright if I come in?"

"Yeah, I can't move."

He hurried inside carrying plastic sacks and opened a red package. "This is a heating pack. It sticks wherever the pain is, and you can take it anywhere. It lasts for twelve hours. Aleve, chocolate, soup, Wheat Thins, and Sprite. Did I miss anything?" He pulled out each thing and set it on my nightstand.

"A new body for me."

He opened his mouth, smiled, and then closed it again. He cleared his throat. "Not something you need."

"The pain says otherwise. Every month."

I had a disorder that gave me extremely debilitating cramps for the first two to three days of my period every month. The doctors said the only thing that would cure it would be to have a baby. For some reason, that would reset things. The other option was birth control, and my mother wanted me to have nothing to do with it. Since babies were not a priority at sixteen, I suffered every month, but Ezra often came to my rescue and took care of me. Heating pads, Aleve, and scorching baths were all that helped. A strict diet of pop, soup, and Wheat Thin crackers were about all I could tolerate.

The meds and portable heat patch he'd brought did wonders, and we went out to my couch, where we watched a movie. He covered me with a blanket, and I rested my head on his lap while he played with my hair. His soft movements against my scalp led me to sleep. When I woke up, he hadn't moved, but a new movie was playing.

I sat up and squeezed my eyes shut to dislodge the grogginess. "Did you not like the movie we picked?"

"It was great, but you slept through it."

"I'm sorry."

"No, it's a good thing. It means the stuff worked."

I slipped out of the blanket. "I'm going to make you dinner. What do you feel like?"

"One of your sandwiches or five. A bonus if you have your pies."

"Now I see why you stick around."

"All the food is a good assumption." He winked.

My stomach nearly bubbled over from the warmth in his voice and face. I darted to the kitchen to quit looking at him. "We could always make a pie together." I opened the cupboard and fridge to study their contents. "Cherry or chocolate cream are what I can do without a store trip."

He stood next to me and examined everything I brought to the counter. "Why not both? But you should probably make it. I'll ruin the entire thing. Are you sure you're feeling up to this?"

"Yeah, the meds and heat are making this doable. You're the best friend a girl could have, by the way."

"Yeah, best friend. Right." His voice trailed off a bit as he looked to the side. "Why don't we start some music?" He messed with the little radio my mom listened to the hymnal music on while she did the dishes.

"As long as you remember to turn it back to the station she had it on."

"It would be funny to see her face with pop music pouring out."

I started measuring ingredients and pouring them into a bowl. "Yeah, until I got punished for the drums she had to hear."

"We couldn't be having that. I'll make sure it's put back." He watched me work for a bit. "Don't you need a recipe or something?"

"No, I put in what feels right based on experience and instinct."

"How?"

I shrugged. "I'm not sure exactly how it works. It just does."

"Hmmm... You're right. It makes no sense, but it always works."

I pointed to the crust I'd made. "You roll it into the pan."

"I what?"

"Like this." I demonstrated halfway. "Finish it. Then you can make pie for yourself."

His left eyebrow shot up. "Why would I want to do that?"

"Because you love pie."

"Yeah, *your* pie. Maybe you should show me again how to do this."

"Why? So I just end up making the entire thing?" I stepped back over to where he stared bewilderedly at the dough.

"Maybe. I wanted you close to do this." He tossed flour at me.

I gaped. "Seriously, Ezra!"

He sprinkled a bunch over my hair. "Seriously."

I shoved a cloud's worth at him, and it started a war. Flour flew in all directions until we were head to toe, covered in white. He picked up an egg and threw me a lopsided grin.

My eyes widened, and I stepped back. "You wouldn't."

He tossed it at me, and I leaped past him to grab two that I smashed over his head. He picked up four, and I took off running, screeching. I flew under the table and cowered behind a chair. He flung the chair next to me and crawled under the table. I shoved the seat in front of me out of the way and took off through the kitchen. More chairs toppled. A thud followed by his cry told me he'd hit his head on the table. I made the mistake of stopping to check on him, and it gave him time to reach me.

He grabbed my waist and tickled me. I leaned into him, laughing, and we both slipped on the egg, landing on the floor. The pain was dimmed by our laughter that we couldn't stop. When we finally got in control of ourselves, we put the kitchen back together and cleaned ourselves up.

I grabbed a rag and soap and helped rinse the egg out of his hair in careful movements not to tug on his scalp. He gently grabbed my wrist and met my eyes. We stayed locked in a gaze that allowed me to take in his soulful hazel eyes. I saw so much kindness and heart in them. They spoke so much of the person he'd proven himself. We blinked out of our trance, and I rinsed out the soap and patted him dry. He helped me wash out flour in a few places I didn't catch.

Ezra sat on the counter, swinging his legs back and forth. His hair spiked out wildly like it had a will of its own. I didn't mind it being untamed, much like the boy himself.

"What?" He furrowed his brow, adding a smirk.

"I like your hair, is all?"

"You like my post-food fight hair?"

"Yeah." I put the cherry pie in the oven and turned the apple-shaped timer on the stove.

"You have to use a timer? Instinct doesn't tell you when to take it out?"

"No, because it's a time-sensitive thing. I daydream, and the timer brings me back in time to save the pie." I took out the sandwich ingredients and got a plate.

"Daydreaming about what?"

I pulled apart the turkey into smaller pieces and arranged them on the bread. "Lots of things. The future and imaginary worlds."

"Worlds to write about."

"Or keep in my head."

"That's pretty selfish."

I paused the knife in my hand. "How do you figure that one? They're my stories."

"And you have to keep them all for yourself?"

I resumed the sandwich-making, but a smile I couldn't stop made me turn my head slightly away from him. "Not sure anyone else would appreciate them."

"I already do."

My smile grew, as did the heat in my cheeks. That boy did crazy things to me.

Chapter Thirteen: Dangerous Drinks

Summer had quickly faded into autumn, which was the time I saw as the crawl to my November birthday. I'd just started feeling better from when Ezra had gone to my house two days ago. I shredded all the leftover chicken, and music boomed loudly from the large stereo on a shelf above my head. Natasha, my energetic coworker, danced as she weighed the chicken in small bags to be frozen for the pot pies.

She wiggled her butt to the ground and popped back up. "Your parents are out of town?"

My hand jerked before it froze. "How do you know that?"

"I heard you tell Carylon."

"I'm not throwing a party, if that's what you're going to ask me. My trailer is too small and frail to handle that."

She waved her hand. "No, that's not what I was going to say at all. I want to bring you to a party. A college one at Adams State."

For being a small valley town, we had a university that was planted in the middle of Alamosa, and it was party central. Natasha went to the local high school but often asked for rides to the college after we got off work.

I threw away the leftover chicken bones and handed her the shredded pieces. "I'm not into parties and would rather get run over with a cement truck than go to one."

She squinted one eye. "You can't be serious."

"Unless it's a small gathering with people I know well and love."

"Well, tonight they are having a massive bonfire, and you need to go. We're going to leave here, and after we shower, I'm going to do your hair and makeup."

"I don't wear makeup."

She snorted and put the chicken bags in the metal rectangle container to carry them to the freezer. "You are tonight."

"This is a bad idea. My parents would kill me."

"Good thing they're out of town. You do this, and I'll go to youth group with you like you've asked a million times."

That grabbed my attention, and for the sake of Natasha's soul, I said yes to something I hated. We clocked out and returned to my house, where she went through my closet.

She threw the last item on the bed. "None of this is going to do. Let's go to my house."

"I don't know. I really want you to go to heaven when you die, but this feels wrong."

"I'll go to two youth groups with you. That's double the chance for you to convince me I need salvation."

I closed my eyes, unable to resist her offer. "Okay. It's a deal."

We left for her house, where more negotiating went on until she talked me into wearing a lavender dress that reached my knees and had spaghetti straps. The temperature still had a summer warmth that made her not let me wear a sweater over it. My shoulders and knees tingled in protest of their nakedness. She catapulted me further out of my comfort zone with foundation, mascara, and eyeliner. She used eyeshadow to give me smoky eyes. The berry lip gloss and curling iron ringlets finished the look.

She turned me toward her wall-length mirror. "You are going to stun at the party." She studied my face. "Don't look like I took you to the strip club for the first time. Nothing shocking here. You're hot. I could make out with you."

"What?" I squeaked.

"I'm just kidding, dear."

I turned the silver purity ring on my finger. "Boys can't see me this way."

"There's going to be no boys, honey. Only men."

I gulped and snapped out of it when she shoved high heels in my arms. "I will kill myself in those by tripping and falling into the fire or something else just as dumb."

"Okay. We want to get you kissed. Not killed."

"I'm not kissing anyone! I want you in heaven with me, but we can't face God by kissing random men on a college campus."

She burst into laughter. "Calm down. Kissing is optional, but you should try it. Making out is the most fun. Well, the start of the most fun."

It occurred to me that if Natasha left with a guy, no one would know where I was, and my parents wouldn't be back for another four days. I took out my emergency phone from my purse. My parents wouldn't let me get a contract for one, so it was a phone that I bought a prepaid card for. It cost a dollar a minute, and if the entire minute wasn't used, it rounded up. For this reason, I only used it when I had to.

I dialed Ezra's number while Natasha went to the bathroom and waited until he answered on the second ring. "Just in case I disappear, I'm going to a party at the college tonight. In the field by the main parking lot. You know that one spot they always have them at?"

"You're what? Why?"

"I need my coworker to go to heaven. I'm sure I'll be fine. Nothing bad can happen when I have good motives. I have supernatural protection. My father says, you're never safer than you are when you're doing God's will. If something bad happens, that was his will." I thought it over a second. "Maybe pray for me."

"I'm not sure what all that means, but you shouldn't go to a college party at night," Ezra said.

"There are going to be lots of people there. I should be fine. I gotta go. My phone is about to go into another minute. Bye." I hung up.

Natasha's black dress met her upper thigh and dipped pretty low on her chest. The heels she wore almost seemed like mini stilts. We took my car to the college and hopped out to the party well in progress. Music flowed from a live band behind the mountain of flames that people danced around and munched on food taken from four long tables. Many chatted in groups with red Solo cups in hand.

A guy in a blue polo, khakis, and slicked-back hair walked up carrying a drink. "Hey, sweetheart, thirsty?"

It was impolite not to accept refreshments from someone, so I took it. I went to sip it to not be rude, and it flung out of my hand.

Natasha jerked me away from the guy, whose smile had turned into a glare. "Never accept drinks! Ever, Mila! I don't care how thirsty you are. Never take a drink from a guy."

"Why? He looks nice."

"He looks like a prick that wants to take you to his dorm room or a back alley."

"You shouldn't say that word."

She grabbed my shoulders. "Promise me no more drinks from anyone here!"

"Okay. I promise. What do I do if someone offers?"

"You say no."

"But they'll think I'm rude."

She shook her head. "Just promise me. You could get hurt in a way you seem too innocent for me to explain."

"Okay. I promise."

"Alright, good. Go have fun. I have someone I need to dance with."

I turned down another drink while I stood by the fire.

The polo-shirt guy walked up to me. "I'm Steve."

I shook his hand and glanced behind me. "Sorry about your drink. My friend is a bit weird."

"It's okay. I can get you another one if you wait here a minute."

I put my hand up. "No, it's okay. I promised her I wouldn't take any more drinks from people I don't know."

"I see." He threw his thumb toward the stage. "Why don't we dance? Then I'm not a stranger anymore." He grabbed my hand and pulled me to the dance floor.

I stuck my heels in the gravel. "You're a nice person and all, but I can't dance."

"Anyone can dance. I can teach you a few things."

"No, thank you. It's against my beliefs."

He laughed, frowned, and laughed again. "We could go back to my dorm and watch a movie."

A familiar heaviness spread across my chest. "No, I'm going to go find my friend now." I jerked my hand away and ran toward the fire, looking for Natasha.

What had I gotten myself into? I couldn't leave without her and didn't know how to contact her. Steve ran after me, and I scanned wildly for anywhere I could hide.

"Mila? Are you okay?"

My head jerked to the buffet table. Val stood behind it, wearing a maroon hat and matching apron.

"Are you alright?" she repeated her question.

"Ummm..." I looked for Steve, but he had disappeared. "Yeah, yeah, I'm good. A little lost, but fine. You're working?"

"Yeah, the party planning company I work for got the catering for tonight. I recommend the chicken sandwiches. The best ever."

"Thank you. I'm not super hungry."

She smacked her forehead and had to exchange her glove. "I forgot you work around chicken."

"It's not that. I'm not super hungry. Would you get in trouble if I stayed around you? I can be useful without pay."

"Sure. I don't think they'll care as long as I still do the work."

Val and I talked as she served food and drinks. We'd grown closer lately, and it helped take my mind off Riley. It wasn't like Val was a replacement for Riley. It was more like I had time to get to know Val again.

Val handed a girl a plate and pointed her chin behind me. "I bet that's for you."

I spun around to see Ezra searching the crowd with significant strides. His jaw looked tense enough to crack.

I leaped at him. "You didn't have to come."

"Your lung-squeezing hug and trembling say otherwise."

"I'm not trembling."

He looked me over, and his lips parted. "Woah!"

Scorching heat moved through my chest and face. "It's a bit much."

"No, it's perfect."

"You like me better this way?" I had to force my lower lip not to pout.

"No, that's not it. That's not it at all. You look different, not worse or better. Different."

My lower lip quivered. "I just want to go home."

"What happened?" He glanced around like he might need to kill someone.

"Nothing. I worked and am tired but can't leave because I brought my coworker."

"I'll wait with you but hold on. I'll be right back." He disappeared toward the parking lot.

Val handed out two more drinks. "Are you sure you don't want anything?"

I walked over to the table. "Ezra will." I started piling food on a plate that I knew he loved.

"You two are cute. I think that every time I see you together."

"Ezra would love hearing he's cute." I grabbed a cup but set it back down. "He can get his own drink."

"I keep telling my cousin Kyra to back off. The only one Ezra sees is you."

"Yeah, we're great friends."

Ezra jogged over with a blanket and put it around my shoulders. "To stop the shivers."

It smelled like him, and I tried not to be weird and bury my nose in it. "Thank you."

The blanket didn't stop my trembles, but it hid them better. We talked for a while until I finally spotted Natasha dancing.

I ran for her to not lose her. "Are you ready to go soon?"

She swayed her hips in a way that looked unnatural and perfect. "No, but I have a ride." She smiled at the guy in front of her.

"Are you sure?"

"Very, sweetie. I'll see you at work." She kissed my cheeks and went back to dancing.

Ezra followed me back to my house, and since my parents were still gone, I invited him inside after he helped me feed my birds. I put it in a movie and sat on the couch next to him.

He put his arms around me. "What happened tonight?"

"Nothing. The party was too much."

"Okay."

We turned our attention to the movie but slowly sank together on the couch. I woke to daylight coming through my living room window. My head rested on a firm chest that smelled like a magical forest. My senses slammed into me.

I rolled off the couch and landed with a hard thud. "Ezra! We fell asleep together!"

He groaned. "Yeah, it was nice. We should sleep longer."

"I'm making breakfast."

"If you must, I won't complain."

I went to the kitchen but stopped to stare at him. His disheveled hair went in every direction, and his face had a peacefulness to it I hadn't seen in a long time. I really liked his face a lot. His eyes popped open, and I dashed into the kitchen.

Chapter Fourteen: Cancelled Birthday

Three months had gone by since Riley had spoken to me, and it was the longest it had ever been. I'd stopped by her house a few times, only to be sent away by her mom. I mailed her a letter to let her know I was having a seventeenth birthday party if she wanted to come. A week later, I got a card from her in the mail on the day of my party. It didn't have a stamp, so she had to have dropped it off.

I rushed into my room to open it and stared at the words inside. The tears hit before the emotions did, and I climbed into bed to sulk. After I had calmed down a little, I dialed Erin's number.

She yawned. "Mila?"

"Riley said she's not coming to my party."

"Good. She doesn't deserve to go to your party. Terrible friends don't belong at birthday parties of the friends they hurt."

"I'm going to cancel it. Thought you should know that."

She blew air through the phone. "No, you're not! We're going to have so much fun without her."

"I don't want to, but I want to go ice skating today. Do you want to? I have to call everyone first to cancel, but then we can go to the pond."

"It's your birthday, Mila. I'll call everyone and cancel."

The card in front of me allowed sadness to creep in. "Are you sure?"

"Yes, very sure. I'll meet you at the pond in two hours."

"Okay." I took a shower where I could cry in peace. Never in my life had I thought I'd lose Riley or that she would pick a guy over me. It cut through me, and part of me wanted to climb into bed for the entire day. Ice skating was peaceful, and it was what I needed.

My mom was in the kitchen when I came out of the bathroom. "You're present is on the table. Happy birthday."

"Do you want me to open it now?"

"Yeah."

I ripped open the paper and smiled at the blue coat with white fur lining. "This is pretty. Thank you!"

"You're welcome. I figured it's been a couple of years, and it was time for a new one."

"I love it a lot. Thank you!"

"I hope you have a great day. I'm off to the Bible study."

"Okay." I put on the coat and watched my mother leave. It was soft, and I knew she'd probably saved for it for a while.

I found my skates buried in the back of my closet and located my hat, gloves, and scarf. There was still another hour until I had to be at the pond, so I drove around in my car, listening to my Lifehouse No Name Face Album. I played the song "Somewhere in Between" over and over. Ten minutes before I was supposed to meet Erin, I arrived at the pond to test the ice.

It wasn't a super deep pond, which was why we picked it. If we fell in, it would only be a frigid inconvenience. Around the nature-made rink grew tall yellow grass, and blackbirds danced in the sky to a melody that seemed intrinsic to them. Like they all came with the same built-in song that allowed them to carry out aerial dances without colliding. I turned on the radio, rolled down the windows, and turned up the volume.

Once it was cranked as loud as it could go, I took off on the ice, gliding and twirling. The thoughts bounced around in my head until I was lost in the music and my mind.

Car doors slammed, and it jarred me a little. I finished my twirl and stared at the shore. Erin stood there, but so did Val and about ten other people we sometimes hung out with.

I swished over to her. "You didn't cancel."

Ezra sat on a rock, tying up his skates. "We wouldn't let her."

Erin grinned and shrugged. "I tried."

I gave her a half-eye roll while laughing. "I'm sure you tried so hard."

"Yep!" She glided out onto the ice.

More people joined us, and I hurried to Val to steady her.

Her skates slid about until she almost did the splits. "This is going to be fun."

I helped steady her and took both her hands, skating backward. "Have you ever done this before?"

"No, Erin let me borrow her sister's skates."

"Well, I appreciate you risking life and limb for me."

"Anytime. You're one of my best friends. You don't have to guide me. I can watch from the shore." She wobbled a little and leaned toward me.

"Unless you don't feel comfortable, I don't mind," I said.

"Okay. I'm fine with it, if you're sure."

I nodded and brought her out to the middle of the ice. She wobbled and gripped my arms, but I knew how to lock myself in place to keep us steady. I'd taught myself to skate when I was eight, and the trailer park I lived at dug five inches out over a large area and filled it with water for people to skate. My grandparents had gotten me the skates I begged for, and each day I went alone to the rink. Back then, no one thought twice about a little kid being all by themselves. I walked all over town alone without anyone saying anything.

I came home with lots of bumps and bruises from using the trailer rink, and I even hit my head a few times. Never once did I tell a soul about my injuries because I wanted to be allowed to keep going, and before long, I could skate well.

Ezra skated over. "Want to spin?"

Val eyed him warily. "I'm not sure. Maybe slowly." She placed one of her hands in Ezra's, and I took his other one.

I'd done this a few times with him, but we'd gone fast together. We took it slowly with Val until she felt more comfortable. Toward the end of the morning, I'd taught her to skate on her own a bit more. While I was instructing Val on proper skate placement, a ruckus was occurring by the cars.

"Happy Birthday to you!" everyone sang.

Ezra and Erin each held one side of the cake and slowly glided it to me. A few of the candles had blown out from the wind, but I made a wish and blew the remaining ones out. Everyone cheered, and a few of my other friends spread blankets out on the ice. We sat there eating cake, letting our butts become numb. My friends all pulled out presents and piled them on me. I took time opening each one and squealed at nearly everything I got.

I opened Val's gift and squeezed the little stuffed blue bird to me. "Where did you find this?"

"The sand dune gift shop sells them."

I hugged her. "I love it!"

Erin had gotten me a few books and a long card that went into great detail about how she felt about me. I looked over one of the books because it looked unusual.

"It's a book to write all about yourself, so you never forget who you were the last year before adulthood ruined your life," she said.

I pulled her against me. "Thank you, friend! I love it."

Ezra sat back a little but said nothing. He was the only one who hadn't given me anything. I met his eyes but quickly looked away, not wanting him to think I noticed. He didn't have to get me anything. We packed everything up, and everyone but Erin, Val, and Ezra left.

Val wrapped me in another hug. "You want to come over to my house next Friday? We can binge on movie store candy and rent some DVDs."

"I'd love that." I watched her climb into her car, and it made me happy that I'd reconnected with her over the last few months. She was quickly becoming one of my closest friends. I hugged the little bird as I thought about her.

Erin collided with me in one of her lung-smashing hugs. "Are you feeling better?"

I frowned at Ezra climbing into his truck. "Yes, I am. Thank you for this."

"What are you talking about?" She threw her hands up. "I tried to cancel the entire thing."

"Right. Love you, girl."

She squished me again. "I love you too. I would totally invite you over, but we're going to the Springs, as you know. Wish you could come. I shouldn't have gotten the tickets for your birthday, but I thought your parents might let you go if I did."

"Someday, we'll go to all the concerts we want together."

She got into her car, and I climbed into mine.

Ezra hopped out of his truck and approached my window. "You want to go for a drive?"

"Yeah, I always want to go on a drive with you." I got out of my car and headed to his truck.

"Do you have a change of clothes?"

"Ummm... You don't like what I'm wearing?"

He laughed. "It's great, like always. But you'll need clothes to change into later."

"I have an extra pair of pants for emergencies."

"That'll work, and you can use one of my shirts." He opened his truck door for me and got in the other side.

We drove a long way, and I didn't ask him about it. I enjoyed the scenery and his hand in mine that we didn't ever talk about. We traveled into a different set of mountains and onto a dirt road. Blue spruce trees crowded out the greener ones and covered most of the ground except for white rock patches and the dusty trail that rumbled the car. A red-tailed hawk flew overhead, and I watched him dive in and out of pines and sky. Smoke rose from a small cabin in the distance, and it seemed wonderful to be the person living there. The ground leveled out into a dirt parking lot. A wooden fence ran along the edge of a large drop-off.

Ezra pulled out a backpack and took my hand to help me out of the truck. He didn't remove it as he led me up a trail. Snow blanketed the land everywhere, and a heavy chill was in the air. Grey clouds warned of a pending blizzard. I didn't complain because the entire thing was my birthday turning perfect.

We hiked so far back that I feared we'd get lost, but the boy holding my hand didn't hesitate for a single step. We pushed through thick trees and went higher and higher until it opened up into a mountain-top. I gasped at the winter white landscape awakened by the tree greens and blue boulders.

Ezra glanced at his watch. "It took a lot longer getting here than I thought. We'll have to come back for one of the surprises, so we don't get stuck here after dark or in the storm."

"I won't complain about having to come back here again."

"You want your presents?"

My chest nearly burst with excitement. "More than one?"

"You thought I forgot, didn't you?"

I rapidly shook my head. "No, no. You didn't have to get me anything."

He put two presents in my lap and sat down, facing me. His knee rested against mine. "There was actually a third, but it was the thing you needed a change of clothes for."

"Next week?"

"Yeah, we can leave early morning and have the entire day." He pointed to the bigger one. "Don't open that one yet."

"When should I open it?"

"Tonight, after I drop you off. You can open the small one now."

I carefully picked at the tape on the shiny purple wrapping and opened the tiny square black box. A little silver bird dangled from a chain. "It's beautiful, Ezra!"

His thumb brushed over my cheek. "Hopefully, those are good tears."

I leaped at him. "Of course, they are."

He relaxed into me as though everything had become right the moment I landed in his arms. "Figured I couldn't go wrong with birds."

I agreed with him, and we started back to his truck.

Chapter Fifteen: Mila's Mix Tape

♥

As we drove back, he squeezed my hand. "Did you have a good birthday?"

"The best."

"Are you okay?"

"Why wouldn't I be?"

He fiddled with the radio until he found the station he wanted. "Erin had said you were upset, and that's why you wanted to cancel your birthday."

"The same thing with Riley. She gave me a card that said she wasn't coming with a list of reasons. Her reasons hurt."

"All lies, I'm sure."

I leaned my cheek against the window, absorbing the icy touch. "No, they were all accurate."

He released my hand to turn on the wipers to keep his visibility in the falling snow that had started about ten minutes earlier. "Like what? If you don't mind sharing."

"Reason five. When we were thirteen, I got a new batch of ducks. Little babies, and half came dead because there had been a blizzard and the post office didn't transport them right. I was devastated. One was sick, but I thought he would live if I cared for him well enough. My mom watched him while I had to go somewhere. I don't even remember where, but my mom watched him. He died while I was gone. Riley came home with me, and when my mom told me the duck had died, I asked my mom how she could let the duck die. That she was never there for me when I needed her, and all she cared about was church things. It made her cry, and I was a terrible person."

Deep shame overwhelmed me at the memory, and it scared me Ezra would see me differently.

"You were upset and said something as an outburst. Can't say I haven't done that."

"I apologized to my mom after Riley left and hated myself for a long time."

He turned the wipers up as the snow grew heavier. "How was that reason five for Riley not going to your party?"

I pushed my thumbnail into the side of my pointer finger. "Riley said she saw my true character come out that day. She can't trust me to know what I truly think about her, and my outbursts about Lonzo have shown I haven't changed. I'll keep everything inside until it bursts out to say awful, unforgivable things to people."

"She said that to you?"

"Yeah, and she's right. It was a terrible thing to say to my mom. My mom couldn't do anything to save the duck, and I'm sure she tried. But instead of realizing that, I made her cry." I sunk lower against the window.

"Maybe you said those things to your mom because you thought they were true, and it took powerful emotion for you to be willing to say them."

I sat up straight and waved my hands. "No! That's not how I feel. You think I'm a bad person too?"

He chuckled, but it had no genuine humor in it. "Mila, I don't think you are a terrible person. Now or then. I think you've felt unseen by your mom during times you needed her. You didn't really think she let the duck die. Not after you had time to think about it. The entire thing wasn't even about the duck, and besides, it happened four years ago. If yelling that at your mom is unforgivable, the rest of us are doomed to never find redemption. You want my opinion about the whole Riley thing?"

"Yeah, I always value your opinion."

"Always?"

"Yeah, I might not agree with you, but your opinion is forever welcomed by me."

He slowed his truck as the visibility neared whiteout conditions. "Riley knows how she's treating you is wrong. Maybe even what she's doing is wrong, but when people want to keep doing the wrong thing, they rarely want to admit it's wrong."

"Okay. That's probably true."

"It's easier to blame you for what's happening because it deflects her actions. She can't stay mad at you unless she keeps thinking up reasons to be mad at you. She can't be having that because you might tell her the truth she doesn't want to hear. You honestly think Riley thinks you're an awful person because you yelled at your mom about a duck four years ago?"

"I'm not sure. It's hard to forgive myself when I explode."

His eyes stayed focused on the winding road that was nearly entirely concealed in white. Most people might have been biting their nails, but it was a typical November for us. "How can you not explode? You push it all down, but emotions weren't made to be pushed down. They were made to be released. Eventually, they get tired and become a geyser. No one can stay fine all the time without some sort of consequence. You're allowed to have all different emotions and express them."

We made it down the pass, and the roads became slightly clearer to navigate. Our conversation halted, but it didn't feel abrupt. It was like we'd both realized we needed reflection and didn't require words to confirm the agreement.

Ezra dropped me off at the pond. "I'm going to follow behind you to make sure you get home safe in this storm."

"Okay, but don't stop in front of my house."

"Yeah, I know."

I lifted the little black box with the necklace. "Thank you for this! It's beautiful."

"You're beautiful. Happy birthday, Mila."

My cheeks warmed right up in the sub-zero temperatures. "Thank you."

He did as he said and followed me home, and while he didn't stop at my house, he crept past until I got inside. My parents were watching something in the living room. Akela jumped on me and did three fast circles. I picked him up, and he attacked my face with kisses. After giving him a good ear scratch, I set him down.

I stood in the doorway. "I'm home."

My mom looked up from her cross-stitch. "Good. Did you have a good birthday?"

"Yeah, thank you again for the coat." I set all my presents in my room and went back out to tend to my birds. After making sure they were all inside, I shut the outside entrance. I plugged in the heat lamps and did a final count to ensure they were safe. "Love you guys. Cuddle close. It's going to be a chilly night."

Back in my room, I put up all my presents and changed into blue flannel pajamas. Riley's card fell on the floor when I lifted my covers. I picked it up and cried again as I read the ten reasons she wouldn't talk to me. I held it over the trash and stopped. It went into my drawer where I kept all the things Riley had given me since we met at eight. Without the card, it would have been the first year she hadn't gotten me anything.

I turned my attention to the bigger present from Ezra and opened it. Inside a nicely wrapped shoe box were a Discman, headphones, and a CD. In black sharpie, "Mila's mix" was written across it.

I popped it in and placed the headphones over my head. "Crazy for This Girl" played first, followed by "Hanging by a Moment." I went through the list. "She will be Loved", "Crash and Burn", "Iris", "Breathing", "I'm Like a Bird", "Slide", "All the Things She Said", "Drops of Jupiter", "You and Me", "Wherever you will go", "Blurry", "Hero", "Be Like That", "Someday We'll Know", "It's Gonna Be Love", "Truly, Madly, Deeply", "Cry", "Everything", and "Only Hope".

More and more, it was becoming a struggle not to cross lines with him, but I didn't know what the songs meant. It was a lot of the songs we listened to together. Did he do it as a nice thing because I loved all of these songs, or did he mean them? He probably didn't have feelings for me. I stared at the wall, wishing Ezra meant all the songs to me. How could I know? All hope that had risen collapsed. No matter what, my feelings for him were wrong, but it was getting difficult to accept that.

One thing was truer than anything else. I could never allow him to get hurt by my actions. I cried myself to sleep with the music he'd given me playing in my ears.

I made sure I was ahead in my schoolwork. Since all my classes were online and it was self-paced, I could do things ahead of time to get a break. It left me with a free weekend, and Ezra was taking me to his surprise—my third birthday present. I'd done the movie night thing with Val but had left a little after midnight.

He arrived at five in the morning but parked a block away. He called my emergency phone and let it ring twice as we'd discussed. I left a note on the fridge that I'd gone to Erin's. In his car, I didn't bring up the CD or the fact I'd listened to it at least twenty times since I'd seen him last. He didn't say anything, either.

We drove back into the mountains. The weather had warmed a little with the way fall tried to hold on to a little warmth before it surrendered to winter. Snow covered more places, and it was clear autumn was losing. We hiked from the dirt parking lot again, but this time, we descended to the other side. We trekked through narrow paths and walked sideways to make it through a small opening.

Steam rose from a pool in front of us with brownish rocks surrounding on all sides. The stone was barren until the top, where pines grew around it, making the barrier around us even taller.

He helped me over a rock that placed us on level ground. "I was hiking with my brother and found this place this summer. Figured I better take you here before he does."

I flinched. "I'd rather go with you."

"Are you sure? He has a motorcycle and is in the Army."

"You have good genetics! What else do you want me to say?" I turned away from his mile-high grin. "What is this place?"

"Hot springs. Like the pool in Mosca, but private."

I'd put a t-shirt and shorts under my clothes and stripped down to them. Ezra took off everything but a pair of shorts. We hurried to the pool and submerged ourselves in warmth.

"Race you!" He took off across the pool.

"Hey! Cheater! You have to give me fair warning." I dove after him.

"I did. I said, race you."

I caught up to him and tapped one side of the pool before rushing to the other. He grabbed my foot and pulled me back, shooting ahead. We made several laps, and on the fifth one, he whirled around and grabbed me. We spun around in the water. He lifted me in the air, and I raised my arms. We floated on our backs with our arms extended over our heads to keep our hands together. We spent most of the morning floating and swimming in the pool.

When we tired, we sat in the shallow part, facing each other and talking. We had our knees peaked and alternated them. That put one of my legs between his and one of his between mine to bring us closer together. The water went right above our shoulders and kept us warm. There never seemed to be a shortage of topics to talk about. We left the pool, and I went behind a large rock to change. I hid all my damp hair under a large hat and met him at the pool exit.

He helped me over the rocks. "Are you warm enough?"

"I will survive, but I think warm enough will only happen when we get to the car."

"We better get you there quickly." His hand stayed in mine unless he removed it to hold my waist over icy spots.

As we drove back, his truck took forever to warm, and he covered me with a blanket from his back seat. "Did you open your second present?"

"Yeah, I loved it. You know all my favorite songs." I waited, hoping he'd tell me they meant something more than that.

"Right. Yeah..." He cleared his throat. "Yep, that's why I made it for you, because you love all those songs." He ran his thumb over his chin.

My heart dropped, and I moved the little silver bird back and forth on the chain that hung around my neck. "The presents you gave me were my favorite."

"Really?"

"Yes, you made my birthday."

"Good. That was the point."

I sighed, wishing I hadn't overthought the songs. That was stupid of me to think he saw me as anything more than a best friend. I watched his profile as he sang to the radio, tapping his finger on the steering wheel to the beat. He looked over and smiled, making my chest ache and feel giddy. Two extremely opposite emotions buzzed through me. A profound longing to be more than his friend played ping-pong with the joy of sitting in his truck while he drove us through the mountains.

Chapter Sixteen: Entertaining

♥

C hristmas time approached, and our church always put on a play. We had a musical group coming in from Denver to help with the songs. I was playing a mother whose child was in the hospital for Christmas. The church group arrived in the evening, and my dad wanted me to greet the teenagers coming with them. Ezra, Val, Kyra, and Hannah were also there to be greeters.

I'd been sitting in the pew, listening to my dad speak to the leader, who had arrived early, about the leader's teenage daughter. As usual, I seemed invisible to the adults around me. They always spoke as though they could say anything in my presence, even about me.

"I have to watch my sixteen-year-old daughter Stacy so closely. She's boy crazy. It doesn't matter how often she goes to youth group. Sometimes I think it makes it worse because there are boys there." The man shook his head and laughed.

My dad messed with the sound system, turning knobs and sending a shrill sound into the auditorium. His voice became enhanced by the microphone. "We've gotten lucky with our Mila. She has no interest in boys at all. Has no desire to date any of them. She's a good girl. Does everything she's told."

"What's your secret?"

"We enforce the rules and don't give her much breathing room for mistakes. Strict rules and consequences make well-behaved children."

I stared at the ground, wishing I could vanish. I didn't want to look up to see what the others thought of my dad's announcement.

"Mila!" My dad's eyes landed on me. "The bus should be about here. Go greet the kids."

"Yes, sir." I went through the back of the church. On the bottom level were the nursery, a pew, the bathrooms, and the door that led to the basement. A small set of stairs went to the fellowship hall, and a taller set led to the upstairs classrooms and attic. I went down the back steps as a blue bus pulled into the parking lot. Around fifteen teens and three adults hopped off.

"Hi!" I waved, plastering on a smile. Interacting with strangers and forcing small talk exhausted me, but I knew how to do it as well as breathing. "Welcome to the San Luis Valley! We're happy to have you."

They waved, and I went over all the instructions I'd memorized. We went back up the steps and into the kitchen, where my mom and several other women were making food for the new arrivals. The fellowship hall had long tables and folding chairs, and it was where I sent the group.

Kyra, Ezra, and I went to the front and led them through some Bible games until the food was ready. I sat in the middle of the new people and asked them polite questions, answering the ones given to me. After the meal, other people cleaned up while I continued to entertain our guests. My anxiety had mounted all night until I needed to escape to breathe. I excused myself and went down to the nursery, missing Hannah slipping out with me.

She followed me into the small room. "We need to talk."

I sunk down onto the floor and rubbed my forehead. "No, we don't. I have nothing to say to you."

"Too bad, because I have a lot to say to you."

I got up to leave, and she stepped in front of the door, shutting it. The widows looked promising.

She crossed her arms. "Really? You're that much of a coward that you can't talk to me for five minutes."

"It's that I'm not interested in anything you have to say to me."

She stepped closer. "You think you have everyone fooled, don't you? Your parents and all."

I stepped toward the window like I was facing a feral ferret. "What do you want?"

"My sister has been hanging out with Ezra lately. His parents and our parents are working on land projects together. They've been getting along really well, and it's time you back off from him. Since you don't like boys and all. Quit making him think you like him."

"Why can't your sister do her own bullying? Is it something you just enjoy, so you find a reason to do it? I'm honestly curious about why your sister can't say these things to my face." I made it two more steps to the window. The nursery seemed bigger than it ever had.

"She can, but I'm helping her out because I'm tired of your fakeness. Everyone likes you because you cater to what everyone wants from you. You're faker than a Halloween mask at Christmas."

I crinkled my nose. "What?" I sighed. "Look, I have no respect for you, which means I'm not going to do anything you want me to. Let's just get that clear. Maybe people like me because I don't back them into a church nursery and boss them around. You should try my method some time to be liked."

"Yeah, because I want to be a plastic Barbie like you. Miss pretty and popular." She rolled her eyes.

"I'd rather be a plastic Barbie than mean."

"Stay away from Ezra!"

"Or what?"

She launched forward and shoved me against the wall. "Or find out! You really don't want to." She gave me one last shove and left the room.

I couldn't breathe as I sunk to the floor. It took a few minutes to gain enough composure to crawl to the door and lock it so no one would find me. I stared at the clock as the minutes ticked by. When I finally exited, the church was dark, and I'd been locked inside. Luckily, it was easy to get out. I couldn't lock the deadbolt but made sure the bottom lock was turned before leaving. My car was a block away, and I drove around for a while. My life had too much drama for me to exist in it.

Everyone was probably at Sonic, and I drove by to see I was right. Kyra was sitting at a table with Ezra, and that made me pull into the parking lot. At least he didn't sit on the table like he did with me. For some dumb reason, that made me feel special. I was angry with him and Kyra, even though I had no right to be. I fixed my hair in my mirror and got out of the car.

Some of the visiting kids were there too, and I ordered an Ocean Water before sitting down with the two girls and three guys I'd sat with at dinner.

Val pulled up and walked to the empty spot next to me. "Is it okay to sit here?"

I zipped up my coat to give more room on the bench. "Yes, please."

We talked about small towns versus big cities, and all agreed there were pluses and minuses for both. I tried to keep my mind on the conversation and did an excellent job of pretending I was all in. My

Ocean Water arrived, and I tried to quit looking over at Ezra, who still hadn't realized I'd shown up. He was too involved in his conversation with Kyra, and my anger was mounting no matter how hard I tried to shove it back down. Hannah noticed me and smiled.

I hugged Val. "I'm going to head home."

"Are you sure?"

"Yeah, but do you want to come over again Friday and have a sleepover?"

"I'd love that."

I headed to my car, and one of the guys caught up to me. "Would you like to catch dinner and a movie while I'm here?"

"I'm not allowed to go to the movies."

"What about bowling? Do you have a bowling alley here?"

"Yeah, okay. When?"

"Tomorrow night." He glanced at his phone. "Seven?"

"Okay. Sure. I have people I can invite."

He waved his hand. "No, I thought you and me could go alone."

My eyes widened as I realized he'd asked me out. "Umm... I'm not allowed to date, either. Sorry."

Ezra noticed me then. Almost like his radar had picked up a guy asking me out.

He got up and threw his cup in the trash as he jogged over. "Hey. I couldn't find you earlier and thought you went home."

I glanced at Hannah's glare. "No, I needed a break. This is..." I turned to the guy. "I didn't catch your name."

"Ricky." He held out his hand to Ezra. "Nice to meet you. I was just asking Mila on a bowling date, but it seems she doesn't date."

Ezra stared at the guy's hand and stepped closer to me in a move that almost looked subconscious. "Dating isn't really something any of us are allowed to do at our church. They let you guys?"

Ricky put his hand down. "I do what I want. Mila, my offer still stands. We could go in a group if that makes it more allowable."

I nodded and took one last look at an angry Kyra and Hannah. "Sure. You guys are here for a few weeks. Bowling would be fun at some point in a group that's not a date. I know we're going on a ski trip, too."

Ezra followed me over to my car. "Are you alright? Why did you need a break?"

"It's a lot entertaining all these people we don't know. Everyone assumes I'll just do it without asking me how I feel."

"That's familiar. It's what happens when our dads are in ministry. Lots of pressure to behave and volunteer. Then people wonder why preachers' kids have a reputation for being rude and rebellious."

I opened my car door but paused getting in. "Yeah, maybe we all get fed up with it at some point and just want to be free."

"Or maybe what everyone calls rebellion for us is everyone else's normal, and people notice it more because we're expected to behave."

"That's probably true. Maybe both."

He rubbed the back of his neck and glanced at Ricky. "Are you going bowling with him?"

"Maybe. You should come. Bring Kyra. I've heard you like hanging out while your dads work on land projects."

His brows knitted. "Yeah, she's alright, but I'd rather go with you."

"I have a present for you for Christmas. We could go to the Christmas festival at Cole Park, and I can give it to you then. Don't worry about getting me anything."

"Too late."

"You didn't have to. The birthday presents you gave me were more than enough."

He shrugged. "I already got you one, so you'll have to deal."

I wanted to ask him if he'd already gotten Kyra a present but let it go. "Are you going on the ski trip?"

He looked at Ricky again. "Is he going?"

"Probably."

"Yeah, I'm going if they'll let me snowboard instead."

"It costs more, but they allow it." I climbed into my car. "Night, Ezra."

"Night. Call me when you get home. We don't have to talk. Let it ring once, and I'll know you made it safe. If you let it ring twice, I'll know you want to talk. Good night, Mila."

I went home and took care of my animals before climbing into bed and calling Ezra. I let it ring twice.

"Hey, what's up?" There was music in his background that lowered.

"I'm not sure. Not sure why I let it ring twice, other than I wanted to hear your voice."

"Call any time for that. Look, if you need a break from entertaining all these people, I can probably convince our dads to let us rotate, so you can have more breaks."

I closed my eyes, starting to drift to sleep. "As long as you don't have a rotation with Kyra, I'm good with that." My eyes popped open when I realized I'd said the words aloud."

"Mila?"

"Yeah?"

"I don't like Kyra."

"Okay. Goodnight." My chest zipped with sharp pangs that wouldn't settle. My fear was that how he felt about Kyra would change with time. A deep gut feeling had settled inside that I couldn't let go of, but for now, I knew he meant the words.

"Goodnight."

We hung up, and I prayed Ezra would never like Kyra. It wasn't clear if God would answer a prayer like that, but I had to try.

Chapter Seventeen:

Festive

♥

The night of the Christmas festival, I could barely sit still because I'd gotten Ezra the perfect Christmas present. I bought makeup and followed what Riley had shown me a while back. My parents were gone for the night, which meant they wouldn't catch me. The nice thing about having a job was that I could afford to buy forbidden things. I curled my hair and looked myself over. My blue velvet dress made my matching eyes pop. My white button-up coat and stocking cap added to the look to make me feel pretty and festive.

I grabbed Ezra's present, that I'd taken time to wrap as nicely as possible, which included a fancy bow made of pine, dried cranberries, and white ribbon. It had taken a bit to perfect it, but I couldn't wait to give it to him. My knee boots went over my black tights. I had a rare confidence and waltzed through the streets, taking in the lampposts decorated with pine wreaths that had big red bows on the bottom middle. Little white lights lit up all the storefronts.

"Silent Night" flowed from enormous speakers that hung over a silver, tinsel-lined archway. Booths were set up with different activities, food, and merchandise, and a cinnamon and oranges aroma flowed from one of them. A sign pointed to where to find Santa and feed the reindeer. I was meeting Ezra at the base of the light-up walking bridge on the east end of the park. I waved to several people I knew and continued to the bridge.

He was already waiting there in his leather jacket and black stocking cap. I took a minute to appreciate him before he noticed me. His furrowed brow relaxed when he spotted me, and he grinned as though seeing me made his entire night.

"Hello, gorgeous." He pulled me into a hug and held tight for a few seconds, burying his nose in my hair. "You smell nice."

"Thank you. You do too."

Our fingers naturally laced together until we remembered anyone could be watching. We pulled them apart and walked into the festival.

Ezra rubbed his chin. "Let me guess. Mila wants to feed reindeer first."

"I love that idea!"

"Not a surprise."

I bolted for the back of the park, and Ezra shook his head as he chased after me. We got in line and hummed to the Christmas music while we waited. I held the food in my gloved hand and let the massive brown animal tickle my hand. We posed for a picture with the reindeer between us and continued to get one with Santa. A woman handed us hot cocoa, and we snuck to the softball bleachers to sip and talk.

When our drinks were finished, we rested our backs on the bleachers, facing the sky. Ezra was one higher and right next to me. The sky was strangely clear for a Colorado December, and the stars spread above in ribbons of shimmering silver and blue. Neither of us spoke for a long time, but Ezra found my hand, concealing our touching in the low lighting around us.

He squeezed my hand. "You want to dance?"

I shot my head to the side to meet his eyes. "We can't dance."

"We're not supposed to hold hands either, but..."

"I have no idea how to dance, Ezra."

"Let's not worry about the how." He sat up and helped me up.

We retreated to the darkest part of the area, but the music still reached us clearly. He pulled me to him, and while I didn't know how to dance, I knew how to align myself with him. It was natural the way we fit. I rested against his firm chest, absorbing his heartbeat pattering against my cheek. We swayed as "Away in a Manger" led us into a peaceful lull.

My emotions zipped everywhere like a bee stuck in a jar. Big feelings pounded at me, wanting me to acknowledge them. What did he feel about me? Was it anything close to what I felt for him? Even if it was, it wasn't like we could give in to things. Maybe we pretended because we knew the us, that could be, was doomed from the start. I let go of thought and let the moment happen. Later, when I no longer had him against me, I could analyze all the questions. We eventually let go when the music faded and people packed up the festival.

Ezra walked me to my car. "Where do you want to exchange gifts?"

"You could come back to my house. My parents are out of town for the night."

"Okay. Yeah."

He followed me home but parked his car down the street like he usually did when he came over. We took every precaution we could. I changed into my red flannel pajamas and braided my hair. I went out of my bedroom and did a little dance as I brought him his present.

He laughed and paused his mouth on a crooked smile. "You can't handle the anticipation. Can you?"

"Not a single bit. Here is your present!" I shoved it in his lap and folded my hands to contain my shaking.

He watched me for a little longer, like he couldn't take his eyes off my amusement. "This is going to be the best present ever."

"Don't put that kind of pressure on me."

"It could be a toilet brush, and I will love it because of how excited you are."

"That's better. If it's at the standard of a toilet brush, this will definitely be better to you."

He ripped off the paper and opened the box. His jaw dropped. "How did you know?"

"When we went shopping, you stared at it longer than the other skateboards."

He ran his hand over the black skateboard with an alien on the other side. "This is beautiful. Dang, Mila, I can't believe you noticed."

"I always notice you."

"This is the best thing ever. I'm serious."

"Better than a toilet brush?"

"So much better than that." He leaped off the couch, scooped me up by my waist, and spun me around. "Thank you!"

I beamed at his happiness. "I made you cookies and pie, too."

"You're way too good to me. Not sure mine to you will be as awesome."

"But I want it, anyway. Even if it's a toilet brush."

He picked up the little box from the coffee table and handed it to me. "I'm nervous now."

"I'm going to love it because it's from you." I gently removed the green paper and pulled a snow globe from a box. "Is that?"

"Mount Blanca. Yeah, it is. So even when you go over that mountain someday, you remember there's always a place to come home to."

My lip quivered, and my tears trickled unhindered. "It's beautiful, Ezra. I love it! I love it so much."

He let me cry into his chest. "Better than a toilet brush?"

"Better than anything." I calmed enough to get up and grab the pie and two forks.

We each started on opposite ends while we watched a movie. Unknown to us, we'd chosen something spooky, and I kept varying between burying my face in Ezra's shoulder to squeezing his hand.

The movie ended, and I stared at the screen. "There goes my sleep for the night."

"Do I need to tuck you in?"

"I wouldn't mind it."

"Okay." He jumped up and threw me over his shoulder. I squealed as he zoomed me to my bed and plopped me on it.

I laughed and took a minute to find my breath again. "My teeth need brushed." I finished my bedtime routine and climbed under my covers. "You don't have to stay."

Ezra sat next to my door. "I have to protect you from the monsters pulling you under the bed and taking you to an alternate dimension."

"Thank you for reminding me of the movie."

"I'm only reminding you why I need to stay and protect you," he said.

"Thank you for the snow globe."

"Thank you for the skateboard. Spring can't come fast enough."

We stared at each other until my eyes drooped, and I drifted to sleep. I woke to the realization that Ezra had fallen asleep on my floor. Snow drifted to the ground outside my window, and I jumped up to get a better look.

"Ezra! It snowed! A lot!" I unlocked my window and pushed it open to stick my head out and catch snowflakes on my tongue.

"Snowman?"

"Snowman!"

We threw on our gear and rushed outside, where we rolled three massive snowballs and stacked them on top of each other. We gave it a cherry nose and rocks for its mouth and eyes.

"Five minutes to build your protection!" Ezra jumped to one side of the yard, pushing snow together.

"What?"

"The battle starts in less than five minutes! Prepare yourself!"

I watched him for a few seconds before I started on my wall. Ezra counted down from ten, and the snowballs went flying. I lifted my head over my wall, and one hit me right on the nose. I grabbed a pile of snow and packed them together, taking my ammunition behind a tree and circling around the yard to pelt him from the back. He jumped up and launched several at me in a row.

I couldn't make the snowballs fast enough, so I shoved piles of the frosty white at him. He copied, and we created a mini blizzard with our enthusiasm. The activity wore out my arms, and I plopped on my back in surrender. Ezra joined me, and we flapped our arms and legs to make snow angels. He rolled over to me and put a pile of snow down my back. I screeched and slammed a bunch into his face. I went to pile more, and he tickled me.

"Cheater!" I gasped through my giggling.

"It's worth it to get you this close." Ezra froze and brushed my hair behind my ear. He ran his thumb over my bottom lip.

I stared back, unable to control the fast thud in my chest. "Ezra?"

He blinked and kissed my forehead. "I should probably get home."

He helped me up, and we went inside, where I talked him into staying for breakfast. My lips tingled from the memory of his thumb, and I did my best to not wish for more.

He hugged me goodbye at the door. "Thanks for breakfast and the best Christmas present ever."

"Thanks for guarding me from interdimensional monsters and for the best Christmas present ever."

He left, and I watched him disappear from my kitchen window. I took the globe to my room and shook it. It went in the middle of my dresser, where I could see it from my bed. I got back under my covers and played "Mila's Mix" for the hundredth time. It was clear I'd fallen for Ezra Henderson, but there was nothing I could do about it. I needed to bury my feelings so deep before things got out of hand. The biggest problem was my room had remnants of him everywhere, making it very tough for me to muster the strength to stay only his friend.

Chapter Eighteen: Black Diamond Tumble

Snow gear covered me from head to toe to protect against arctic mountain temperatures, and sunglasses to ward against snow blindness made me challenging to recognize.

Ricky still did and took the seat next to me. "Hey."

I opened my mouth to tell him I was saving that for someone else when the youth leader from the other group and Mr. Thompson stood at the front and went over the rules. Ezra hopped on, and his eyes darted right for Ricky and me. His jaw stiffened, and he took the seat next to Kyra. I sunk against the window as Ricky told me about his life the entire hour and a half up the pass. I kept pushing back tears at Kyra and Ezra chatting. By the time we arrived at Wolf Creek ski lodge, I was an emotional mess.

I watched Ezra exit the bus with Kyra and wanted to go home. We went to the equipment rental, where a worker set me up with my boots, skis, and poles. The lodge offered the option of taking a class, but I'd gotten good over the years and no longer had to take any.

Log cabins and ski lifts were the only signs of civilization. Besides that, the mountain looked untouched, with its deep powder and abundant trees. People in blues, oranges, yellows, and other bright colors popped against the snow. A group of children held plastic rings attached to a rope as they followed behind their instructor. Several people sat on the lodge balcony, eating breakfast.

Ricky walked up next to me. "Want to go on a black diamond with me?"

"I'm more of a blue square girl."

"Come on. You have to be a better skier than that. You live right by these resorts."

I watched Ezra and Kyra walk to a lift and get in line. "I don't have enough skill for one."

"Come on. It'll be fun and help you get better."

As I watched Kyra and Ezra get closer to the lift, something shifted in me, and I no longer cared. "Fine. One black diamond, and then I'm back to blue."

Deep inside, I knew this was a terrible idea, and I wasn't experienced enough to take on a black diamond. The main reason for my lapse in judgment was I knew Kyra and Ezra wouldn't be on a black diamond, and I wouldn't have to watch them interacting. Worst case, I'd slide on my butt on the way down.

The way it worked was the lift that led to the closest black diamond would run next to the lift that led to the blue square Ezra would be on. That might have also been another reason I decided to go for it. While I didn't want to see them interact, I wanted him to know I was skiing with Ricky. The sheer terror of the situation didn't hit me until I was already well on the lift.

"Hey, Mila!"

I turned around to see Val on the lift behind me. "Hey! You're going on a black diamond alone?"

"No, I saw you get on and was hoping we could ski together."

"Yes! That would be great. Do you have much experience with these?"

"Yeah, a ton. Don't you?"

"Umm... A little," I lied.

Ricky continued to talk about himself, and I had no idea how a person could tell someone they had just met so much about themselves. The stuff he told me would have taken someone months to get out of me, but because I'd perfected pretending to like small talk, he thought I was listening.

"Mila!"

I looked over to see Ezra with his hands cupped around his mouth, yelling at me from his lift.

I waved. "Hey!"

"What are you doing?!"

I dramatically shrugged, and he frowned. He was all too aware I belonged nowhere near a black diamond. I could ski well, but I was no expert.

"Be careful!" he shouted. He watched, looking horrified, as our lifts moved farther apart.

It was too late for careful, and my anxiety rose at the same speed as the lift. We exited the lift and waited for Val. Val and Ricky skied down easily, and I followed them more cautiously. Val and I discussed the future as we swished back and forth down the first part. We found ourselves laughing and trying to talk over Ricky, who was still going on about his life.

All went well for a while until the trail steepened significantly, and rocks jutted above the snow, creating obstacles along with narrowed tree paths. The wind had also picked up, blowing snow and limiting visibility.

It would be okay, was what I told myself exactly when there was a sudden drop, I hadn't seen from the blowing snow. My body flung forward, popped me out of the skis, and I tumbled. My hard plastic boot slammed into my head, and my foolishness hit me full force when I landed against a tree.

"Mila! Oh my God! Mila!" Val stood over me. "Mila! Say something!"

"Ouch," I whimpered.

She pointed at Ricky. "You, boy! Go get ski patrol!" She turned back to me. "Don't move. Stay put, Mila. We're going to get help."

I blinked, trying to shake the dazed feeling and understand more of what was happening. "I'm... Fine."

Ricky skied over. "She says she's fine."

"She's not fine! Look at her eyes! Go get ski patrol!" Val sounded like she was going to shove Ricky off the cliff nearby.

"Let's get her up, and I'll help her down if need be."

"Go get ski patrol, you moron!" Val somehow found my sunglasses and put them back over my eyes.

"Why don't you if you think she needs it so bad?"

I lifted my hand, and it flopped back down. "I'm fine."

Ricky thrust his hands toward me. "See, she's fine."

"You're going to get ski patrol because she is clearly not fine, and I'm not leaving her with you!"

Ricky snorted. "Fine. Whatever. I'm getting hungry."

"Real great person you are! Get going, and I swear to God almighty, I will kill you if you don't send help quick!" Val took my hand. "Talk to me, Mila. Tell me about the animals at the shelter."

I stared at the grey sky and the birds flying through it. "I'm sorry, Val." A few tears rolled down my cheeks.

"For what?"

"I'm an idiot. I knew better than to take on a black diamond."

"Let's not worry about that right now. What's done is done. I want to hear about your shelter animals."

"We had a good adoption day two weeks ago outside the Big R. Five dogs and two cats were adopted."

"That's amazing! Which is your favorite?"

"This golden retriever named Trevor. I keep thinking someone will pick him, but he's been passed over the last three adoptathons." I groaned as I tried to sit up. "I'm probably fine. Just stunned myself. There's no reason for a big fuss."

"You were knocked out cold for a good five minutes. You need looked at."

"What? I didn't get knocked out."

"Yes, you were. That moron was no help at all. He was like, give her a minute, and she'll be fine."

I scrunched my face. "Are you sure?"

"Yeah, I've never been so scared in my life. We talk about heaven all the time in church, and it's this wonderful place. But no one is in a hurry to get there or have anyone they know get there."

"That's true. I'm sorry I'm ruining your ski trip."

She shook her head. "Sitting here, talking to you is the best. You only would have ruined it if you hadn't woken up. I've enjoyed getting to know you again these last few months."

"Same. It's been really nice. You remember when we were kids and played at Devil's eye?" I wasn't sure why I brought it up other than my mind not functioning right. It seemed to fly through random things more than it normally did.

"Yeah, it really did look like an eye made of dirt, and we caught those grasshoppers that landed on it because we thought it made them magical."

I smiled as I recalled the dirt patch next to our school playground. "I miss those days."

"Me too. They were a lot less complicated."

"If something happens to me, can you tell Ezra I love him?"

She laughed and squeezed my hand. "Mila, everyone, including Ezra, knows you love him. And nothing is going to happen to you. Too many people need Mila in this world."

"He doesn't know, and if he does, he doesn't care. He went skiing with Kyra."

"Probably because you were with Ricky. You really need to kiss him already."

My eyes shifted. "No, we're... It's not..."

"Yes, and denial is your entire problem. For both of you. Between denial and doubt, you two have a road ahead."

Shivers had sunk into my bones. "It's getting so cold. We should probably try to get down the mountain. Who knows if Ricky is sending anyone? I think I'm okay."

She glanced around. "You would have thought someone would have come by now. Maybe I should go get someone myself."

"You should get warm somewhere. I'll be fine."

"Not getting warm until you are, but I may need to get help." She got herself up with her poles. "I promise I'll be back soon. Stay awake. Sing Sunday school songs."

She left, and I grew sleepy. My head throbbed and my body ached.

"Mila! Can you hear us, honey?"

I opened my eyes to see a red-headed woman in a blue ski patrol uniform standing over me. Val had been quick. Blankets were wrapped around me, and a brace placed around my neck.

A man shined a light in my eyes. "Can you tell us your name?"

"Mila Sadler."

"How old are you, Mila?"

"Seventeen. I could probably walk out of here. There's no need for all the trouble."

"We'll let the doctors decide that. You've taken quite the tumble." He helped the woman get me on a stretcher, and they skied me down to first aid, where they decided they should transport me to the local hospital to be safe. My parents were going to kill me over the ambulance bill alone.

Pain shot through my skull as I sat up. "I really feel fine now. No need for an ambulance. Really. I promise to get checked out, but no ambulance."

Val sat in the chair next to me. "You really should get checked out as soon as possible."

The medic wrote something on a clipboard. "Let's call your parents and let them decide."

"My girlfriend is here! Mila Sadler! I need to see her right now!" Ezra said from somewhere in the other room.

I sank under the covers. Both wanting to see him and embarrassed by my stupidity. "I think I can just leave. There's no reason to fuss over me." It hit me then that Ezra had called me his girlfriend, but then my swirling head might have imagined it, sourced from wishful thinking.

A medic popped his head into the room. "There's an Ezra that would like to see you. Should I send him in?"

My cheeks heated, but my desire to see him grew stronger. "Sure."

The other medic left to call my parents, and Ezra burst into the room, making large strides to my side.

Val stood up. "I'm going to go get some lunch and give you two a minute. I'll check back soon."

When the room emptied of everyone but Ezra and me, he leaned forward. "Dang it, Mila! I told you to be careful!"

"I'm a terrible listener."

"What were you thinking going on a black diamond? Was that to impress Ricky?"

I closed my eyes and yawned. "No, it was to not see you with Kyra."

"I only went with Kyra because you were with Ricky, and I thought I'd be interrupting something."

"Why would it have been a problem to interrupt?" I opened my heavy eyes to meet his.

He ran his fingers through his hair like he always did when stressed. "What are they saying? How hurt are you?" His voice broke a little.

"I'm fine. They said I'm fine."

"Your forehead doesn't look fine, and why are you still here if you're good?"

I closed my eyes. "That's a great question. But honestly, please don't worry about me."

"Way too late for that."

"You should go spend the rest of the day with Kyra."

He tangled our fingers together. "You really did hit your head hard if you think I'm going anywhere right now."

The medics talked to my parents, who wanted me to ride back with the group and go to our local hospital. Since I was conscious and coherent, they figured it wasn't an emergency. The staff wanted to keep a close eye on me as a precaution. Ezra spent the rest of the day with me in the first aid building, talking and watching old black and white movies on the large tube TV. No matter how many times I tried to convince him to get his money's worth with snowboarding, he stayed. He wanted to carry me to the bus, but my legs still worked. I hobbled with his support.

Ricky walked past us on his way to a different spot. "I see you're no worse for wear."

Ezra jumped out of his seat. "No thanks to you."

"Clearly, she's alright."

"You won't be in a minute."

I grabbed Ezra's arm. "Let it go."

"He went and got lunch while you were hurt on the mountain!"

"It's okay. Helped me decide not to go bowling with him."

Ezra sunk back in his seat. "Only good thing that came out of any of this."

The verdict back home was a concussion and a sprained ankle. I owed my rescue to Val, who had gotten me help quickly when Ricky had flaked out. Things could have turned out badly for me if Val hadn't gone with us. I would live on with a lesson learned the hard way.

Chapter Nineteen: Skateboarding and Books

The Denver group left a few days before Christmas after the play's closing, and winter carried on with Ezra babying me for a while. I had recovered well after a few weeks, and the ski trip was long behind us. Spring arrived with Riley still not talking to me, and I'd gotten to the point I'd accepted it. My free time was divided between Ezra, Val, and Erin. Sometimes, all four of us did things together.

The most exciting thing of the year was the library sale, where they would have old books for ten cents. The library sat in front of Cole Park, along with city hall and a few other government offices. Between the buildings and the playground was the skateboarding area that was Ezra's second home during warmer weather. I often walked to the park to enjoy the fresh air and watch him do flips off the ramps. It was magic seeing him in his element.

I bought a ton of books that filled three bags and took them to my car. Music boomed from a stereo someone had set on the grass. Brown plastic benches rested in front of the skate park, and I sat on one to watch Ezra and his friends skateboard. His blue hat was turned backward, and he had on a white shirt and black jeans.

He flew up the wall, came off his board, and landed back on it without stumbling. It was like he had wings, and some force kept yanking him back to the skateboard for perfect landings. He slid over a railing, flipped his board, and landed back on it. Several times, I stiffened, thinking he would collide with concrete, but he stayed steady.

I watched him for a good hour, wondering if he ever wore out. He gave his friends a weird handshake, where their chests collided.

A couple of them walked my way, and one did a chin nod. "What's up?"

I waved and waited to see if Ezra would notice me. He took a swig of his water bottle and did a few more stunts before tucking his skateboard under his arm and leaving the ramps. He put his headphones in and messed with his Discman. His relaxed mouth and bright hazel eyes popped, giving him a contented appearance.

His face lit up when he spotted me. "How long have you been there?"

"About an hour."

He removed his headphones and stuck them in his pocket. "What? I could have introduced you to everyone."

"I was having too much fun watching you do tricks."

"I lucked out today. No collisions. You want to get some ice cream?"

"Yeah, isn't that always a yes?"

He laughed. "Right. Next time, I'll tell you we're going to go get ice cream."

"Sounds good, because I won't complain."

We walked around to the front of city hall.

Ezra stopped at the library sale sign. "Now I get it. That's why Mila came to the park today instead of reading in her bedroom."

"I had to get a new stockpile."

"To go with the other thousand you still need to read."

I threw my hand up. "Don't judge! They will be read."

"Sure. Don't you have enough to read for school?"

I gaped. "What?"

"Right. Sorry. That was dumb to say. I was thinking we should go camping. Maybe up by the hot springs. It's been warm lately."

"We could hike up those trails that are above Zapata. Estimate where we want to put our house."

He put his skateboard in his car. "I thought you wanted it on the top. That'll take a long time to hike all the way up."

"All we got is time."

"Says the girl with fifty million things she's juggling."

The temperature made it the perfect walking weather, and downtown was busier than usual. A live band flowed from Milagros's coffee shop on the corner, diagonal from the bookstore I often had to sneak into. My father had publicly condemned some of the bookstore's selection choices, but I didn't believe in censoring literature. He wanted an outright ban on many of the books inside. My father had a war on stories while I lived for them.

We decided on cookies and hot cocoa in the coffee shop instead of ice cream. Milagros was a coffee shop with purpose and helped fund La Puente, the only homeless shelter in town. Their mission was to help struggling families get back on their feet. The shelter was directly across the street from our church.

The jazz music made eating our snack entertaining, and we sat, watching the band play. It was something I appreciated about Ezra; he could sit in a moment with me and not have to talk about it.

My emergency phone vibrated in my pocket, and I pulled it out with a frown.

I darted outside. "Hello?"

"Mila, it's Ruth. You know, from the humane society."

"Yeah, did you get a new bird in? I can head right over."

"No, nothing like that. You know our president, Linda Hill?"

I thought for a minute. "Yeah, I met her once at the fundraiser banquet."

"She passed away, sweetheart. Such a terrible thing. She was an animal champion. We lost one of the best."

"I'm so sorry, Ruth. Is there anything I can do?"

"I was hoping you'd come to the funeral. I'm calling all the volunteers so we show what she meant to all of us."

"Yeah, I'll be there. Do you know what her favorite flowers were?"

"Purple petunias, I believe, or maybe daffodils. Bring whatever you think is pretty."

I turned around to see Ezra. "Okay. Will do."

"It's tomorrow at three. They buried her quick. Not sure why, but they did."

"Okay. See you then." I hung up and turned my attention to the inquisitive boy beside me. "The president of the humane society died. I need to go pick up flowers and go to her funeral tomorrow."

"I'm sorry, Mila."

"I didn't really know her but should pay my respects."

"Do you want me to come?"

I shook my head and went back inside to take care of the food I'd left. "You don't have to. It's more of a formality out of respect for the woman who helped so many animals. We could do something after, but maybe we should start planning the camping trip. I'll work ahead in school, so we can have a few days."

"I can do the same, but what will we tell our parents?"

I shrugged. "That we're going camping, but we'll just have to change who we're going with. Erin will cover for me. If you don't want to risk it, I get it. We could always climb to Zapata and back for a day."

"Don't worry about me. I'm worried about you being punished if we're caught."

I threw away my trash and grabbed a bag for the leftover cookies. "We can stay gone a couple of nights. I doubt my parents will notice."

"Alright. Next week then?"

"Yeah, that works." He walked me to my car, and we parted ways.

I went home to care for my animals and get some schoolwork done. Ruth called me a few more times with things she'd forgotten to tell me. I had to have spent twenty dollars or more on her calls alone, and I looked forward to the day I could buy a contract phone like my friends had. It rang again, and I sighed. Riley's name popped on the screen, and I gaped for a few seconds before fumbling to answer it.

"Hello?"

"Mila, hey, I know I'm wasting your minutes."

I waved my hand about even though she wouldn't see it. "It's okay. Don't worry about my minutes."

"I'm house-sitting and was wondering if you'd like to come over tomorrow night so we can talk. If not, I get it completely."

"Yes! I'd love to."

The phone stayed silent for a few seconds. "Okay. Good." She gave me the address, and the call ended.

I sat back on my bed, working through the shock. Riley hadn't talked to me in months, and now she wanted me to come to the place she was house-sitting to talk. The last part made zings zap my stomach on constant repeat.

I walked into the large white church. It looked like the kind out of books and movies with the bell steeple, making it a pillar in the small town it resided. Inside, royal blue ruled the way red did in my church. The carpet and pews were covered in the bright color. At the front was a lavender, grey open casket with flowers and plants decorating around it. A girl in a white dress handed me a paper with Linda Hill's picture and details about her life. I signed the guest book and glanced around the room. The church was packed, and I slipped into one of the few empty spots toward the back.

The music started, and Carter flung himself into the seat next to me. "Hey!"

I scowled. "What do you want?"

"I'm here for the funeral. But damn! Mila cleans up nice. No ponytail or loose clothes. You're hotter than usual. That dress!" His eyes ran over me.

"And you're an idiot! We're at a funeral!"

He threw his hand toward the front. "Casket tells me that. We should go out. Why don't you and I go to Burger King tonight?"

I pressed my lips to give my scowl emphasis. "I have plans."

"Okay, another night. I'm on a personal mission to make you my girlfriend, baby."

"Call me baby again, or pursue your mission, and I will kick you in the shin."

He put his hand up. "Woah! Hey now. No violence at a funeral, though that could be hot."

The service started, and I ignored Carter's whispers through it. I paid my respects to the family and headed out to my car. My birds would need to be taken care of before I went to see Riley in case she wanted me to spend the night. The thought seemed crazy after she hadn't spoken to me in so long. It hit me then that maybe I should be worried about what she was going to say. This most likely wouldn't be a happy little reunion, as I'd envisioned all day. Something had to have happened for Riley to talk to me again out of nowhere.

"Hey! My offer still stands. I'll take you on the best date ever. It'll be fun." Carter jogged up to my car.

I paused, opening the door. "We're at a funeral. Someone died, and all you can think about is landing a date with me."

"I have to make a move before Ezra does."

"Carter, you're terrible. I'm not going out with you."

"This is going to make it awkward for us to volunteer together, isn't it?"

I got in my car. "Working with you is already awkward. Go ask someone else out at the most inappropriate time ever." I slammed my door and drove off.

My mind stayed on Riley for the rest of the day. My phone rang right after my shower, and at the rate things were going, I'd have to hand my paycheck to the phone company.

Ezra was on the other end. "I know this is costing. I'll give you money when I see you, but I wanted to make sure you were okay after the funeral."

"I'm fine, but thank you. Like I said earlier, I really didn't know her. I met her once briefly. It's sad she died, but she lived a long life helping animals."

"The reason I didn't call your house phone is I want you to know I got it all arranged with my parents to be gone two days next week. They think I'm camping with a friend. They didn't even ask which friend, so I'm not going to add anything. I'm sure they assume it's Lance."

"I'll do the same thing and make sure Erin knows to cover for me."

"Sounds good. Night, Mila."

"Night, Ezra." I smiled and hung up my phone.

I let my mom know I was going to Riley's for the night and brought up the camping trip.

"Yeah, that's fine, as long as you're caught up in your schoolwork. Have fun at Riley's."

I slipped out the door, thinking that had been too easy.

Chapter Twenty: Unclear Promises

♥

I squinted at all the houses to figure out the correct address. The even houses were on the left, and I crept down the street like a scouting burglar. All the houses were cookie-cutter white and two-story. I pulled into the driveway. Riley's Geo showed me I'd found the right house. I knocked and tried not to gape when she answered.

She'd grown her usually spiky hair to her shoulders. "Hey, come in." She wore a white tank and jean shorts that stopped at her upper thigh. "I got chocolate. Lots of it and those fruit gems you love."

"Thank you." I stepped inside, taking in the Aztec statues on three adobe archway shelves between the living room and the kitchen. "This place is nice."

"Yeah, my mom's coworker went to Denver and wants me to be here for her love bird."

My eyes widened. "Love bird."

She chuckled. "Yeah, I thought you'd like to see it. We could make tacos. I bought the stuff."

I took off my jacket, draping it over my arm. "That would be fun and yummy."

She held out her hands. "I could hang that up for you."

I handed the coat to her and glanced at a fancy painting of cowboys riding horses while driving cattle. There were lots of other artwork, and it seemed this person was either an artist or had lots of money for non-necessities.

Riley had gotten all my favorite things, and it wasn't clear what she wanted from the meeting. We went to the enormous kitchen that seemed larger than my entire trailer. The granite countertops and stainless-steel appliances were the fanciest I'd ever seen. Massive space stood between everything and a grand kitchen island.

Riley got out a pan and all the ingredients for tacos. "I thought we could watch a movie. If you want to."

"Yeah, that would be great."

"I have one in mind if that works?"

"Okay, yeah." In old times, I would have asked her if it had Keanu Reeves in it, but this wasn't old times. What this was, was confusing.

We munched on our tacos on a big fluffy black sectional couch in front of a sizeable flat-screened TV. The only other person I'd seen own one was Erin's family. She put on the movie, and we watched while devouring all my favorite snacks that felt like a bribe for something. The film was called *Enough* and featured Jennifer Lopez. She played an abused wife who saved herself and her daughter from her violent husband by learning to fight.

When it ended, Riley shut off the TV and grabbed a pillow. "How have you been?"

"Alright. Same stuff as always. What about you?"

She nodded. "Same."

Silence descended on us, lined with an awkwardness Riley and I had never had before.

She sat back and stared at the floor. "I wanted you to see that movie."

"Oh... Yeah, it was a good movie."

"It was. Look, I know we haven't talked in months, but I watched this the other day, and it made me think about you."

My nose crinkled. "Me?"

"Yeah, what I yelled at you the last time I saw you was said wrong. What I said was true, but I didn't say it the nicest. The world will hurt you, Mila, and that scares me. I'm hoping you'll make me a promise. Not that you owe me a thing, but I'm hoping you will, anyway."

"Okay. What promise?"

She got up and sat next to me, taking my hand. "I want you to promise me the first time a guy hits you, you leave. The first time he calls you a name, you know he shouldn't, you leave. And I want you to know that no matter how things are between us, you call me if you're ever in trouble. Anytime day or night, and I will come to get you. I'll get you out of the situation."

"Okay. Same for you."

She squeezed my hands and let them go. "But promise me. The first time a guy abuses you, you leave him. No matter how much you love him. No matter what your religion says. You get out."

"Even if we're married and I didn't listen to him?"

She closed her eyes as her shoulders sank. "Yes, Mila, even if you've been married to him for ten years. Promise me." She reopened her eyes. They were bright green and golden. Her cat-like eyes were some of the prettiest I'd ever seen.

"Okay. I promise." Something sunk in my gut because I didn't fully understand what I had promised her. At what level did my husband have to be mean for me to leave? What if I'd done something to make him mad or disobeyed him? What contingencies did this promise come with?

"Then you call me. I don't care if we live a thousand miles apart or down the street from each other. I'll come to get you. No questions asked."

I nodded. Things grew quiet for a few minutes as we sorted through our thoughts. She showed me the love bird and let me hold it.

After that, she got my jacket for me. "I'm technically not allowed to have anyone over here."

"Oh, okay. Thank you for this." I pointed to the kitchen. "Shouldn't I help clean up first?"

"No, I got it." She opened the door. "It was good seeing you again."

"Yeah, my number is the same. Don't worry about the dollar a minute. Really, I don't mind."

"Have a goodnight, Mila."

"Ummm... You, too." I went out to my car but only drove a block away. I pulled my car over in front of a fancy blue house and stared out my windshield at the clear night sky, wondering what had just happened.

I double-checked everything I packed for the camping trip. My neighbors were going to feed my ducks and chickens while I was gone. They would get spending money, and I'd get time with Ezra for three days and two nights. My parents were busy with ministry, and I was confident they'd never notice enough to question more about where I was.

My mom was sitting in her vintage blue chair. Her feet were up on the matching footstool. She threaded the needle through her cross-stitch. It was her favorite pastime, and she had given me one when I was eight. It was of a ladybug standing in front of a cottage with flowers around the scene. Nine years later, it was still a work in progress.

I popped my head into the room and waved. "I'm off to the camping trip."

She glanced up for a second and returned her attention to her project. "Okay. Have fun."

I hiked my red duffle bag up on my shoulder and rushed out the door. My ducks, chickens, and geese were chomping happily on their food as I checked on them one last time. Ezra had parked two blocks over, and I strolled to the location we'd agreed on.

I leaped into his truck and tossed my bag in the back seat. "This is so exciting!"

He grinned. "Yeah, I have to say my excitement might match yours."

"Not sure that's possible!"

"Yeah, you're probably right." He switched on the radio and turned his truck toward our mountain.

Birds danced against a grey sky, twirling and diving like the freest creatures. The terrain morphed from rolling tumbleweeds and yellow foliage to pines, boulders, and vibrant life. Ezra had reserved our campsite and crept his truck along the spots filled with mainly RVs. A few had tents like we had. The campground made a nearly perfect circle, and we could cut through a middle path that led to bathrooms.

Ezra set up the tent while I pulled everything out of the truck. I unfolded the blue canvas chairs and set them in front of the fire pit, placing everything to start the fire and our cooler beside them. By the time he had our sleeping area set up, I had the camp put together.

"Now what?" I peeked in the tent to see our sleeping bags next to each other.

"Whatever we want. Maybe some of the hiking trails."

"We go as far up the mountain as we want."

I made sandwiches, which made Ezra happy that I'd packed him three. We turned away from the sand dunes and went up a trail that led into the eastern mountains. A crispness formed in the air, giving it a green, earthy aroma. Pine trees that had started out scarce grew close enough to touch in most places. Bare patches still had a lot of beauty with silver rocks and yellow grass. A few flowers flourished with determination among several boulders. Chipmunks scurried out into the open, chasing each other, and crows cawed overhead.

Despite the nature sounds of rustling leaves and bird songs, a stillness surrounded us that we took in without words. My fingers brushed his, and he took my hand. Handholding was the simplest intimate gesture between two people in love. My chest fluttered at the thought of being in love. A heavy ache replaced it at the pretending we had to do. I longed for so much more with him, and it would be easy to lose control. Chaotic feelings scared and excited me. How wonderful would it be to let go with Ezra? To allow ourselves to act on what we felt when we wanted to.

The air grew chillier, and I zipped up my jacket. Snow littered the ground like patches in a quilt. Rocks made up the spaces in between. The trail grew steeper, and we walked until our legs ached and our stomachs demanded we make use of our picnic. We found a ledge free of snow, and I laid out our blanket. Ezra downed his sandwiches faster than I did my one.

The sky had faded into night with glimpses of stars speckling an indigo sky. We talked about everything like we always did on the barn roof and got lost in conversation until my teeth chattered and Ezra demanded we return to the tent. He seemed unwilling to let me come close to freezing.

He got the fire going, pushing logs around with a stick for an optimal blaze. "It's a campfire. That means it's time for a story."

"What kind of story?"

"Any. Start talking like you normally do and let plot fall out."

I sat back in my chair and stared at the sky. "Once upon a time, there was a girl, and she loved a prince. She loved him so much, but she was cursed to be encased in glass. That glass meant that even if she could get him to love her back, they could never touch. She set out to find a way to break her crystal cage and was told by a wise squirrel—"

He scrunched his face. "A wise squirrel?"

"Do you want the plot to fall out of my mouth or not?"

He spread his arm in a sort of bowing gesture. "By all means, continue."

"The wise squirrel told her there was a magic lake that would erase any curse. She went and bathed in the curse-breaking waters. Sure enough, her glass dissolved, and she hurried to find the boy but found him in another's arms. She'd waited so long, thinking she wasn't good enough for him, that he gave his heart to another."

Ezra grabbed the bag of marshmallows next to him and handed me a metal stick with a wooden handle. "I got one."

I straightened myself and paused stabbing my marshmallow. "You're going to tell me a story?"

He shrugged one shoulder. "I give no promises to be Mila good, but here we go. Once upon a time, there was a girl. She was the prettiest girl a lowly stable boy had ever seen. He wanted to take her in his arms and kiss her, promising her through every terrible storm he'd never let go. But he knew if he gave in to his desires, it would anger a terrible monster. That monster could hurt the girl a great deal. Night after night, the boy watched the stars, praying for the perfect star to wish the monster away. Until that happened, he had to protect the one he loved, which meant keeping her an arm's length away. Their love could never be the reason he lost her."

I dropped my stick and took in a sharp breath. We stared at each other because we understood our stories' meanings.

We went to the tent, eventually. Long after the air had become too cold to endure without my coat and several blankets. We wouldn't freeze, but it could be uncomfortable. We went inside the tent and into our sleeping bags. On our sides, facing each other, we talked far into the night.

Chapter Twenty-One: Fueled by Anger

♥

The campground bathroom also had showers, and I got up early to take one. It felt nice to stand under the water, and I took a bit of time to enjoy it. I dressed in a fresh pair of clothes and exited the bathroom.

Ezra had beaten me back from his shower and was cooking bacon and eggs on a little battery-operated griddle. I mixed the pancake batter and used a second griddle to make them. After our big breakfast, we drove in his truck to the Zapata entrance and climbed the trails above the waterfall. The dirt trail curved sharply in places, and one side dropped straight down to an enormous white rock platform. No guardrail or fence prevented tumbles.

In some places, a dirt and rock wall rose next to us, and in other areas, it became level ground of yellow grass and wildflowers. We stopped at a higher platform, and I wove two flower crowns while we talked. I placed the first on Ezra's head. His left brow popped, but he left it on. I made a second for myself and sunk into the yellow grass. The clouds overhead had perfected themselves worthy of a magazine with their fluffy appearance against an azure sky.

For a long time, we stared upward. Ezra tugged my hand, and I rolled over into his arms. We remained buried in the wildflowers. He asked for a story, and I gave him three short ones. One thing I loved about him was that he listened to me talk about the characters and kingdoms stuck in my head. He would add comments and questions that showed he'd taken in everything I said.

It was peaceful and how I wished to spend every morning for the rest of my life. My mind wandered into dreams grounded in reality. They weren't about some magical land or legendary creatures. They involved a mountain home, Ezra, and calm mornings. Yet, it seemed they were still a fantasy. The simplicity we'd never share because I was destined for Bible college, so I could have tons of children and homeschool them. That was what I would use my teaching degree for.

My mother reminded me to put as much of my work money aside for this thing she wanted me to devote my life to. I would pay for college, but it would be where they demanded I go. Each paycheck, I stocked away money, but my savings felt like a harsh life sentence. More and more, I wanted that money for my escape plan, and lately, that plan had taken shape into a form I didn't fully understand yet.

I turned on my side. "Ezra."

He tore his face from the sky. "Mila."

Heat flooded my chest at the sweet way he said my name. He always said it like it was his favorite lyric in the music he loved. "Would it be crazy if we eloped? I mean, not now or anything, but when we turn eighteen. No one could stop us from making choices because you'd be considered my umbrella. Only God would be above you." The heat from my stomach rose to my face. "That's a stupid idea. Sorry."

"Mila." My name came out as laughter this time. "Stupid is not the word for it."

Watching a cloud shaped like a horse made me think of the horse painting in the house Riley met me. Ezra would never hurt me. He'd have rather died before he saw me suffer. His actions and words had always told me that. I'd never have to keep that promise to Riley if Ezra married me. The promise wouldn't need to exist. Our life would be cloud watching and mountain climbing. That's what life with Ezra would mean. It would mean peace.

I met his eyes again. "What's a good word for it, then? Ridiculous, insane, terri—"

"Perfect. It would be perfect, Mila. No one could touch us then, but I don't want to be your umbrella."

My face fell. "Oh."

"I want to be your equal. Not that I won't protect you like that whole concept teaches. Not that I wouldn't provide a good life for us, but you and I have always been equals. Different. Balanced. But never one above the other, and why would I want to change that to spend the rest of my life with you?"

My eyes fluttered, and tears slipped out. He kissed my temple, and I relaxed my head against him. Perfect was definitely what we had. It was everything around us that created storms.

In the afternoon, we found a little stream. It only went up to our ankles, but we splashed in it. Our feet slid against the coppery rocks, but we kept our balance and practiced hopping over each stone. The sun moved close to the western horizon, so we turned back. The wind had picked up and chilled my damp clothes even more.

Ezra unzipped his bag and tossed me a hoodie. "Can't have my fiancé catching pneumonia on my watch." He grinned and winked.

I laughed while putting on the hoodie, shrugging my shoulders to bring the lingering fabric scent closer to my nose. "Your clothes always smell the best."

"That's good to know that learning to do laundry well at a young age has paid off."

"It's more than that. It's you."

His eyes shifted to the ground. "Me? I smell?"

"Yeah, it's my favorite."

"Really?"

"Yeah."

"I guess that makes sense. I love to smell your hair."

I crinkled my nose. "Does the rest of me stink?"

He shrugged. "I'm not sure. The hair distracts me from finding out."

I giggled at his smirk. We made it to the Zapata parking lot and returned to our campsite. I brushed my teeth and used the bathroom while Ezra got our campfire going. We watched the stars and told more stories. The night cooled further, and we got in our sleeping bags. My teeth chattered, and it seemed colder than the night before.

Ezra stood up. "You're going to freeze, aren't you?"

"I... d-don't... know."

"We should zip our sleeping bags together, but only if you're comfortable."

I leaped up. "That works. For survival purposes, of course."

"Right. It's a necessity." He zipped our bags together.

I snuggled up to his warm chest and drifted to sleep with the weight of his arms removing all the things that made me anxious.

The next morning, we packed up camp early and drove to the cafe on the college campus. They were famous for cinnamon rolls as large as plates. We each got our own. The flaky pastry melted in my mouth with the perfect combination of butter and icing. The richness stayed at a delightful level, but I could only eat half of mine. Ezra didn't complain when I handed my leftovers to him. The boy was always starving. He burned it off skateboarding nearly all day.

He dropped me off a block from my house, and I went straight to my birds. The neighbors had already fed them, so I sat with them a bit before going inside. My parents had already left somewhere for the day, and I logged on to school to get ahead for the week. The front door opened, but I kept my eyes on my computer screen.

"Mila!"

I jumped at my dad's stern voice and stood to face him. "Yes, sir."

"Can you come and sit in the living room with us?"

I studied my parents' faces and sunk onto the couch. My thumbnail dug into my finger to allow the pain to ground me and hold off anxiety until I got through whatever this was. My mom sat in her chair, holding her little terrier dog on her lap. His name was Frisky, and he had a little white beard that stood out against his wiry sandy coat.

My dad remained standing. "Mr. Mondragon said he saw you at the sand dunes campground."

I nodded. "Yes, that's where I was camping. Mom knew about it."

"What your mom didn't know was that you went there with a boy."

"W-what do you mean?"

"He saw you with a boy but didn't get a good look at his face. He'd seen you in the morning, then that evening, he saw you go into a tent with a boy."

"Maybe he thought Riley was a boy because she has really short hair."

My mother scratched her dog's ear. "You said you were going with Erin."

"But Riley showed up at the last minute."

"Mr. Mondragon said the boy had dark hair, and he was confident you entered a tent with him."

I reached for an excuse but stuttered and stumbled as I pleaded for a believable lie to pour from my mouth. "He must have seen wrong."

"His wife saw it too." He shook his head. "And now you're lying about it. I gave you a chance to come clean with the truth. Go to your room and wait. You know what happens next."

I rushed to my room and considered going through the window but didn't.

It seemed an eternity and two seconds when he entered the room. "Tell me who the boy is, and this will be easier."

I realized then that all that mattered was protecting Ezra. "A boy I met at the campground. We went hiking together, and he came back to my camp to make S'mores."

"And he went into the tent with you?"

"Yes, to play card games."

"You know the rules."

And I did, and that's why I took my punishment without resistance. I put my hands against the bed and remained still while the belt hit my back and butt. It was the first beating I'd gotten since I was thirteen.

He stood in the doorway, folding his belt in his hand. "You realize if the church doesn't think I can handle my own family, I lose my entire ministry. Next time you think it's okay to be alone with a boy, think about how you're feeling right now."

He left, and I didn't cry. The pain grew anger inside me, and I let it sit there. I soaked it in until it became a part of me. I stared at the can that had my savings, and it couldn't be a life sentence. It had to be my escape plan. The anger gave me the strength to wait until my parents went to bed. I limped out to the computer and flinched when I sat down. College websites weren't something I had bookmarked, so I googled them all. I applied to six, three for veterinary medicine and three for creative writing and journalism. Whichever one accepted me would determine my fate.

I got a warm bath to ease the pain and planned everything in my head.

I stayed angry for the next week and avoided Ezra at church for the next two. He'd called my phone several times, but I hadn't answered. He knew better than to stop by my house, but I swore I heard his noisy truck more than once. Not that I didn't want to talk to him. I didn't want him to find out what had happened because he'd have taken the blame for it all. It would have angered him, maybe more than it had me. He never held back when someone hurt me. I tried to focus on school, work, and my birds.

Riley had also stayed on my mind. After the strange few hours with her, I thought our friendship might get fixed. However, there had been no word from her. I called her a few times, but she never answered. It left me even more confused by her odd behavior. The conclusion I'd arrived at was that she needed to soothe her conscience somehow. Like she felt somewhat responsible for me, but didn't want me back as a friend. That made it hurt more somehow.

My phone rang, and I hesitated a few seconds before hitting the green button. "Ezra? What's up?"

"Hey. It's been a while."

"Sorry. I know. The camping trip put me further behind than I thought it would."

"It's church workday, and there's no Mila here."

"Yeah, my dad let me out of it because I have a big school project due soon."

He gasped. "That's a shocker."

"Yeah, I know. Sorry."

"Actually, you're kind of needed here. I hate to interrupt your project."

I clicked on the screen to close out my school portal. "No one else can do whatever it is?"

"We've all tried. David even ran down to Jack's market and got some bologna."

I furrowed my brows. "What?"

"It's going to be cold tonight. Is there any way you could come now?"

I felt better enough to keep Ezra from noticing anything was wrong. "Okay. I'll be right there."

Chapter Twenty-Two: Phoenix

♥

I drove to the church and parked on the street because the parking lot had filled with everyone already working. Work days happened every other month, and all the members came out on a Saturday to do building repairs and deep clean the inside. The Welsh family cleaned the church weekly, but it was purified during the work days.

The air had taken on a chill even though we neared May. A few men were taking items in and out of the basement. Ezra, Kyra, Hannah, Val, and several others from the youth group stood around the lattice that covered underneath the rickety wooden staircase leading to the church's back door. Hannah rolled her eyes when I walked up, and Kyra crossed her arms. Val smiled and waved. Ezra gave me what might have qualified as a smirk if it hadn't looked tight enough to crack his jaw open.

I studied all their faces. "What's wrong?"

Hannah's nose twitched. "What makes you think anything is wrong?"

My keys dangled from my hand, and I used them to point at Ezra. "He said I was needed here."

Kyra's eyes dashed to Ezra, and her lips parted. "If we can't get it to come out, there's no way she can."

Ezra took a step toward me and away from Kyra. "If Mila can't get it to leave, it will freeze because no one can."

Kyra pushed her lips together. "Sure. Let's see little miss perfect give it a try."

I stuck my keys in my pocket. "What's going on?"

Val, crouched in front of a small opening in the lattice, looked up at me. "It's a dog. Small one and no one can get it to come out. According to the deacons and your dad, it's been under there since Wednesday's service. They keep hearing it barking, and it's supposed to be below freezing tonight. I shined a flashlight, and there's a drippy spout it's probably been getting water from."

"Okay. Everyone, go stand at least ten feet away."

Hannah stuck her chin in the air. "Who made you boss?"

"Unless you want the dog to freeze to death for the sake of your pride, I suggest you step back about ten feet."

The others had already moved. Hannah and Kyra stayed planted.

I sighed and sat in front of the hole. "Hello, baby. Hey, sweetie." I continued talking to the dog in a high-pitched but quiet voice, making no moves to startle it."

"There's no way this is going to work." Kyra's tone made it easy to picture her scowling.

I sat there for a long time, talking to the dog. Ezra got me a flashlight when I asked, and I shined it in to see a Jack Russel terrier-type dog cowering in the far-right corner. Many of the others got bored, but

Kyra and Hannah didn't move from the spot I figured they'd die in if it proved some ambiguous point they wanted to make. The next step was me on my stomach. The parking lot gravel pressed sharply into my belly, but I remained flat on my stomach, slowly reaching my hand forward. A cold, dry nose sniffed it and licked my fingers.

I watched him for signs of upset, and when he licked my hand again, I scratched his ear for a few seconds. He whimpered as I removed my hand, and I called him while keeping my tone upbeat but quiet. He crawled out the hole and into my lap. His white body with tan spots trembled, and I removed my hoodie to wrap him up. He wagged his tail and licked my cheek. Patience was vital for trust, so I didn't get up for a few more minutes. I scratched his ears and continued to talk to him. He cuddled up close, and I carried him to my car, ignoring the glares from Kyra and Hannah.

Val followed me over. "That was amazing, Mila. No one had gotten him to budge an inch from the corner."

I shrugged. "Gaining an animal's trust is something I do all the time. It takes a lot of patience. They're like people. When they've been through a lot, it takes a ton to get them to relax."

I got in my car, and the dog jumped on my lap. Usually, I would have taken it to the humane society, but for some reason, I headed home instead. My mom had come home from the work day early, and I carried the dog in to find her. The door to her room was open, and she was lying on her bed.

She glanced over. "Mila, you startled me. What's that?"

"The dog under the church stairs. I was told Dad knew about it."

She sat up and blinked a few times. Most likely, she was having another migraine. She had a lot of them, along with stomach problems, including terrible ulcers. People told her it was because she worried too much, and she would tell them about the doctor who discovered bacteria caused ulcers. The church said anxiety was a sin, after all.

She held out her hand and let the puppy sniff it. "Let me see him."

I set him in her lap. "He's pretty skittish but sweet."

"Poor thing. It doesn't look like it's eaten in a while."

"Do you think I could keep him?"

She pressed her lips. It was the same almost glare she gave me the hundred other times I'd brought home a hurting or lost animal. The variety of animals had extended from a cricket with a broken leg to lost dogs. The frogs and lizards were her least favorites, and she hated I took spiders outside rather than squashing them. I would scream the entire time I carried the jar out but felt better when it was free to live its life.

She let a big breath go. "We already have two dogs and lots of fowl."

"I know, but he's special." I grabbed the dog as he jumped back into my arms.

"It's up to your father. Do you really have time to take care of another dog?"

"Yeah, and Akela could have a friend."

Mom pointed to her geriatric terrier, who hadn't even acknowledged a new dog in the house. "Akela has Frisky."

"He's at the end of his life. He can't even really see or hear anymore."

She looked at the new dog for a bit. "If your father says it's okay. But this is the last animal. I mean that, Mila."

"Yeah, definitely."

"We can't take in all the homeless animals out there. It's not practical."

"Right. That's why I work at the humane society. To make sure they have a home somewhere."

I took the dog to the bath and washed him with flea shampoo. He didn't appear to have any, which would help me convince my parents to keep him. "What should I call you?" I rubbed my chin, cycling through choices. "Phoenix. I'm going to call you Phoenix because you've risen above your problems today."

I dried him off and went into my room to find Akela. He hung out in his giant plastic igloo most of the time. It was made for the outdoors. Akela was only around twenty pounds, but I'd gotten him the largest one and put it in my room. He had a sizeable setup with an enormous bed, toys, and blankets. His food and water bowls sat right outside his enclosure on a mat. He peeked out, lowering his head and sniffing.

I sat Phoenix on the ground, but he growled and hopped back in my lap. Akela dashed back into his igloo. It would take some time. My mom called me for dinner, and my dad was already at the table. I took my seat and waited for him to give the lengthy blessing before telling him about the dog.

He dished the mashed potatoes onto his plate. "I might have considered it, but your behavior lately is why I'm saying no."

"I already got punished for that."

"Are you talking back now? I'm not sure what has gotten into you, but it will stop now. Am I clear?"

I pushed my green beans around with my fork. "It's clear."

"Yes..."

"Yes, sir."

"Unless you want another whooping, you need to straighten your act up and watch your mouth."

"Yes, sir." I picked at my food and cleaned up before returning to my room. It would do no good to argue. I called the humane society director and told her about Phoenix.

"You think he's a short-haired Jack Russell?" she said.

"Yeah, and probably a couple of other things. He's pretty timid. Will only go to me."

"Him and about half the animals here, it seems. There's a Jack Russell rescue in Denver. It would be perfect for him. If you want to bring him in, we'll get him checked out and make sure no one is looking for him."

Okay. Thank you. I took Phoenix back to my car and drove to the pet store, where I bought him a bunch of things to take to his new life. After I got him settled, I drove around, listening to sad music. My phone rang, and I hesitated when Ezra's name popped up. He called back a second time, and I answered, worrying it was an emergency.

"Mila." A melancholy had set into his voice. "We need to talk. Can you meet me?"

"Where?"

"Sonic."

"No, somewhere more private."

He stayed quiet for several seconds. "Okay. The softball field?"

"Yeah, there shouldn't be a game today." I drove to the field and found him already there.

Most likely, he'd been at the skate ramps on the other side of the park.

He sat up from where he'd been staring at the sky. "Hey."

"Hey."

"What's going on?"

I gave him an update on Phoenix, leaving out my dad's words.

"No, why have you basically ignored me since the camping trip?"

"I've been busy," I said.

He nodded slowly. "Right. Even for a phone call."

It occurred to me then I needed to tell him something that would help him get it. "My parents found out I went camping with a boy. Mr. Mondragon saw us, but he couldn't tell who you were."

"Okay. Well, that explains that."

"Explains what?"

"Amber said you were caught with a guy in an unholy position." He put his hand up in a shrug when my face scrunched. "Those were her words. I thought maybe it was someone else."

I sunk onto the bleachers. "That's nice to know rumors are so easily spread among church folk."

"I gave her a Bible verse on gossiping. That shut her up."

"But you believed her. That's why you're here."

"No, I wasn't sure. That's why I'm here. It wouldn't be a shocker if someone found you beautiful and wanted you," he said.

"You think I'd do that?"

He leaned back and returned his gaze to the sky. "I think if you did, it's no one's business but yours."

"Then why bring it up?"

"Because I'm nosy when it comes to you. I don't always do what I should." His smile faded as something seemed to hit him. "Wait. Did they punish you for the camping trip?"

"Why do you think I haven't been talking to you?"

"Oh... I'm sorry, Mila."

I didn't elaborate on the punishment and let him think grounding was what it had been. The bruises had started to heal, and the fading pain of sitting had lessened the reminder. I wanted to put it behind me, except for the little motivation I needed to create my escape plan. I held on to the anger from it, so I wouldn't lose the nerve.

He tugged at my hand and pulled me close when I leaned into him. "Are you okay?"

"Yeah, we just need to be more careful. If they had known it was you, I don't know what would have happened."

"We will. It'll be okay. We're almost eighteen."

"You sooner than me."

"Not by much."

We didn't move for a long time, but his hug healed something sad that had taken shape since the camping trip consequences.

Chapter Twenty-Three: Banquet

♥

Summer was approaching, and I crossed off days on the calendar, waiting to turn eighteen. Our youth pastor decided we needed to have a formal banquet on the same night as the high school prom. He hoped it would discourage the teenagers of Alamosa from attending a worldly dance. We had a pretty large RSVP rate, which showed teens maybe did want an alternative.

Val looked at my dress. "It's beautiful. Ezra took you dress shopping?"

"Yeah, he snapped pictures of me like I was in a fashion show." I set my dress on Erin's bed.

"I'm sure those will go right on his wall." Erin swished in her maroon knee-length dress. "What do you think?"

"Gorgeous as always." I changed into the sparkly blue dress that I'd settled on. The dress I'd really wanted was one my parents would have killed me for wearing.

We put on our dresses and did each other's make-up and nails. We rode together in my car. The adults had transformed the auditorium into a banquet hall with ten round tables. The pews had been stashed somewhere. Tall blue candles stuck out from short round vases with betta fish in them.

I picked one up and studied the turquoise fish. "What do they plan on doing with all the fish when this is over?"

Val picked up a red one. "Maybe we'll get the option of keeping one."

"They all need bigger spaces."

"I thought small spaces made bettas feel safe?"

"No, they want places to hide. This was a poor choice to spend the budget on." I set mine down and made a note to find out their fate.

People came in the entrance, and my heart sped up with each one. Finally, the boy I'd waited all day for stepped into the room, wearing a black dress shirt and light grey pants. He was more of a jeans guy than a suit wearer, but he looked good in anything. His gelled hair made my stomach do happy somersaults. Guys and girls were kept separate, but Ezra and I cheated by choosing tables next to each other. His chair backed up to mine.

He leaned his head back. "Hey, Beautiful. You're stunning.

My stomach somersaults intensified into cartwheels rolling down a mountain. "Thank you. I like your hair."

He chuckled and straightened himself in his chair as the adults came in. They served us salad, garlic chicken with mashed potatoes and green beans. Bread and condiments sat in the middle of the table to be shared. Tea, lemonade, and water all sat in glass pitchers. We gave our dessert selection of either strawberry or chocolate cake. The church spared no expense to keep their young people from sin.

Val finished her bite of salad. "You're really worried about the fish, aren't you?"

I looked up from where I was leaning in to ensure our table betta was okay. "It's unclear what's going to be done with them when this is over."

"I'll help you take them to your car when this is done."

"We have to be stealthy about it."

She gave me a light elbow nudge. "I have your back on this."

Erin munched on her dinner roll like it came from the Greek god of bakers. "This is so good! I'm totally in for a fish heist too. Should we dump them in the Rio Grande?"

I paled. "No! You can't put an invasive species in rivers or lakes. If they survive, it's bad for the entire ecosystem. People like to mess those up as it is."

"You're not going to keep them all, are you?"

I chewed on my lip. "I'm not sure."

Val let out a giggle. "We all know she's thinking that."

I took pictures with Erin and Val in front of a backdrop with white Christmas lights around it. I wanted one with Ezra, but the best we got was a group one where one of the Thompson boys sat between us. Everyone dispersed, and I had one goal.

I found the youth pastor, Mr. Thompson, talking with other men about the cleanup plan.

The other men left, and he turned to me. "Can I help you, Mila?"

"I was wondering what you were doing with all the fish."

"I'm not sure. People can probably take them home, or we'll dump them?"

"Dump them. Like they're streamers?"

"They don't live long, anyway."

I pushed down rising anger. "What about the containers? Can I give them to people and let them keep the containers until I can get them better setups?"

"Yes, that's fine. You can have them all."

I hurried to the fellowship hall where the little card table was and hauled it to the exit where everyone was leaving. One by one, I picked up each of the fifteen fish, blowing out the candles and setting them on the table. There had been ten tables, but they must have overbought fish. Val and Erin caught on and helped me. Ezra had disappeared somewhere, and I told myself not to worry that I couldn't see Kyra either. Fish lives were at stake. I grabbed a pen and paper from my dad's office and pulled up a chair. Val and Erin sat next to me.

The first person walked by, and I jumped up. "Would you like to take a fish home? They are easy maintenance, and if you give me your contact information, I will bring you a better fish set up soon."

They shook their head and left. I found three homes before everyone left. Now the problem would be getting the rest home without my parents seeing. The important thing would be to get them safe. Then I would see if I could take them to the humane society for the next adoptathon.

We left them on the table but covered them with a blanket. The three of us awkwardly carried it together out a side door. We got it to my car, and they helped me set the fish on the floor.

Ezra ran down the back steps. "Where are you going?"

I double-checked to make sure they were on stable ground. "The fish need dropped at my house."

He grinned and snickered. "I should have known you'd rescue them all."

"Three found homes."

Val held up the list with the contact information. "She's buying them aquariums too."

Ezra seemed to do a quick count. "What will you do with ten fish that can't even share a tank?"

"Twelve. Give them each their own tank."

"Mila, the fish farmer."

Everyone laughed.

"Why don't we go out to the rink?" Val suggested.

I closed up my car and pulled my keys from my pocket. "Hasn't it thawed for the year?"

"Not completely. We got that late spring snowstorm last week, and I've been practicing since your birthday."

"We should say forget the skates and slide around on our shoes," Ezra said.

I glanced at the sky. "It might rain, but I guess we can leave whenever."

We all agreed, and I took my fish home after stopping briefly at Wal-Mart to buy fish food, a net, and water treatment. Erin rode with me and helped me take them all inside. Val and Ezra were already at the rink when we arrived. Ezra pulled a retro boombox from his trunk and cranked up the radio. We slid over the ice and took hands in the middle, spinning. Val and I knocked into each other, and we collapsed in a pile on the ground. We stayed there, and Ezra and Erin joined us to look at the stars.

Val squeezed my hand. "You have a beautiful heart, Mila, saving all those fish."

I rolled on my side and gave her a hug. "Not any more beautiful than yours and the help you give at Le Puente. Or than Erin and the secret notes she leaves people to make them feel good about themselves."

Erin's eyes flung to me. "Who says I do that?"

I sent her a knowing smile and looked at Ezra. "Or Ezra's and how he defends the defenseless or brings my neighbors treats."

He popped an eyebrow but kept his gaze on the sky. "It seems Mila is a spy."

Val met my eyes again. "No, she just sees all of us."

"Not any more than you all see me."

"Can't you just take a compliment?"

Ezra rolled his eyes. "It's not possible for her without her throwing one back at whoever gave her one."

Erin let out a dramatic sigh. "How bad do you think adulthood will be?"

I slipped my hand into hers to help soothe the melancholy that always settled when she thought this way. "I think it may have bad places but also good. It will be pieces of life. We'll have more freedom, but that will also bring more responsibility. Maybe the freedom is worth that."

"We're going to lose each other," she nearly wailed.

I rested my head next to hers. "Never."

We talked about what we wanted to do. Ezra said he was probably going into the army, and I froze. He hadn't told me that before. Val wanted to travel for a while and help on mission trips in poor countries. Erin wanted to freeze herself at almost sixteen, so she would never have to bear the burden of an elapsed childhood. The ice bled through our coats and cooled our backs, but we stayed and watched the stars.

Val's phone rang in her pocket, and she frowned at the screen. "Hello?... Are you sure there is no one else?... Okay. I'll be right there." She put her phone in her pocket and sat up. "Sorry, guys. I just got called into work. A late-night party for the college, but it's in Monte Vista for some reason. Two of my coworkers didn't show."

Erin sat up. "Can you drop me off on the way to your house? My parents said I must be home by ten tonight to watch Charlie. I'm getting paid, so it's not the worst thing."

"Sure. No problem."

Ezra hopped up and gave both girls his hands to help them up on the ice and followed that up by assisting me. We walked them to Val's car. I hugged Erin goodbye.

She touched my cheek with her yellow yarn mitten that she loved. "Stay safe, my beautiful, wonderful best friend forever."

"You, too."

Val threw her arms around me. "I know we were supposed to have a sleepover tonight. It's a tradition."

Val and I had been having sleepovers often with Erin on Friday nights for the last several weeks. We'd scare ourselves with the latest horror and talk until the sun rose.

"That we can resume next week." My chest clenched as the words came out, and I pulled her back for a second hug. "See you soon."

"See you soon." She got into her car and drove back toward Alamosa. "Kryptonite" from Three Doors Down was playing as the car drove away. For some reason, I would always remember that, and whenever I heard the song again, I would think of that night on the ice with Erin, Ezra, and Val.

Ezra studied me. "Are you alright?"

I blinked my attention away from the disappearing car. "Yeah, I miss them already."

"Luckily, we have youth group in two days. Do you want to spin some more?"

"Yeah."

And that's what we did. Ezra picked me up and did some kind of odd spin on his heels. I squealed as he increased the speed. He spun us dizzy, and we plopped back on the ice. The sky broke, drenching us. We hurried under a willow tree. We heaved to catch our breath, and a bit of moonlight lit up his face through the rain clouds. Our eyes met, and I touched a raindrop falling down his cheek.

He cupped my face, and his hazel eyes looked strangely bright in the darkness. I'm not sure who moved first, but our lips met halfway. He was warm somehow in the cold, and we paused for a split second as we tried to work through what to do. I surrendered thought and soaked in the gentle pressure he moved against my mouth. Our movements became natural after that, and he deepened the kiss. I shuddered and pressed closer.

We slid to our knees. Icy mud squished into my legs, but it was an afterthought. I didn't know what first kisses should be, but it felt like Ezra and I had waited so long that everything we'd ever felt for each other poured out through the kiss. We moved intrinsically through it.

We broke apart and rested our foreheads together, heaving differently than when we'd first gone under the tree. My swollen lips zinged with pleasurable tingles.

His arms yanked me against his chest, and he kissed my temple, then my head. "I love you, Mila."

"I love you, Ezra."

It felt like a sealed promise neither of us would ever choose to break. He kissed me goodbye at my car, and I went home in a dreamy state. Ezra Henderson was the first boy I ever loved, and I wanted him to be the last.

Chapter Twenty-Four: Breathing

I was floating from the formal. It had been such a good night with Erin, Val, and Ezra, Especially Ezra. It had been a great night other than Val having to leave early from getting called into work. I'd have to call her later and tell her about what happened. About Ezra finally kissing me. I touched my lips, recalling the entire thing. Life was perfect, and with giddy contentment, I drifted asleep.

The phone startled me awake, and dread seeped in when I realized it was only two in the morning. Something had gone wrong with a church member, and my dad needed to go be there for the family. That's what late-night phone calls always meant.

My dad answered the call. "Oh, no! That's... Wow... Okay. We'll be right there." My dad had his broken voice. The one that made me realize he could have strong emotions other than anger. His voice shook as he said something to my mom.

I sat up, staring at the wall because the ice had seeped into my muscles. Somehow, I knew this phone call was very different, and there was a before and after of my mom knocking on my door that night. It would forever remain a deep desire to live in the before.

"Come in," I called.

She stepped part of the way in. "Honey. There's been an accident."

"Accident." The word came out to stall discovering the who behind the accident.

"Yes, one of the girls from youth group. Vallery Thompson."

"Oh. Is she alright?" I pressed my back into the frigid wall.

"No, she went to Jesus about an hour ago."

I stared at her and blinked. "That doesn't sound right."

"We have to go to the hospital and be there for the family. I'm not sure when we'll be back."

"Okay."

My body realized what had happened long before my mind did. I trembled and wobbled when I walked. Without any thought, I grabbed my keys and drove south. I pulled my car off the road and walked a mile, still feeling nothing, not even the pebbles piercing my bare feet. The cold air didn't touch me because I felt nothing. I made it to Ezra's trailer and had to concentrate extra hard on which window was his.

The curtains gave it away, and I knocked. They were blue. His favorite color. It took a few times because I was trying to stay quiet enough that no one else in his house would hear. He pushed the curtains back, rubbing his eyes and yawning.

He pushed open the window. "Mila? Why are you walking outside with no coat?" He studied me for a few seconds. "What happened?" He tugged me up. "Come inside."

I used a wooden box off to the side to boost myself, and he helped me the rest of the way.

He shut the window and locked his door. "Mila, you're scaring me. What's wrong?" He touched my arms. "You're freezing. Where are your shoes?" He got a blanket off his bed and wrapped it around me.

"Ezra."

He pushed back my hair and cupped my cheek. "Mila, what is it?"

"I can't breathe! I can't breathe!" My knees gave out, and I collapsed.

He picked me up and carried me to his bed. "Whatever it is. I have you. I'm here."

"Ezra, Val died."

He flinched and stared with a furrowed brow. "What?"

"Vallery Thompson. Our friend passed away."

"That's not right. We saw her a few hours ago. There must be a mistake."

"She was in an accident." The words tumbled out as a wail that I tapered to not alert his family of my presence. The numbness seeped into agony, and I screamed into his chest without letting the force of the noise grow. They were silent screams.

He was blurry through my tears, but I could see his falling with mine. They were mixing and staining his bed. After a little while, he turned on Lifehouse's No name face Album, and "Breathing" came on first. We played the album on repeat until our tears led us to exhausted sleep sometime later. Some moments of that night stayed hazy, but the most significant things that would lock inside me forever were Ezra's scent, the feel of his arms, and Lifehouse playing in my ears. All three things would remain potent for the rest of my life.

Knocks on his door woke us early, and he grabbed my face with his hand, stroking my cheek. He kissed the top of my head. "Hide the best you can under the covers."

He adjusted the pillows, and I scrunched down as flat as possible.

His door squeaked open as he answered it. "Yes, sir?"

"There was a motorcycle accident last night. Vallery Thompson forgot something for a party, and a coworker offered to take her on his motorcycle to get it. He was going 90 when he hit gravel. Killed them both instantly."

Ezra said something I couldn't make out.

"Your mom and I are going to see if we can do anything for the family. The Sadlers are already with them. I'll let you know the funeral details when I know."

"Okay. Thanks." Ezra shut his door and got back into bed with me, where he held me most of the morning. We cried off and on, not really speaking.

At some point, he got up and returned a while later with a plate of food. "You need to eat."

I sat up and hugged his pillow. "I feel sick."

"At least drink something." He left and brought back a Sprite. "This should help."

I sipped it and stared at the collection of skateboards on his wall. He had the one I had given him in the middle. On his dresser were lots of pictures. Most were of the two of us together. A few had Val and other people in them. His room was simple and not cluttered. It wasn't what I thought I'd find in a teenage boy's room. It smelled clean and looked organized. Processing his room took me away from reality long enough to choke my drink down.

My back rested against his headboard, and he sat with his arm around me. His chin rested gently on my head, and I held his other hand. He turned back on Lifehouse, and we listened to it over and over again, sometimes crying and other times staring numbly at his skateboard collection. He checked his house a while later, and when it proved empty, he drove me to my car.

He pulled me to him and kissed my forehead. "I love you, Mila, and I'm so, so sorry."

"I love you, Ezra."

Three days went by with me in bed. My parents were gone a lot. I wasn't sure they knew how close Val and I had been. I wasn't sure which would be worse, that they didn't notice or didn't care. Ezra called and reminded me to at least drink something. He knew me well. Erin came by on my third day in bed. We cried together, and she had to leave. The funeral arrived on the fourth day.

I wore black again like I had on the day Kendra's baby had been buried. That day Val had sat next to me, and Ezra had held me in the barn. That day I'd prayed, I'd never feel a more profound grief, but the prayer had gone unanswered. As Val's casket was set up at the front of the church, I didn't dare look inside. Instead, I kept staring out the church window. Ezra and I had a hymnal between us again.

He nudged my arm in a movement so subtle no one would have seen it. "What are you seeing?"

I brushed my tears with the heel of my hand. "I really wish a bluebird would sit on the sill right there. Like it did that one time."

The funeral started, and they talked about how it wasn't a goodbye. It was only a "see you later" because we had hope. I'd never felt more hopeless. Songs were sung, and many wailed. I cried silently while Erin fell onto my lap and shook in my arms. Ezra had his head lowered, and his tears trickled into the pew and onto the ground. I wanted nothing more than to hold him, too.

When most everyone had left, I approached the casket where I saw my sleeping friend. I slipped in a postcard with something I'd written her. It had a picture of the mountain bluebird on the other side.

Ezra drove me to the graveyard, not caring about what people thought of us alone together. We got out, and the sky was blue. Not a cloud in the sky, and it made little sense. If there was one truth I had, it was that it rained at funerals. That cliché from books and movies was one that was real. It had rained at my grandpa's funeral, and the day we'd buried Kendra's baby. But the sun shined brightly on the day they lowered Val into the ground.

We stood at the back next to a willow tree, and Ezra slipped his hand into mine. His touch steadied my legs and continued to do so after he took me home and tucked me in bed. My parents were doing things for the family, and he'd parked a block away. He went out and took care of my birds without me asking.

He'd taken the fish to the shelter for me three days ago. They were something I no longer wanted to think about but wanted them to be okay. I got up and made him dinner while he was outside. He ate but gave up trying to get me to join him. We spent another night in bed, holding each other, crying, and listening to Lifehouse.

Over the next few weeks, I barely ate and kept going over everything in my head. I'd taken a leave of absence from work and did the bare minimum with my schoolwork. My birds forced me out of bed, but I no longer helped at the animal shelter. Erin noticed and called me frequently. She came over even more, trying to get me to go places with her.

Ezra called, reminding me to eat, and often brought my favorite foods, but still, I barely ate and focused only on hydration. He knocked on my door and entered when I said to.

He opened a pizza box. "Pizza Den! I rushed it over here because it's the best when fresh."

I sat up and threw my covers off. "I better shower, so you're not scared away."

"No way that will happen." He looked me over. "Mila, you're scaring me. You're bones. I'm scared."

"I'm going to go get a shower." When I got into the bathroom, I caught my reflection in the mirror and realized he was right.

I stepped on the scale, and the red numbers glowed at 90. The warm water washed away the grime of the days I hadn't showered. Typically, showers were a daily thing for me. I sunk to the ground with hot water pouring over me, scared if I couldn't snap out of things, I'd lose Ezra and Erin in an entirely different way than I had Val.

Ezra was gripping his hair when I walked back into my room. He smiled, but it stayed stiff. "Hey. You ready for pizza?"

"Yeah." I took a slice and nibbled it as I fought through nausea.

"Tell me how I can help. What can I do for you?"

"You've done more than I could ever hope for." I hugged my stuffed bluebird. "I keep thinking how cruel life is. Val wanted to travel the world, and all she ever saw was the valley. Why did I survive the ski accident and Val die because of some speeding idiot? My stupidity was forgiven, and that moron's got my friend killed."

Ezra rested his arm over his one-peaked knee. His ball cap was backward like the boy he'd always been, but his pressed lips and watery eyes made him look like he'd aged years since Val's funeral. "You know, I keep thinking about you on that mountain, too, with Val making sure you got help, and I thank God for the years she lived. Because I don't know why God took Val to heaven and let you survive falling down a mountain. But what I do know is I am thankful every day that I don't have to put flowers on your grave too."

"How is this even possible that we have to put flowers on her grave? How do we get through this? We aren't supposed to have friends die at seventeen. It makes me angry, sad, and numb. The pain is so bad that all food is like eating paper." I set the pizza down.

Ezra leaped across the room but stayed on his knees as he took my hands. "Mila, look at me. You need to eat because what I'm trying to tell you is you're slipping away from me, too. I'm in so much pain, but your pain feels so much worse. If I lose you, Mila... I can't handle that much pain. I can't... I'm not strong enough. Some days, I don't even know how I'm breathing through any of this." His shoulders shook. "Mila, if you can't eat for yourself, eat for me. Eat for Val because you know she would hate this. I don't know what else to do!" He fell on his side, letting his hands slip from mine.

His cries broke me, and I dropped next to him.

I held him against my chest until his cries faded into sobs. "I'm sorry, Ezra, for not seeing your pain through mine."

He lifted his hazel eyes that had turned a murky brown. All joy had escaped from them some time ago. "Your pain is my pain, Mila."

"Same, Ezra, same." And for the millionth time, Ezra and I fell asleep crying.

Chapter Twenty-Five: When Bluebirds Can't Fly

❤

Life moves on, no matter what happens to you. The entire world felt like it should have stopped, but people continued to do everything they did before my life spun out of control. I worked hard on eating at least one meal a day. It was forced, and sometimes I forgot. My mind still sank into a sludgy abyss, but on the outside, I did my best to appear fine. My grief stayed stuck inside, so I wouldn't have to extend it to anyone else. Depression would take other people away from me when they got tired of me staying in bed for days.

At night, my thoughts turned the darkest, and I pondered what it would be like not to exist. I eyed the medicine cabinet when I went to the bathroom, thinking only about not feeling any longer. The problem was I'd been taught my entire life that death wouldn't mean nothingness. It would mean everything forever. Riley always said you worry about the ones that say nothing. I never understood that until I did everything I could to hide my pain.

I'd exhausted myself by being social in youth group and had taken a long bath. My cotton pajamas with ducks all over them were cool and comfortable against the summer heat. We didn't have air conditioning. A swamp cooler did its best to cool our house, but about half the time, it chose not to work. The Colorado summer air cooled drastically in the evenings, and I opened the window, which allowed me to use a light blanket. I did my evening wall staring that I could safely do because everyone had seen me look happy a couple of hours ago.

My phone rang, and I reluctantly answered when I looked at the screen. "Hello, Ruth. How are things going?"

"Good for me. How are you? Everyone misses you. The animals too. I can tell."

I closed my eyes. "Maybe I'll come to a clinic soon."

"I hope so. Doc keeps asking us to get you back here. But I'm hoping to offer you a little transition back. I know you've turned the last three birds down, but this is your specialty. A broken wing."

I sighed and flopped onto my back. "I'm not sure I'm ready yet. What kind of bird?"

"A mountain bluebird."

I sat up and gasped.

"Are you alright?"

"Yeah, I'm fine. I'll be right over."

Mountain bluebirds were common in the valley. This wouldn't be the first I'd cared for, but it still felt like something bigger. I needed bigger to help me out of the slump I couldn't break free from. All the animals they'd called me with, I'd turned them down. This one was different. This one was for Val. It gave me a tangible way to grieve and remember her.

I washed my hands in the sink as soon as I arrived in the wildlife room. We were one of the few licensed wildlife centers in the area and received most of the wildlife that got called into officials. I sometimes helped with other animals, but birds were my thing. They liked giving them to me because they were fragile. Often one would look like it would pull through, only to die unexpectedly. It took skill and patience to get one to fly away day.

I walked over to where Jasmine, the vet tech, was standing in front of a clear tote. "How's it doing?"

She smiled. "It's good to see you. We've missed you with these birds. I was sorry to hear about your friend."

"Thank you."

"Broken left wing. Do you want to tape it?"

"Yeah, I can." I went over to the supply closet and grabbed the vet tape. It was a special type that would prevent it from sticking to the feathers and skin. That would save a lot of potential problems when we went to remove it. "Is it drinking, or do we need to start an IV?"

"She does well with a dropper."

I looked at the tiny panting bird and could tell instantly it was a girl. She was a bluish grey with a rust-colored belly. The male of the species was a brighter blue, but a few of her wing feathers came close to that shade. "She's beautiful."

"She is. Ruth thought she'd get you back here. Apparently, she was right."

"She was." I took my time wrapping the wing, using all the tricks I'd learned to cause the least amount of stress on the bird as possible.

Jasmine inspected my work. "That's a well-done wrap."

"Thank you."

"Do you want to take her home?"

"No, it's too hot. Our swamp cooler is out again. I'll make trips here as much as I can."

I went home but returned often. One night it struggled to drink, and I slept on a cot next to it. I didn't have school, and I had limited shifts at KFC. The bird became my primary focus, and it healed. We released it into the sky, and my chest soared and sank. We'd saved the bird, but what purpose did I have now?

I cleaned the area and prepared for the next bird we'd get in.

Jasmine walked in with medicine for a sick squirrel. "Doc wants to see you before he goes back to Denver."

"I'm finished here. I'll go see him now."

My stomach zapped at what Doc might say about me being gone for the last three months. His main clinic was in Ft. Collins, Colorado, and he traveled to help us at the valley. I went around the vet side and found him inspecting a Pitbull with severe mange.

He glanced up. "Mila! A long time since you've blessed us with your presence. How are you doing?"

"I'm alright."

"I'm sorry about your friend."

"Thank you." I pointed my thumb behind me. "Jasmine said you wanted to talk to me."

"Yeah, how are those college apps going?"

"I got in."

"To which one?"

"All that I applied for."

"That's our girl!" He wrote something on a tablet. "You're going to tell me CSU is your choice, right?"

I chewed on my lip. "It's confusing now, because I don't know what fate wants. I'd decided I'd go to whichever I got into, but now I don't know what to do since I got into all of them."

"How many did you apply to?"

"Twelve. Originally it was only six, but I got worried that wasn't enough to get into one. Half writing and half veterinary."

"You know my vote. As I've told you, you're already hired if you go the CSU route."

"Thank you. It's definitely high in the running," I said.

"Good."

I assisted him with the dog by keeping it calm during treatment and started toward home. I drove past the turn to my street and kept going to the sand dunes road. The shallow river at the base of the dunes cooled my feet as I crossed it into miles of sand. The summer heat did well to cook the ground, and I put my shoes back on. Trudging and climbing burned my calves, but I continued until the sand opened into a large pocket.

It made me feel closer to Val because this was the place our friendship had restarted—the day we'd built a sandcastle and climbed to the top of the dunes. She'd brought me back from when Hannah had confronted me for the first time. It was this soothing power she had that healed the wound Riley's absence had brought me.

Bluebirds flashed through my eyes—the one we'd seen here, the one on the church window, and the one I'd recently cared for. Val had called them brightness amongst the dull. What happened when bluebirds couldn't fly like the most recent one? The world lost beauty. The entire world didn't notice it, but it still lost something. What if we lost all the mountain bluebirds? What if they all couldn't fly? Would the world even notice? Probably not, but some would. The entire world didn't know Val, but the world lost something big when she died. It lost a lot of beauty, including the amazing things she would have done.

My wings felt broken. The ones Val talked about us using to travel the world, but the truth wasn't as grim as it felt because I still could change the world for the better and leave beautiful things behind me. I needed to embrace life and live the way Val no longer could. The thought rocked me with sorrow, and I sunk into the gritty sand as I thrashed about, trying to release everything pent up inside.

Sorrow had become me, wrapping itself so tightly I'd suffocated in shadows. Further up the dunes, no one was around. I screamed with everything I had and did it ten more times until my voice left me. I curled into a ball and realized while life had no meaning anymore; I needed to give it some.

Chapter Twenty-Six: A Slow Crawl Back to Normal

♥

Ezra and I had long forgotten our kiss. At least, it appeared that way. It made me think that maybe we'd always remain good friends, and the kiss had been a caught-up-in-the-moment kind of thing. Perhaps it was that we'd used up all the emotions we'd ever have in the last few months. He called me every few days to see how I was, and I did my best to call him on other days. Our phone calls never lasted long, but we still checked on each other.

The end of summer left me numb but with a new resolve to make my life count. That threw me deeper into the humane society, and I served meals a couple of times at Le Puente like Val used to do in her spare time.

The last youth group of the summer was a cookout at the Thompson's house. I arrived late and sat in the back. Ezra was at the front with Kyra, Hannah, and a few other kids. Kyra kept touching his arm, and he stiffened each time. No one else probably noticed the subtle movements, but I knew him well. I spent the entire youth service watching them interact and slipped out before it came time to eat. I'd only gone there to check my name on the sheet, so my parents knew I attended.

Life made a small crawl to normal, and my eighteenth birthday was only a couple of months away. Erin and I had started hanging out like old times ago, but I'd barely seen Ezra. I wanted to see if he wanted to go to Zapata for last time before summer ended. He didn't answer when I called, which meant he was probably at the skate park.

I walked from my house rather than driving, and it took about half an hour. Makeup had restored life to my face, and I put on a cute blue sundress that met my knees. It tugged at me that I might have lost my best friend. People always said tragedy brought people closer, but in my short, almost eighteen years, I'd realized it could also tear people apart. In the case of Ezra and me, it had caused a slow drifting, like we'd clung to each other in a violent storm. When the storm had lessened, we'd grown too tired to hold on as the aftermath ripped us apart through gentle waves we underestimated.

I went to take my usual spot and found Hannah sitting in it, and I tried to retreat.

She jumped up. "Ezra's with my sister. They're going to be together soon, so you're wasting your time."

Something had changed in me, and I stopped walking away. "I never told you how sorry I am about your cousin. For your loss."

She gaped and sat back down, turning away from me. "I'm sure you really care. You only care about yourself."

I took a bench a bit away from her to keep a safe distance. "I could see how you would think that. Especially lately."

She rolled her eyes. "You're trying to dig at me by agreeing. You want me to think you're perfect like everyone else does."

I let out a sharp laugh by accident. "If everyone thinks I'm perfect, they don't know me at all."

"But I do. I see who you are. You're a snob and exclude my sister and me from everything. You even got more time with Val."

That stung on another level, but Hannah's pain had set deep into her brown eyes.

I closed my eyes a couple of seconds. "You're right. I have never even invited you and your sister over to my house. Would you like to come over to my house?"

Her face twisted. "No! Why would I ever do that?"

I shrugged. "Because maybe life is unbearably short to not find peace."

"I'm not going to your house!"

"Okay. But if you ever want to talk about Val, I'd love to do that with you."

"Stop talking about her!" Several tears fell down her cheeks.

A couple of mine fell because this conversation hurt us both, and I cried as much for Hannah as I did myself. "I'm sorry," I whispered.

She turned away again, and we both sat waiting. I watched the skateboarders do tricks on the ramps. Ezra and Kyra rounded a corner, laughing. It tore something in my gut to see them looking happy together. This had been a terrible idea. I'd tried to make peace with Hannah but had only hurt her. She was right about my selfishness. I got up and slipped behind a tree, waiting for the perfect opportunity to dash away.

"It's Mila, right?"

I spun around the see a guy with shoulder-length brown hair. He had on an opened blue button-up with a white shirt underneath. A skateboard rested under his arm, level with the top of his cargo shorts.

I crinkled my nose. "Yeah? Do we know each other?"

He laughed. "You don't know me, I guess."

I took a step back. "How do you know me, then?"

He pointed at the skate ramps. "My boy has your picture all over his room. A few are in the glove compartment of his truck. He talks about you so much I feel I know you."

I peeked around the tree. "What about the girl he's talking to? Does he talk about her?"

He smirked. "No, I have no clue who she is, but she hangs out here a lot. I don't think you have much to worry about there."

"Who says I'm worried?"

His smirk grew. "Your face and questions say a lot."

"I'm curious more than anything."

"Right. That's why you're spying behind a tree rather than talking to him."

"Wouldn't want to interrupt."

He gave me a two-finger salute. "Suit yourself." He walked over to the ramp and said something to Ezra.

I cringed when Ezra looked my way. He took off in a jog my direction, and I froze.

The boy jumped in front of me. "Why are you hiding behind a tree?"

"Your friend is a snitch."

"Yeah, and I'm glad he is in this case."

"I wanted to go to Zapata with you, but your day is pretty set with Kyra. Congratulations, by the way. I heard you guys are almost together."

"By who?" He looked around the tree like it might give him an answer.

"It's not important."

"It is because it's not true."

"Oh, okay. Well, do you want to go to Zapata with me?"

"I do. There's something I've wanted to show you. Why don't we go tomorrow? We'd get more time and what I want to show you is at my house."

"We need to go to your house?"

"No, I need to pick it up from there." He tossed his head to the side. "Want to come watch me skate for a while?"

"Kyra probably wouldn't like it."

"Who cares?"

"Okay." I took my spot back on the bench diagonal from the sisters.

They both sent me glares, and while I might have imagined it, it seemed harsher than usual. My shoulders drooped as I realized Hannah had probably told Kyra I'd brought up Val. Ezra hit the end of his board and flipped it around, taking off down the ramp. Each time he did any kind of trick, Kyra leaped up and cheered. Hannah clapped. I silently enjoyed all the ways he moved.

Ezra and I drove separately and decided to meet above the falls in the wildflower field. It prevented anyone from seeing us. I arrived first and made flower crowns as I waited. He carried a guitar case and set it down.

I stared at the instrument like it was from a foreign planet. "You learned to play the guitar?"

"Yeah, I needed an outlet to express myself." He positioned the orangish brown, shiny guitar in his lap and strummed a tune that took me only seconds to recognize. He played it a bit. "I don't mind spending every day. Out on your corner in the pouring rain. Look for the girl with the broken smile. Ask her if she wants to stay awhile. And she will be loved. She will be loved!" He sang the last bit of Maroon 5's 'She Will be Loved' and leaned forward, pushing a strand of hair behind my ear. "Been practicing that for a few weeks. I can't wait to see you smile again, Mila. I miss it more than most things. Maybe I only miss time with you more."

I widened my eyes to slow my tears. "I've missed you so much it hurts to breathe sometimes. Like when I think about you, I wish we were close again."

He put his guitar away and flung himself at me. His arms wrapped around me tight, and I returned his embrace with all I had. We didn't need words because our hug's strength clearly spoke about how much we'd missed each other. We rested in the grass, and he kept his arm around me while we watched the clouds.

We explored the mountain for the rest of the day and returned for the next three days. It became a little like old times, though he seemed older, which he was. A boy—or rather the law considered him a man at eighteen. But he seemed older than even that, and I wondered if I did too. Our world had crumbled three months ago, and one thing was for sure. We'd never be the same.

We dangled our legs off a rocky cliff. The wildflowers, yellow grass, and waterfall were far below. I rested my head in his lap, and he curled himself over me to kiss my forehead. I'd grown wiser than the six-teen-year-old me had been. What Ezra and I had was more than best friends, but it didn't really mean we were together. We talked about everything in the universe but about what we were.

It worked for us in a way. We existed together with no terms and did what felt was right at a safe level. My lips often tingled when he was close, but we didn't pursue another kiss. Maybe kissing him scared me all over again because it had created the best day of my life that led into the worst.

Our senior year started, and it meant we wouldn't see each other as often, but we were close again. My eighteenth birthday would arrive soon, and I went fully back to work. My hope increased as my savings grew. I spread all my college acceptance letters across my bed and stared at them. They'd grown to fifteen, which scared me enough not to apply for anymore.

Options in abundance were what I had in front of me, and each would lead to a different life. How did a person decide that? My parents had left three hours ago to take my brother back to college. I called Ezra to come over because he needed to know about my plan, and I wanted to know his.

He walked into my room as I'd told him to on the phone. "What's all this?"

"I've gotten into all these colleges but don't know what I want. My mom has been pestering me to know which Bible college I'm going to and how my applications are going. I haven't told her I'm not applying to them. Might have to apply to one to get her off my back until I'm ready to leave. There's one in Iowa. My parents didn't go to it, but they are alumni because the school they did go to in Denver merged with the Iowa one. It'll make her happy, and she won't question it. No way I'm going to live in Iowa, though."

"That's probably a good idea. It'll buy you some time." He looked each one over. "These are all over the place."

"It won't matter where I go, will it? You're going into the army."

He nodded. "Yeah, I think so. We should elope. It has a lot of benefits for spouses."

"You really want to do that?"

"Yeah, I do. As long as it's what you want. I know we're young. It won't be easy, and we'll probably be long-distance for a while."

"But we can make it work."

"Yeah, we always do. We have a strong foundation." He put his arm around me. "Let's narrow down these choices."

He spent the next hour with me going over all the schools' pros and cons. We got it down to five choices. Three were for writing, and two were for veterinary college. If I went the vet route, I'd definitely go to CSU because I had a guaranteed job with a team I already knew well, including a boss I loved and worked with for years. I took another one away. That left three writing colleges and one vet.

Ezra put the losers in the drawer I asked him to. "You have plenty of time to decide."

"But I'm a lot less overwhelmed now. Thank you."

"Our future will be great, Mila."

"As long as we have each other, I'm not afraid."

My mom called to let me know they were two states away already. Ezra and I went out to the living room and watched a movie. I fell asleep on his chest, knowing I wanted a life with him more than anything.

Chapter Twenty-Seven: Options

❤

My eighteenth birthday arrived and went. My friends threw me another surprise party, but this time it was warmer, and we went to a park. I tried to stay in the moment and not think of Val missing. It became tough to think about how much the last year had changed everything. My mom gave me another coat. She said I could use it when I went to Iowa for college. I'd made the mistake of telling her I'd gotten into the Bible college there. Her excitement over it was the most I'd seen in a long time. Going there was the last thing I wanted but seemed to be her greatest desire.

I told Ezra everything she said. He listened and often shook his head but didn't say much. We climbed above Zapata. At least once a week, we'd hike somewhere. Sometimes it was several days in a row after we got all our other responsibilities out of the way, even when winter grew cold. We played hide and seek among the trees, and sometimes we'd climb to snow to throw it at each other.

We had an amazing winter and spring and had grown closer than we'd ever been. Our days also included time on his barn roof and conversations until sunrise. We discussed big dreams we knew we'd live together. Our graduation was only a few weeks away, and I had everything for school wrapped up. I'd narrowed my choice to a writing college in Ames, Iowa, or veterinary school at CSU to work with Doc. I'd done everything with both options to keep the process going and would have to decide for sure soon.

Ezra tapped his knee up and down and kept glancing around. He'd slipped into youth group ten minutes late, which was unlike him.

As soon as we got through everything and had snack time, I approached him. "Are you alright?"

He blinked. "What?"

"What's wrong?"

"Nothing. Not really. I was hoping you'd go to the recruiter's office with me. I need your opinion on all of it."

"Yeah. When?"

"Tomorrow."

I wanted to rub his shoulders to ease his tension, but we were at church. "Are you sure you want to?"

"Yeah, I do."

"Okay. Yeah, I'll go with. Nothing else is bothering you?"

"No, it's a big step."

The recruiter's office was relatively small, with a set of computers on one side and cubicles on the other. A small waiting room was where we signed in and sat in plastic chairs. A tall man with broad shoulders and buzzed hair shook our hands.

He grinned like we were a reappearing relative he'd loved dearly and lost. "Let's have a seat, and we'll have a chat." He shook our hands and gave us his name.

Ezra introduced himself. "This is my fiancé, Mila."

I tried to recover from his words quickly, but the more I processed them, the more they made sense. We planned to get married when he joined, and he probably wanted the guy to know that.

"It's nice to meet you both. What are your ages, and have you graduated high school yet?"

Ezra pulled out my chair for me. "We're both eighteen and graduate in May. We're getting married right after that. I plan on joining once we are."

The recruiter turned to me. "What about you, Mila? Have you thought about joining? We're currently highly encouraged to recruit women and minorities. There are a lot of benefits."

My eyes snapped to his. "Women soldiers?"

"Yes."

I closed my gaping mouth, not wanting to bring up that it was against my religion. "I hadn't thought about it."

"Do you two have time today? You could take the practice ASVAB and see where you're at."

"That sounds fun! I like tests," I said.

Ezra grinned, almost laughing. "Yeah, we have time. Unless Mila doesn't."

"I cleared my schedule for this."

He led us over to the computers and gave us instructions. I flew through the tests because I found them fun. I smiled at the screen triumphantly. "I got an "A"."

Ezra did his one eyebrow lift. "You're done already?"

"Yeah."

The recruiter came over and looked at my screen.

His eyes widened. "You got a 96."

"Yeah, that's an "A" right?"

"Something like that. Why don't I show you what the army has to offer? With your score, you could have a pick of almost any area."

Ezra finished his test, and the recruiter seemed happy with his score, too, but Ezra wouldn't tell me what it was. We watched some videos and got up to leave.

The recruiter shook his hand. "I'd love to talk to both of you about the next steps. Here's my card." He handed one to each of us. "You seem pretty set, Ezra. What about you, Mila?"

"I'm not sure. It's not really in my plan."

"It can help you pay for the colleges you mentioned. You may decide you like it. If you stay in for twenty years, there are a lot of benefits to it."

"I'll think about it."

He nodded, keeping his wide smile on. "That's all I can ask."

We went out to Ezra's truck, and he stared out the windshield, not moving for a few minutes. "Dang! Mila."

"What?"

"What just happened in there?"

"I'm not sure. You clearly passed. That's good."

"I got an 84."

I sat up straighter. "That's awesome! That's a "B", which is above average."

He chuckled. "That's not what the score means."

"Oh. But it's still good, right?"

"Yeah, it is. Enough to get in and have decent options."

"You look mad. Shouldn't this make you happy? The army is what you want."

He turned on the radio and backed up his truck, driving onto the main road. "Yeah, it is. Even more so after talking to him."

"What's wrong?"

He sighed. "Nothing is wrong with Bible college."

I locked up, terrified he was jumping on the bandwagon with my mother. "What?"

"Nothing is wrong with going to Bible college. If it was what you wanted, I'd be the first to encourage you to pursue it. But it's not what you want. You scored a 96 on the ASVAB practice test, Mila. A freaking 96! And your parents think your potential is Bible college so you can be a better homemaker because you were born a girl. As I said, nothing would be wrong if you wanted it. But your dreams are so big, Mila, and sometimes it scares me that your parents will convince you that you should accept less than those grand things in your heart and soul."

I stared out the window at the passing road cracks and grooves. "It scares me too."

He took my hand. "That recruiter wants you to sign up bad. When you went to the bathroom, he asked me to try to convince you."

"I know. It seemed like he'd get bonus points for recruiting a woman."

"I think your score added to that."

"Does he get bonus points for higher scores?"

He shrugged. "I have no clue."

"Are you sure you're okay?"

"Why wouldn't I be?"

"You seem... Tense. Upset, maybe."

He flipped the radio to another station. "It's a little scary to think about everything. I'm starting to think Erin's fears of adulthood are valid."

"It is scary, but I'm ready for it. For our adventure."

He retook my hand and rubbed his thumb over the top of it. "As long as I have you, I'll be good. I could lose everything else and still be good."

"Same."

He let out a breath and relaxed. "We should go somewhere crazy. Maybe the Springs."

"I want to go to the hot springs."

"Let's do that!"

"Now?"

"Yeah, unless you have somewhere else to be," he said.

"Nowhere, but I don't have a change of clothes. Only my emergency shorts and pants in my bag."

"You can use one of my shirts."

"Okay."

He drove to the hot springs, and I relaxed against the window to take in the perfect drive up the winding mountain. We stopped at a little cafe to grab lunch. We hiked back through the mountain and into the tight area that led to the steaming water. I changed behind the rock into my shorts and Ezra's blue shirt that swam on me.

His eyes widened, and his grin faded into something intense. "Looks good on you."

We got into the water to race, but it quickly turned into him chasing me. He trapped me against a rock wall, and I turned around. Water dripped down his face, and he brought his thumb up to my lip, cupping my chin.

I shuddered as he pressed closer, and his mouth captured mine, moving slowly. He parted my lips, and we both sparked to life, moving without thought. He rested me on his hips and carried me over to a ledge. Heat moved through my body as he kissed down my neck. I leaned into him, and he tugged at my shirt. I removed it, putting us skin to skin. His hand gripped my upper thigh. Small layers stood between us and giving each other everything.

He undid my bra but stopped before removing it, gasping for air. He rested his forehead on mine. "I've never wanted anything more. Not anything more than you."

"I want this too. Ezra, so much I want this."

He kissed me slowly and pulled back, holding my face. "Let's do this right. We can elope this weekend. I'll pick you up on Saturday, and we'll go. Then we can finish this."

"What about graduation?"

"We can still attend married. I won't mind having my wife there. Then no one can stop us from doing what we want. Unless you don't want to."

I wrapped my arms around him. His heart thudded, and I listened to the rhythm for a bit. "I want it."

"It makes sense, right?"

"Yeah, it's everything."

"Everything." He kissed me again.

We took our time hiking back to his truck, and he let me go on about the birds, and I listened to him talk about skateboarding and music. I hummed as I ran inside to pack for the weekend.

My mom was flipping chicken at the stove. "Did you go swimming?"

"Yeah."

"Your dad and I want to talk to you when he gets home."

My stomach flipped. "About what?"

"I'll let him tell you. It's good news."

My clenched body loosened. "Okay."

I took a shower, and my mind drifted into the memory of Ezra's kisses. I was in love with him. More than ever before. He was in love with me, right? I frowned, not sure. Maybe he was only marrying me to help me out. People not in love could kiss like that. I thought they probably could, but wasn't sure. Panic settled in the back of my mind. What if Ezra didn't really love me? I shoved the thoughts away. It didn't matter at that point. What we had was worth it.

I got dressed, and my parents knocked on my door a short time later to ask me to the living room. Despite my mom saying it was good news, nausea threatened to consume me.

Dad took his chair. "Your mom and I have decided to move to Iowa with you."

My eyes shifted between them. "You're moving to Iowa?"

"Yes, I've always wanted to go back and get my master's. This will save you money. You won't have to pay for room and board, and I got a job for you."

I stared at him, finding words difficult. "You want me to live with you while there?"

"Why wouldn't you? We should stay close to keep an eye on you and save you some money. We'll get a two-bedroom apartment. It works out since I'm technically an alumnus of the school. I talked to an old friend. You're hired for the IT department. They need a female student to go into the girls' dorms and fix the computers."

"I don't really like fixing computers."

He threw his hand out. "It's not a forever job and will help you pay for college and give you a discount since it's working for the college. It'll be perfect while you get your degree. A great skillset to have."

"You accepted the job for me?"

"Yes, they want you to come down early to help set up the network for the year."

I chewed on my lip. "I know nothing about that."

"They'll teach you. It's a great opportunity. I'm resigning tonight at church. The deacons already know."

A dull ache had formed in the middle of my forehead. "You guys decided you would move with me to college, and I would live with you? Then you proceeded to accept a job for me that I have no interest in?"

"Yes, this will be our way of helping you with college, since we aren't paying for any of it. You'll get used to the job."

I nodded slowly. "Okay." It didn't matter because, in three days, I'd be married to Ezra.

That night at Wednesday service, my dad announced he was stepping down, so they could follow me to college and he could get his master's degree. He told them about the blessing of my new job that came about by God arranging things for me.

I sank into the pew and thanked God that wouldn't actually happen.

Chapter Twenty-Eight: Elope

♥

Ezra and I made out under the softball bleachers, and I enjoyed this new level with him. Soon we'd be able to go all the way, and not even God would be mad at us.

He gave me a long and gentle kiss. "You're the best thing that ever happened to a simple Colorado boy. I had no idea that little 'girl in the red dress would become mine ten years later."

"The day we met."

"Yeah, you looked so cute in your pigtails and white tights."

"You caught a trapped frog with me after church. That made me like you."

He laughed. "That's right. It couldn't get back up the outside basement steps. We did teamwork well back then, too. You put holes in the knees of your tights. Your mom loved that."

"But we saved the frog."

"We did. Who knew saving a frog would be the best decision of my life because it led to the best friendship I've ever had?"

"Deciding to rescue an animal is always the best decision," I said.

He rested his forehead on mine. "Saturday will be the real best decision."

"Agreed."

He held me against him, and then we went to the skate park. Kyra and Hannah showed up, but it didn't matter because Ezra was mine. Things went well for a while until Ezra did a flip wrong on the ramp. His board went out from under him, and he slammed onto the concrete. I screamed and bolted for him.

He stared off dazed but stayed conscious.

I dropped to his side. "Ezra!"

He blinked and shook his head, gasping. "I'm... fine..."

"You're not fine! You can barely breathe." I could barely breathe.

His buddies helped him up, and he reassured me he was okay. He went back to skateboarding, but I went to the restrooms to hyperventilate.

Hannah came in and paused as she went into a stall. "You shouldn't be sitting on the floor. It's filthy. Gross."

The room spun, and I thought I'd suffocate. Hannah gawked at me some more before she left. I worked through the panic and got myself up. Ezra skated a little longer and walked over to me.

Hannah grabbed her purse from the bench. "You probably should avoid hugging her, Ezra. She sits on dirty bathroom floors." She pointed to the public restroom.

"I'll take my chances!" he shouted.

We walked toward my house, and he nudged me with his elbow. "Are you okay?"

"Why are you asking me? Are you okay?"

"I'm fine. Not the first time I've gotten the wind knocked out of me. Why were you sitting on the bathroom floor?"

I rolled my eyes. "I went to the bathroom for privacy. Hannah shouldn't have said anything."

"Why did you need privacy?"

"I panicked. When you hit the ground, I saw Val's casket. Her sleeping in it. Then I saw you in one. I couldn't survive that."

He stopped walking, and his arms eased the aftershock of my anxiety. "I'm fine now." He took his jacket off and wrapped it around me to probably stop my trembling.

"I need you to stay that way."

"I promise."

Most of me knew he couldn't really promise that. No promise on earth would have kept Val with us.

I waited for the phone call from Ezra for me to run to his truck. The call that would lead to the rest of my life. I gripped the bumpy handle of my bag. When his name appeared on my phone screen, I squealed and bolted for my front door. For one night, I would rebel and go crazy.

My mom was sitting in her chair doing her cross-stitch. "Where are you headed?"

"Going to Erin's. We're going to the Springs, and I'm not sure when tomorrow I'll be back."

"Okay. Try to make it back for Sunday night church. I got you some boxes to start packing. Dad is getting a storage shed, since we won't have room for everything in an apartment."

"Did he find one?"

"Not yet. He figured we would once we got up there. We'll just stay in a hotel until we do."

"Separate rooms?"

"No, that's too expensive. We'll get two queen beds." She went back to her hobby.

"For how long?"

"Until we find a place."

"Okay. See you later." The conversation gave me extra momentum to get to Ezra's truck. When I returned, Ezra and I would be the biggest scandal ever in our church, and I didn't care a single bit. I ran the entire block and flew into his truck, panting.

He looked me over. "You alright?"

"Yeah."

He started driving. "You still want to do this?"

"Yeah, you?"

"Yeah."

"They're going to notice when we miss church tomorrow."

He tapped the steering wheel to the radio beat. "We'll be married by then, and it won't matter what any of them think."

We listened to music but didn't talk much. Ezra gave short answers to anything I said. It caused a nagging at the back of my mind. Something was off, but I ignored it because I wanted everything perfect. We stopped at landmarks and took pictures. We made it into Nevada, and my eyes came alive at the lights and bustle of Las Vegas. Elaborate buildings towered everywhere. We checked into our hotel, and I got ready while Ezra went to find our options for getting married.

I looked myself over in the mirror. My brown curling iron ringlets framed my face, and I did my makeup in a smoky look and put on berry lip gloss. I felt beautiful in my simple knee-length white dress. Ezra took much longer to return than I thought he would, and I worried enough to call him. He didn't answer.

Panic had set in deep when he finally stumbled in near midnight. He knocked over a lamp and staggered onto the bed.

"Ezra! What happened?"

"Nothing," he slurred.

I gasped at the potent stench coming from his breath. "Are you drunk? How did you get alcohol?"

"They don't card everywhere."

"Why would you get drunk when we're about to get married?"

He ran his fingers through his hair. "I needed to make this easier."

"What does that mean?"

"I can't marry you, Mila. I thought I could, but I can't do that to you. Look how beautiful, smart, and wonderful you are. You deserve so much better than me. You're brilliant. Look at what you scored on the ASVAB and all the colleges you got into. I look at you and think how could someone so gorgeous ever want someone like me? You stop my breathing all the time, and I don't deserve that."

"How can you not see you're that most amazing person I've ever met? How easy it is to love and want you? There's no way you can't see that because it's obvious! Our scores weren't that far apart!"

"I'm going to hurt you in a way I can't stand." He plopped back on the bed and snored.

I didn't know what he meant by his last sentence. If he meant not marrying me would be the pain he'd cause me, or if he wasn't marrying because he was afraid, he'd cause me that pain. Maybe both things were meant in his sentence.

I stayed up, watching him and thinking most of the night, crying and raging. He woke up the next morning, and I had Advil and breakfast waiting for him. It was what the internet said would help a hangover. We packed up without a word and drove back toward the valley. Anger and confusion played over every other emotion trying to be felt.

He pulled into a rest stop with red rocks in the background. "Let's take a walk."

I wanted to stay planted in the car because I knew this would be the end of Ezra and me. He waited until I finally stepped out of his truck, and we walked up a trail.

Then one sentence from him shattered my heart. "I can't marry you, Mila." He'd said the same thing the night before, but it stung worse with him sober.

I crossed my arms like I was warding off a chill in the eighty-degree weather. "Why not?" I knew the answer. He didn't love me, exactly as I'd feared.

"I went back to the recruiter. There's a good chance I'll get deployed. Something could happen to me, and I couldn't put you through that. Not after Val. Not after seeing your face at the skate park."

My head turned to the side a tick. "You think if we aren't married, it won't hurt me?"

His shoulders drooped. "Yes, and if we don't sleep together, it'll be easier for you to move on. I'm thinking we go our own ways. Figure out who we are. I do the army thing for a while, and you go write. Get your degree, and in four years, if we're still both in a place to, we try this again."

"I need you, Ezra! You were supposed to protect me from being forced into a life I don't want."

"You're already doing that, Mila. All on your own."

"Okay." I took off walking and made it all the way to the highway.

Ezra ran after me. "What are you doing?"

"Walking home."

"It's hundreds of miles."

"I'll catch the bus in the next town." I picked up my pace.

"Come on. Get in my truck. It's not safe to walk on the highway alone."

"What do you care anymore?"

"You're not even going the right way."

I looked all around and realized he was right. I had no clue where I was going. "Fine! I'll ride back with you, but I'm not talking to you."

"That's fair." He let out a long breath.

We drove all the way back to Alamosa in silence. He dropped me off a block away from my house, and I went home. My parents had bought my lie about going to the Springs with Erin. I got a bath and cried. The crying didn't stop until I fell asleep hours later.

Ezra and I didn't talk for weeks. His gaze shifted away from me every time he saw me. It could have been because I glared at him a lot. He'd broken my heart, and the anger from that grew until it was bursting, needing an outlet to explode on. It mixed with a desperation to get him back. I both hated and wanted him. It made no sense.

It took me a while to think up, but I devised a plan. I would join the army too, and we could get deployed together. It didn't occur to me that was not how it worked. It probably wouldn't have mattered if I'd known. Desperation often created the foolish. It also created the brave, and my plan had both those things well inside it.

I marched to Cole Park, where I knew he'd be to tell him all about it. Hannah was sitting on the bench again, but Kyra was nowhere close.

Hannah beamed like she'd won a vacation to Paris. "Hello."

I narrowed my eyes at her cheerful greeting. "Hi."

"You should go look over there." She pointed to the softball field.

There are moments when gut feelings scream at you not to do something, like a child sticking a fork in an electrical socket. But a dusty, old gut feeling returned. One I'd had about Ezra and Kyra since the first time I'd ever met the sisters. My legs moved all the way across the park. And there, under the bleachers, both of my gut feelings came together to be correct. Ezra was kissing Kyra.

My legs gave out the minute I tried to run, which broke their kiss. I leaped up and took off running over the river bridge. I ignored the stabbing side pain. At five foot three, I didn't have the longest legs, and Ezra caught up to me.

"Mila!"

I whirled around. "Leave me alone before I push you into the river!"

"Wait. It's not what it seems."

"You mean you were making out with my arch-nemesis in the same place you did me? That's not what it was?"

"We haven't even talked in weeks. You and I aren't together."

"And we never will be!" I marched away from him and stopped. "I hate you, Ezra Henderson. I hate you so much and love you so much, and I hate that I do. I've never loved anyone more, and this hurts! Go be happy with Kyra."

He cringed like each word I'd sent him had stoned him. "It wasn't anything with Kyra. Something to take the loneliness of losing you."

I picked up a rock and ignored him. He flinched because he most likely expected to be my target, but I just need to throw something at the stupid universe that had clearly cursed us. I launched it into the river. "I hate you! You coward! You give me all the reasons in the world to love you, then smash them for stupid reasons. You cut me deeper by giving them to Kyra. I hate you! Good luck with your life!"

My tears started when he screamed for me to come back and talk to him, but I ran faster than I ever had away from him. Anger once again fueled my escape.

Chapter Twenty-Nine: Hidden Danger

♥

I'd decided I would never forgive Ezra. It had to be that way because if I forgave him, I'd plead for him to be my best friend again. I'd beg him to love me, which would only create a fake infatuation. He clearly didn't want me, and his mind had been made up. It reminded me of my seventeenth birthday. The day after, when Ezra had told me, Riley had to keep making up reasons to be mad at me. I had actual reasons to be mad at him, and I wanted very much to hang onto them to strengthen my resolve.

Since I was eighteen, I no longer had to go to youth group, so I didn't. I went to church, but Ezra had stopped showing up. Kyra always watched the door, and I assumed she was looking for him. Hannah had returned to sending me glares, and it told me things probably hadn't worked out for Kyra with Ezra either. I might have felt bad for her if she hadn't tormented me since she'd met me.

We got regular visitors at church. Potato farms around the area would attract workers from other places. A group of five had started coming regularly. One, Mark, talked to me a lot after church for several weeks in a row. He had black spiky hair, a large nose, and brown eyes. He wore a white t-shirt and black pants most of the time and smelled like cigarette smoke. I refused to judge him on that. People smoked for stress, and it had nothing to do with their character. Riley's chain-smoking mom had taught me that. The rest of the church most certainly did judge him on that. I'd heard it more than once from several. His left eye had a constant twitch.

After one Wednesday night, he approached me. "Hey. How has your week been?"

"Good. I'm getting all packed to move."

"Where you headed?"

"Iowa." I'd decided to go to the writing college in Ames but hadn't told my parents yet. They still assumed I'd be living with them in the apartment.

"Nice. Friendly part of the country. I was wondering if you could do me a favor."

"Sure. I mean, what is it?"

"I'm having a housewarming party." He chuckled. "I'm not sure about the way I've arranged things. Do you think you could come over and help me decorate?"

"Yeah, I like to help. When?"

"I can pick you up on Saturday. Around five? The party is at eight."

"I can drive over, so you don't have to drive me back."

He waved his hand. "No need to spend your gas on a favor."

"Okay." I gave him my address and added a note to my calendar.

Saturday arrived quickly with all the goodbyes I was saying. Erin was crushed I'd chosen to go so far away. I had my last shift at work and went home to shower before going to Mark's for the party. My mom was packing her stuffed koala bear collection in a large wicker basket in our living room.

She grabbed something from a shelf and brought it over to me. "I got you a new Bible. For Bible college. Also, your new boss called Dad. He wanted you to study a few things before we get there." She handed me a note.

I set the Bible down and decided enough was enough. My anxiety ripped apart my insides, but I forced the words out. "I'm not going to Bible college, Mom."

She giggled. "Of course you are."

"I'm not. I got into a writing college in Ames, Iowa. It's about forty-five minutes from where you guys will be."

"That's not an option for you. We have everything set up."

"You don't have anything set up for me and expect me to live in a hotel with you and dad for who knows how long. You got me a job I don't even want! Did it occur to you I don't want to work with computers? It should have because I told you four times, and Dad still announced in church about me having the job. I'm going after what I want for once in my life!"

"You're going to Bible college. You don't have a choice!"

"I'm eighteen! I have all the choices in the world."

"Not in God's eyes. You're still under our umbrella until you get married."

"I'm running as far away from your umbrella as I can get! You are so busy with church things, I'm sure you won't notice a difference."

She sobbed into her hands. "You can't do this to me! To your father! This is the life God wants for you."

"It's the life you want for me! You! Not God. Sure as anything, not me! I want to be a writer! Did you even know that? I want to write novels and tell stories. Stories are my language. I understand them better than I do real life!"

"You can tell godly stories at Bible college and read them to all your children. That's what you're destined to do as our miracle baby!"

"I don't want to be your miracle baby! I'm just Mila. You know how much pressure it is having the name I do! I'm your heaven-sent miracle who is supposed to shake up the entire world for God! You know what that feels like to be told that over and over my entire life while remaining background noise to you. I'm supposed to move mountains for *your* religion, but you have no idea who I am!"

She wailed at that point, and it usually would have made me shrink into myself. This time, it didn't.

She touched her stomach. "God cured my ovarian cancer, so I could have you. Two months before I knew you were on the way, they were going to remove my entire reproductive system, but when they went to do the surgery, the tumor had disappeared. They told me we'd never have children again. Then I got pregnant with you right after that miracle."

I closed my eyes to gain control. Anger rose that I'd had to hear it again. "God cured your ovarian cancer, so you could live your life. That was your chance to change the world. Not mine. You've put this grand mission on my back, and it is pushing me into the ground. You and Dad may be disappointed in me for the rest of your lives. But Bible college. Marriage to a man I have to submit to is a life sentence. A life sentence in a prison that will destroy everything I love about myself."

I walked away, and she screamed I was going, proving she'd listened to nothing I'd just told her. I'd never heard my mother raise her voice, but she did that day.

I showered and changed. When I came out of my room, my mom had left, probably to get my dad to yell at me. I decided if he tried to hit me with the belt, I would get in my car and drive to Iowa alone. My savings was enough to set me up, and I had a dorm room picked out. I'd gotten a grant and a few scholarships that would pay most of my tuition for the first year. It was the perfect plan. I'd move on from Ezra and have a great life without him. Even as I thought that the heaviness hurt my heart.

Mark honked, and I got in his car. The party would be a nice distraction. The fact I thought that and hated parties spoke to how much I needed to be away from everything. We drove about fifteen miles out of town and down a dirt road, followed by a second and then a third. Many of the potato workers lived in trailers in the middle of nowhere. He pulled up to a rusted white and brown single-wide trailer with several holes around the skirting.

The windows had thick black curtains on them. He had a rottweiler on a chain, and it made me frown. It didn't have food, water, or shade close. It panted, growled, and barked.

"Do you leave him outside all the time?" I stepped close to the dog and crouched.

"No, just left him out while I went to get you. Never seen anyone approach a snarling rottweiler before."

"He can't reach me from this distance. I'm giving him space to build trust."

He shook his head. "You're something else."

I reached into my purse and pulled out a dog treat from the bag I kept them. "Can he have a treat?"

"You keep dog treats in your purse?"

"Yeah, you never know when you'll meet a dog that needs one."

He undid the chain from the stake. "Yeah, Rufus can have treats."

I tossed the dog one, and he gobbled it down. We were buddies after I gave him two more. Rufus closed his eyes with my expert ear scratches and licked my hand. Mark put Rufus in his kennel and invited me inside.

"That kennel is tiny. I can bring you a bigger one. He's really scrunched in there."

"He's fine."

I stared longer at the dog and moved closer to look at something on his legs. He had what looked like round burn marks in several places. He whimpered, and I pet him the best I could through the bars.

"I'll get you out of here," I whispered.

The trailer stank of rotted food and cigarette smoke. I frowned, thinking about all the work it would take to get ready for the party. Trash sat piled on his countertops. He had nothing on his walls and only a couch, chair, and tube TV sat in his living room. Cigarette burns covered his chair and the carpet around it, and it hit me then the dog had them too. Nausea settled in my gut.

He opened his fridge. "You want a drink?"

Natasha's words from a couple of years played in my head. "No, thank you."

"Are you sure? Maybe something to take the edge off."

"The edge off what? Where are your party decorations?"

He stepped around the couch and stood a few feet from me. "There's no party."

"Why did you get me?"

"I thought we could spend some time together."

It occurred to me then that the fight with my mother had taken my focus from where it should have been. It wasn't until that moment clarity hit me sharply. I stepped back, but he was between me and the door.

He took a step towards me. "You're very pretty. I've had my eye on you since I first stepped into that church. You can't be looking that good and expect me to behave."

"Thank you for inviting me. I'm going to leave now."

He charged me.

The July air was scorching. It hadn't cooled even though night had fallen, but I shook violently as I walked down the dirt road. Rufus walked beside me. Mark had placed my phone in a cup of water and put his dog back on the chain. He'd fallen asleep, and I had left, freeing Rufus and running until I'd made it to the third turn. The dog had stayed with me. He whined and nudged my hand every so often.

It would take a long time to make it into town, and I didn't know how long I could keep going. I'd already walked for what had to be close to an hour. Images of Mark waking up and speeding in his truck kept me going. My mind remained blank of everything else. A gas station appeared ahead, and I stopped outside of it.

I scratched the dog's ear and took him around the back of the station to keep him out of view. "Sit and stay."

He listened, and I went inside the station, opening the door and relaxing when I saw the clerk was a woman.

She had her grey hair in a bun and looked me over. "Honey, do you need me to call 911?"

I shook my head. "Can I use your phone?" I whispered.

She leaned forward. "What was that?"

I pointed to the black phone on the wall behind her.

"Normally, I refer people to the pay phone outside, but yes, you can use it."

"Thank you."

I dialed Riley's number, which I still had memorized. I was good at remembering numbers and facts. It took me calling her three times for her to answer.

"Hello?"

"Riley?"

"Yeah?"

"It's Mila."

"What's wrong?" Her tone had changed from annoyed confusion to something that might have been fear, but I didn't understand how she knew to be scared.

"You said I could call you if I needed you. If I needed a ride."

"What happened?"

"I'm at the corner gas station on that one road before you get to La Jara." I gave her the gas station name.

"I'll be right there. Give me thirty minutes. That's how long it'll take me to reach you." If she was at her house, she was more like forty-five minutes to an hour away, but she had a speeding problem.

"Okay."

The lady got me a chair to sit behind her counter and put a jacket she got from her office over my shoulders. "Are you sure you don't need an ambulance? You look like you do."

I stared at the door, making my mind blank. "I'm fine."

Riley arrived at some point. She ran in the door and covered her mouth when she saw me. Somehow, we ended up at her car.

"I need to get the dog." I walked around the back.

"What dog?"

"Rufus, we're leaving now."

Riley stared at him for a couple of seconds before she ran and got the dog in her back seat, helping me into the front.

She started her car but didn't drive away. "Mila, what happened?"

I stared straight ahead. "I'm fine."

"We need to go to the hospital. "

"No, my mom will find out."

"You need her to."

I shook my head, and several tears streaked my cheeks. "She can't. She'll make me marry him."

"Mila, what happened?"

I told her, and I remained strangely stoic while she sobbed and held me.

"We have to get you help."

I shook my head. "They'll make me marry him, Riley. They will!"

"They would never."

"They would. You know it. Kendra and Rachel."

Her eyes said she didn't know it. "That would never happen. I'll protect you. Drive you a thousand miles away from them, but we have to go to the hospital."

"No, let me have this choice."

Riley's entire body sagged. She closed her eyes. "Okay."

"We need to take Rufus to the shelter. I can't go in. Can you?"

"Yeah."

I texted Ruth about the dog and told her not to release him to the owner and the abuse I'd seen. That would open an investigation, and I knew from cases I worked on it was enough for him not to get his dog back. Riley took Rufus in. I sat in the car, not feeling like a real person. It made no sense, but it was how it felt. Like I didn't exist. I had no emotions.

She drove me to her house, helped me into the shower, and left to get me fresh clothes and a towel. I scrubbed myself with hot water and soap before changing into the soft blue pajamas Riley had gotten me. She wrapped me in a blanket and held me until I fell asleep. It reminded me of when we were little girls and had watched a scary movie we shouldn't have. We'd cling to each other and feel safer. I'd wake up, and everything would be a bad dream. That was why none of it felt real.

Chapter Thirty: Numb

♥

My mom and dad had called me several times. I'd already answered once and told my mom I was fine at Riley's and needed space. They still called, leaving messages that I needed to come home and talk to them about Bible college.

The day after Riley picked me up from the gas station, she left for a bit and returned with a white paper bag.

She handed it to me. "Take that."

"What is it?"

"Plan B."

I narrowed my eyes.

"It prevents pregnancy after the..." Her voice trailed off, and her eyes lowered to her turquoise carpet.

"An abortion?"

"No, it's time-limited. Please, Mila, take it."

"Okay." I opened the box and did as she said.

I stayed at her house for another three days, and we didn't talk much. She mainly asked me questions about my needs and wants. She also didn't go anywhere other than to get me food, drink, or clothes, and I wondered if she worked at Subway anymore. We watched all the movies we watched as kids, including *Gold Diggers*. That one made us both cry, and we watched it again twice, crying each time. My mind stayed on that and far away from all the things that hurt too much. I'd ignored things my entire life. I was an expert at burying pain. This wouldn't be any different.

On the fourth day, I told her I was ready to go home. We got in her Geo, but she drove me to a clinic.

She pulled into a spot. "Hear me out, Mila."

"No! You agreed I didn't have to tell anyone."

"You still don't. They don't have to know what happened, but it's important you get checked out."

"You can't make me go in."

She took her keys out of the ignition. "You're right. I can't, but this is important. For your health. I'll be with you the whole time."

I finally agreed, and Riley held my hand throughout the clinic visit.

She took me home. "Are you sure you're ready?"

"Yeah."

She wrapped me in a tight hug. "I love you, Mila. You call me for anything. I don't care about the time. It doesn't matter if you are all the way in Iowa. I'll hop on a plane or drive."

"Thank you for everything."

"Think about talking to someone. There are places that are anonymous. Please consider it."

I nodded and went into my house. I took my tenth hot shower and went to bed. In the morning, my mom knocked on my door. I stayed facing the wall when she came in.

She sat on the end of my bed. "I know you're mad, but we need to talk about Bible college. If you go for one year, I will never bug you about going anymore. One year, and then you can go wherever you want. All I want is for you to try it."

"Okay."

"Okay?"

"Yeah, I'll go to Iowa with you and Dad."

I didn't tell her my decision was because I was terrified to go to a college campus full of men I didn't know. The smaller religious campus felt safer, and going home to my parents every night would be safer. I no longer wanted freedom.

The church had a goodbye party for us, and I didn't go. I didn't plan on ever going back to the church because Mark might show up there. It was another reason I wanted to move as soon as possible. Riley came over and helped me pack. We loaded my car while my parents went to the goodbye party. She stayed with me whenever my parents left. She had pepper spray, a bat, and a knife. Someone rang the doorbell, and I jumped into the corner.

Riley grabbed her bat and pepper spray. "I'll go check." She handed me the knife. She returned about a minute later. "It's Ezra. He's pleading to see you."

I shook my head. "No."

She went back out. "Got him to leave. He said to give you this." She handed me a wrapped box.

"I don't want it. Can you throw it in my trash?"

"You sure?"

I nodded, and she tossed it. We went to bed, and tomorrow, I would leave for Bible college.

My dad had taken the last load to the storage shed. They were letting the new pastor use our house and furniture. My grandparents were going to take care of Akela and Frisky until we got a place that would allow them, and the Thompsons had taken my birds a few weeks ago. Originally, my mom had promised she'd care for them while I went to college, but now that they were moving too, I had no choice but to give them up. I was in no state to care for them.

I kept a few pictures of Erin, Val, and Riley. I sent everything to do with Ezra to the shed. The only thing I kept of him was the bird necklace and a picture of us on the mountain. I buried them at the bottom of a bag, put it in my trunk, and went inside to grab one last thing. Ezra's gift stuck out the top of the trash can. I tucked it under my arm and put it in the back of my trunk.

Riley hugged me. "Call me when you get there."

I hugged her back. "Thank you for everything."

"I'm sorry, Mila, for everything."

"Me too."

Erin ran up, panting and holding her knees. "I made it! I made it." She waved a card in the air. "So you never forget how I feel about you." She wept into my shoulder. "Why did you have to grow up?"

"Time stops for no one."

We all three hugged, and it brought back a thousand memories.

"You two take care of each other. Life is too short to stay mad at each other." As I pulled away, I saw them watching me leave with their arms around each other. Val's stuffed bluebird sat on my dashboard, Lifehouse played in my CD player, and Alamosa slowly disappeared behind me as I headed up the pass to Iowa.

My purity ring had weighed heavily on my finger for the last several days. It reminded me I shouldn't wear it anymore. I pulled off at a lookout and stared at the yellow flowers that met up with grey and white rock. I chucked it to a river far below. It bounced for a while until it dropped from sight.

I got back in my car and drove. When I stopped, I made sure a lot of people were around and only used the bathroom. I went in after several women did. Riley had given me the knife, bat, and pepper spray. The bat stayed in the seat next to me, and the other two were in my purse. I drove straight to Iowa, where my parents already were, because I was too anxious to stop anywhere alone. I constantly shoved away anything resembling an emotion. Anxiety was different. It shouted its presence when ignored and hogged everything, even oxygen.

I took a shower and changed when I arrived, climbing straight into bed. My parents were thrilled I was following through with their plan for my life. They didn't even notice all my dreams had died. I had none left. I only wanted safety.

Mr. Jackson was my new boss. He had the energy and strangeness of Willy Wonka and bustled around at full speed like he constantly drank from his chocolate river. I thought perhaps he had an IV drip of it up his sleeve. He was eccentric but kind. I could tell that right away. He introduced me to my coworkers—Archer and Melvin. They both wore navy blue polo shirts and khaki pants.

I was given a shirt to match them, but my dress code would have to be a skirt. A dress or a skirt were my only options on campus. They put me through training, and I set up all the computers in all the girls' dorms. I didn't mind the work because I was alone in a place men weren't allowed to go. It was repetitive, but it meant I didn't have to think. Thinking was something I no longer wanted to do. I avoided it at all costs and kept myself busy.

Riley called and texted me frequently to check on me. I could hear the continual worry in her voice, but I never acknowledged it. My parents got us an apartment and gave me the address. It was a block from campus where all the seminary students getting their masters stayed. They were all in their mid-twenties, except my dad.

They gave me the address, and I walked to it after work. When I went inside, I noticed it was quite small. I rechecked the door number and found it the right one.

My mom walked in carrying a box. "Home sweet home. This will be better than a dorm. Save you some money."

"Where am I going to stay?"

My mom pointed to the couch. "That will be yours."

"I don't have a room?"

"It's only temporary. Maybe six months. We're on a waitlist for a two-bedroom."

I marched out of the room and to the admissions office to get into the dorms, but it was too late, as all the spots had filled. It made me angry, but I buried it and accepted my fate. Nothing mattered anymore, anyway. I just needed to be safe. That's all that mattered.

Dr. Newcomb was my academic advisor. She was part of the Biblical counseling department, which was what I'd chosen to study. It frustrated my parents because they didn't believe it was a field that should exist at Bible college. That made me like my choice more. My parents and home church believed mental illness was sin and needed to be dealt with through prayer, not therapy.

Dr. Newcomb sat behind a mahogany desk in a high-back leather chair. Six bookshelves provided a backdrop for her, and I stared at her abundance of books, missing my personal collection that now sat in storage.

She had brown curly hair that reminded me of Erin, and her pink glasses were tipped to her nose. "What has made you choose Biblical counseling as your major?"

My parents hate it.

I cleared my throat and spit out a different answer. "The mind fascinates me. The way people think and why they do what they do. I also like helping people. It seemed a good way to combine those two interests. Also, it's not a teaching degree."

"Why don't you want to get a teaching degree?"

I fiddled with my fingers and met her eyes. "I don't want to home-school my future children."

She grinned like she knew exactly what I meant and handed me a folder of papers. "This has your class schedule. You just need one more. It's an elective, and you missed it when you picked your classes."

"What are my choices?"

She handed me a list. "One of these."

My eyes scrolled down and landed on one that broke a tiny bit of excitement out of the cage where my emotions lived. "Creative Writing."

"Creative writing? Hmm..."

"Is that a bad choice?"

"No, not at all. I've just never had one of my students pick it before." She studied me like she was trying to unlock my secrets. "We'll meet once a week and make sure things are going okay for you. I'm a licensed counselor, so if you ever need any emotional support to help you through the year, I'm here. We can even set up sessions if you need more than the once-a-week time. It will all stay confidential between us. As long as you aren't a risk to yourself and others, no one will ever know what is said in this room."

I nodded. "The once-a-week thing to check on my classes should be enough."

I couldn't interpret the look she sent me. It was almost like she knew I needed a lot more of what she had to offer. As though Dr. Newcomb saw my pain that I was sure I'd hidden well. What I wouldn't admit was the rebellious field I'd decided to go into was an attempt to save myself.

Chapter Thirty-One: Penguins

♥

Classes started, and I sat at the back. All freshmen were required to attend a 7:00 a.m. doctrines class. Half the class fell asleep, and I wondered who made the rules about classes. The rest of my morning was filled with music appreciation that would only include studying classical and hymnal music. Anything modern was not to be discussed or appreciated. Drums were also of the Devil in this place.

Music class was followed by the study of the Old Testament. We'd break down every sentence in the Old Testament, and next semester we would do the same with the New Testament. Chapel was the last thing before lunch and was like going to church every day. I was already going to a lot of church services because they required that we attend three services on Sunday and one on Wednesday night. After lunch, it was English, which brought me to life a little.

The one I lived for was only on Tuesdays and Thursdays at 2:00. On the other three days, I had to endure the importance of missions where they tried to recruit everyone to be a missionary.

The Creative Writing class was held in a building across the street in a tiny room. Five other students and Dr. Stanley were the only ones present when I arrived on the first day. Dr. Stanley was a stout man with greying hair and wire-framed glasses. I took the fourth and last row in the far back corner. As in all my other classes, I wanted to be as far away from everyone as possible.

We went through introductions, which I had deep-seated hate for long before I started not liking other humans. That's what I wanted. I wanted to not like anyone and keep my distance from them all. Then a burly boy burst through the door.

The boy rushed into the room carrying a notebook with cartoon penguins all over it. He plopped in my row but kept several chairs between us and sent me a grin and a wave that I pretended I didn't see. He almost took up two chairs and had a round face with piles of brown hair above it. "Sorry, I'm late. It's a problem I have."

Mr. Stanley nodded as though he understood. "Why don't you tell us about yourself? Then everyone else can give their introduction again."

I glared at the late arrival because all I wanted was the writing part, and he was making me relive speaking.

He stood, causing the empty chair in front of him to scrape forward on the tile floor. "I'm Louis King. I'm a sophomore here at FBBC. This is the second time I've taken this class. Not because I failed, but because it's the only writing class they have here. I'm a preacher's son, so I'm expected to become one. My dream is to open a comic bookstore, but here I am." He sat down.

The cliché of gentle giant could fully be applied to him, and the moment he met me, he decided he was going to be my friend. But his tactics weren't invasive or scary, not even to a girl who hated men and wanted to avoid them for the rest of her life. Each day after that, he would come into class, sending me a wave and a grin. He would talk to me when we got little breaks, and I stared at him.

One day, he caught up with me after class. "Hey, Mila, right?"

"Yeah."

He dug out his syllabus as if to show me something I didn't know. "We're supposed to pick partners to make the short story for the final project. I write 5,000, and you write 5,000. We meet in the middle."

"I'm going to do it on my own."

"You'll lose ten points." He pointed to where it said that.

"It's worth it for the alone part."

"Hmmm... I guess I'll have to lose the points too, then."

"Isn't there anyone else?"

"No, Paul dropped out, so that makes six of us and the other four have already paired off."

I sighed and silently cursed the universe for whatever reason made Paul drop out. "Fine, but we don't have to meet about it. I can write my half, and you write your half. One sends it to the other, and it can be copied and pasted as one thing."

"How will we make it cohesive?"

"We're two different writers with different voices. It'll never be cohesive."

"People collaborate all the time in writing. Are we even going to talk about the plot and characters? Make an outline." He got out his penguin notebook and opened it to a blank page.

"I don't make outlines. The story falls out as I write. Usually very quickly."

He snapped his finger and pointed. "Now I get you. You're a pantser."

I scrunched my face, and it left my nose twitchy. "A what?"

"A pantser. You write by the seat of your pants. I'm a plotter, which means I don't have the magic you do to let the plot fall out of my brain. I have to sit down and really think about it before writing."

"That sounds like a waste of time."

He laughed, and it came from somewhere joyful. "Definitely a pantser. Why don't I outline things for us? I'll give you whichever half you want. You will deviate from it in some unexpectedly grand way, but you will know the way I'm taking my story. What should our main plot be? The characters?"

I shrugged and continued my walk toward the campus cafeteria known as the multi. "This is your rodeo."

"Okay. I got it. What if we do a war between penguins and aliens?"

"Why penguins? Your obsession?" I jerked my chin to his notebook.

"Penguins are important to the brain."

"How so?"

"Statistically, there is a pause in a conversation every seven minutes. When that happens, everyone thinks of penguins."

My eyes shifted to the ground. "I don't."

"I bet now you will." He sent me the same wide grin he sent me every day in class. "You want to grab a bite? I'm not looking to fulfill your M.R.S. degree or anything, but as friends. I think we could both use one of those."

"My M.R.S. degree?"

"Come on. You've never heard that?"

I followed him over to the food line. "No."

"It's a dumb joke but somewhat true here. A lot of the girls come here to get married."

"Because we're girls, and that's all we're destined to be." I grabbed my plate and placed an apple on it.

"No, that's not what I believe. I want to open a comic bookstore. I'm all in favor of women becoming Wonder Woman and Black Widow. Whatever dream they might have. They could easily take over the world because they are superior to the male species in every way."

"What is a guy who wants to own a comic bookstore doing at Bible college?" I started to reach for a banana but stopped. The apple would be enough.

"I don't know. What's a girl who can write the way you can doing at a college that only has one writing class?"

"Not to get my M.R.S. degree."

"Good. We're on the same page about our friendship lunch date. You know what's the absolute best here? The pie." He picked up two slices and set one on my tray. "You don't have to eat it, obviously, but I highly recommend it."

We sat down, and Louis kept three chairs between us, almost like he knew I needed that. He started talking about writing, and I joined him. That was how Louis became the first person I wanted to talk to in Iowa.

I sent Louis my draft, which was the second half of our story. I figured it would work better with his outline because I could line up the story better at the beginning, before my mind did what it wanted with the plot. If I had taken the start, it would have ended up a long way from where his portion started.

About an hour later, he messaged me back, telling me I'd slayed it. He'd taught me that kill and slay were good things when they referred to an accomplishment. It seemed strange to me, but he knew a lot more about the outside world than I did, so it was probably true. I ate lunch with him every day, and he made me laugh. He started sitting only three chairs away from me in class instead of five.

It made me feel like a hurting animal—like Phoenix. I was cold, lost, and scared, and somehow Louis knew I needed a lot of patience to trust him. He made no sudden movements to spook me.

I lived for creative writing and hated pretty much every other class. It had long become clear that Bible college wasn't for me; in reality, I always knew that. I had no space but my car because my parents would be in the living room a lot, and I would have to wait for them to go to bed to have any alone time at the apartment. For this reason, I practically lived in my car but parked where there were many people.

Riley and Erin continued to call me a lot. Ezra couldn't have called me if he wanted because I had changed my number when I got a new phone. I didn't want to hear from him. It felt as if he had married me, things wouldn't have happened the way they had. That kept my anger toward him ignited into an eternal flame I refused to extinguish.

The last present he'd given me still sat unopened in my trunk, and I planned for it to stay that way until I died.

Louis and I went through the cafeteria line, and I grabbed my apple. He piled mac and cheese, mashed potatoes, three dinner rolls, green beans, and fried chicken on his plate.

He picked a pizza slice and set it on my tray, followed by pie for both of us. "You, of course, don't have to eat these, but they're delicious. In case you change your mind, you won't have to go through the line again."

I'd gotten used to him doing this every time we had lunch. "Thank you."

He finished his mac and cheese next while I nibbled on an apple. "What's your biggest dream, Mila?"

"I don't have one."

"Okay. What's your smallest dream?" He brought his thumb and pointer finger close.

"I don't have one of those either. Life is about making it to the next day until you die."

He dug into his mashed potatoes like my answer was normal. "That's one way to look at it. My brother died last year."

I dropped my apple on my plate. "I'm sorry."

"I was angry for a while. I didn't have a lot of support. My parents were busy grieving for themselves, which is understandable. He was their son. Firstborn. I also didn't have a lot of friends. The ones I did have kept me around because I'm funny. If you haven't noticed, you should have by now."

I nodded. "You are funny, but you're more than funny."

His eyes widened slightly. "Sure, Mila, sure. But I got angry for a while, and no one noticed until one day at dinner. I lost it. I'm not sure what set me off. But I exploded and threw a fork into my dad's big-screen TV. It wasn't my intention. A dramatic hand gesture got out of hand and shattered the costly screen. I walked out of the house, went to our shed, and grabbed my fishing pole because that's what I used to do with my brother.

"I caught this big bass, and I felt happy for the first time since he died. Then I felt guilty for feeling happy. But it was like he sat down next to me and said, Louis, what are you doing? I'm dead and can't fish anymore. Embrace the happiness of that fish because that is what's important to the living. Breathe in every moment you have while your heart still beats. I have a challenge, Mila, for you. Do something. Anything that makes you feel alive and not like you're just trying to survive until you die."

My eyes watered, and I bit my trembling lip. "Feeling alive hurts."

"That's the beauty of it, Mila. That we can feel. We're alive and get to experience what that feels like." He grabbed an unopen tissue package from his pocket and slid it my way. "Sorry. I seem to be superb at making girls cry."

I laughed. "Yeah, but also laugh."

"Told you. I'm the funny guy."

I picked up my pizza and took a bite.

Chapter Thirty-Two: Buried Anger

I sat in front of my counselor for the fifth week in a row. Little by little, she'd chipped away at my mask.

She was only required to talk about my academics, but she took an interest in me like Louis had. "Why do you think you forget to eat?"

She'd commented I looked thinner and wanted to ensure I knew how to access the multi or if I needed financial support for food. She said it tactfully. I'd told her I forgot to eat a lot.

I made little tears in the paper in my hand. "There's a lot I have to do. I forget."

"When you remember, what do you eat?"

"Fruit. Sometimes a salad or chicken."

"I see." She wrote something down on her notepad. "When did this forgetting to eat start in your life?"

I shrugged and read the spines of the two books on her desk. "When my friend Val died is the first time I remember it being a problem. It was probably before that. Maybe. It just happened a lot more when she died."

"What was the longest you went without eating?"

"Two weeks, I think. I stayed hydrated. People can live thirty days without eating."

"Yes, that's true for some, but under normal circumstances, calories will help you gain energy to complete your classwork and keep you a healthy weight. We have a nutritionist here on campus. Would you be willing to meet with her? She might have some suggestions for fast meals that will be easier to take with you and remember."

"Okay. Sure."

She handed me a card with the lady's name and a pamphlet. "Mila, did you ever talk to a counselor about your friend's death?"

Tears edged to my eyes, but I sucked them back in. "No, my parents and church didn't believe in it. It's a sin to be depressed."

"Over someone you love dying?"

"Yes, I mean, you can feel sad and cry, but you should be happy for them because they went to heaven."

"Were you happy for Val?"

I met her eyes. "No."

We discussed Val a little more. She thought I had unprocessed grief, and I thought I'd processed it too much. It didn't end there. Week after week, she did more than talk about academics until one day, I told her about Mark. It was by accident.

"What are you angry about, Mila?" she said.

"I'm not angry. Why would you think I'm angry?" A tear betrayed my control.

"If my friend had died suddenly at seventeen, I'd be furious."

"Anger is wrong."

She wrote something else down. "If anger is wrong, why did Jesus destroy the temple when he was angry at them for commercializing God's house? Was Jesus wrong?"

"No, he never sinned."

"If he never sinned, how could anger be a sin? What are you angry about, Mila?"

My crossed arms and pursed lips were probably my main giveaways. "Everything and nothing."

"What's your everything?"

"I'm angry my friend died at seventeen. My parents barely know I exist unless I do something wrong. They promised me an apartment with two rooms, but they picked a one-bedroom because there were none as close as my dad wanted to the campus. So, I sleep on a couch every night and never have a space that's mine except for my car. I live in my car. I'm a million miles away from everyone I care about, and the boy I love didn't love me back. He ran the first chance he got. He kissed my arch-nemesis at a spot that was important to us. The place we first danced. I'm angry he didn't marry me. That he didn't protect me."

"Protect you from what?"

I stared out the window, watching the wind throw around the autumn leaves. "From Mark. If he had married me, I wouldn't have been at Mark's house. I probably would have never even met Mark."

"Who is Mark?"

I swallowed and glanced at the clock. "I have to go."

She said something I didn't hear as I bolted from her office. I didn't go back to see her for three weeks. She sent emails asking me to come to see her. I ignored them.

Worry about not graduating crept in, and while I hated all my classes except creative writing and sometimes English, I'd never failed any class. I showed up at her office four weeks after I had run out.

She smiled. "Good to see you, Mila."

I relaxed when she didn't make a big deal about my return. "Things are good in class. Sorry I missed the last few appointments. Things have been hectic."

"There's a lot to get done in all your classes. I understand. Do you want to pick up where we left off last time? You can skip anything that makes you uncomfortable."

"What were we talking about last time?" I very much knew but wanted her to think it hadn't been a big deal for me.

"The things you're angry about."

"I've worked through all that. I'm good now. Really fine, actually."

She opened her desk drawer and handed me a pink book. "Do you journal?"

"No, I used to all the time."

"Why did you stop?"

"I don't enjoy writing what's in my head."

"How about you write a list of everything that's making you angry?" She gave me a blue and gold pen from a white mug. It matched the dozen or so others around it.

"I have to do that now?"

"No, before our next session. Then you can show me or not. Your choice. You can even read it to me, and we can only talk about the ones you want."

I left, and it took me four days to sit down and do what she said. All the things I was angry about filled five and a half pages. It extended into my childhood. Starting with being born a miracle baby when I currently felt I was a mistake.

Christmas break was approaching, and I'd decided to go back to Colorado to see Akela, Riley, and Erin. The last session with my academic counselor came two days before I was set to leave.

I handed her the book. "That's everything I'm angry about. Mark is on the bottom."

She read through and gave no reaction. "You're most angry at yourself?"

"It's my fault it happened."

"How is it your fault?"

"My parents told me all my life never to be alone with a boy or man. I didn't listen. I froze and said nothing to him. I didn't tell him to stop or no. I just shook and cried. Then when I left, I felt nothing. I didn't wail or scream. I felt nothing, only cold, even though it was summer. That's not normal. I don't think. But I didn't tell him no, so it's my fault. I dressed in a way I shouldn't have that day. My shirt was too tight, and my skirt was above my knees. I wore makeup. All of that makes it my fault."

"That's a trauma response, Mila. All of what you said was a clear response to extreme trauma. People tend to think that people scream and wail after things like that. They think it would make people hysterical. It causes problems with law enforcement because victims aren't believed. They often seem unbelievably calm. The police that aren't trained in trauma often say there's no way this woman went through that when she's this calm. You froze from the fear, and you coped by shutting down. Escaping mentally from reality. That's very common. You are definitely not alone. Tell me, Mila. Do you think he would have stopped if you had told him no?"

I closed my eyes because I didn't want to cry. "No, he wouldn't have."

"And it didn't matter if you were in a bikini. It's not about what a woman wears or does in these situations. It's almost always about power. Control. You have no shame or guilt in any of this."

We talked a little more, but her words would sit with me but would take some time to sink in. They would take time to become true to me, but it was the start of healing, something that would never fully heal. It was the start of coping skills I needed to survive the trauma I'd buried.

The biggest thing I learned by talking to Dr. Newcomb week after week was that talking about my feelings freed the bondage I'd placed myself in. By denying my trauma's existence, it grew into something that made me want to give up everything. It dragged me to a dangerous cliff that I almost plunged off. She acknowledged my feelings and called them valid and reasonable. I'd never had anyone but my friends do that. Between Louis and Dr. Newcomb, I somehow survived my first few months in Iowa.

I went to creative writing class and would leave for Colorado right after. I'd finished all my finals, and Dr. Stanley was throwing a Christmas party with cookies and hot cocoa. The room was covered in icicle lights and a Christmas tree made from books. He gave each of us a notebook and pen. Louis and I had gotten an "A" on our story. Dr. Stanley said we should consider publishing it.

Louis followed me out of class, putting on his blue stocking cap to ward off the chill from the newly falling snow. He handed me a wrapped gift box. "For you."

I stared at the lobsters wearing Santa hats paper. "There's no way I can take that. I didn't get you anything."

"It's a gift. Not an exchange. If I wanted an exchange, I would have brought it up at our last friend lunch date." He pushed it to me.

"Okay. Thank you."

"Open it."

"Now?"

He nodded very slowly. "Yes, I need to see your face when you see it. It's the value I get from gift giving."

"Okay." I unwrapped it and tried to rile myself into excitement to pretend I loved it, even if it was awful. It turned out unneeded as I burst into laughter. "A stuffed bearded penguin with a top hat?"

"He's Abraham Lincoln in penguin form."

I laughed harder. "Why?"

"Because it's the best thing I've ever given anyone."

I hugged him. "Thank you. Thank you for the gift, pie, and conversation."

"No, the fact you're still talking to me months after meeting me makes me grateful. I'm an odd duck, if you haven't noticed. It scares people away."

"That's the best thing about you, Louis. Don't let anyone ever change you." I put the penguin back in the box to protect him from the elements.

"Remember to find things that make you live. That makes you forget to only survive."

I nodded and walked to my apartment. My plan was to go to Alamosa and see Riley and Erin for a week. Then I'd head to my grandparents' house in Denver on the way back to spend Christmas with my family. My old church would be avoided at all costs, as well as anywhere I could possibly run into Ezra. He'd probably joined the army and was long gone. There was no way I'd run into him while I was there.

Chapter Thirty-Three: Tiny Plant

♥

Riley and Erin surprised me with a little Christmas party at Riley's house with a few of our old friends. I'd gotten them all presents in advance, which was a relief after they surprised me with a bunch.

Erin hugged me for the fiftieth time. "This has been the worst four months of my life, Mila!"

I squeezed her back and held on. "I missed you too."

Erin had called me nearly every night, and on the nights she didn't, she texted or emailed me. "It's like life was mediocre! Do you know how terrible a mediocre life is?"

"I can imagine it's pretty close to how mine is without you."

Everyone else went home. Riley, Erin, and I hung out in Riley's room, and it was like when we were kids before they had stopped talking to each other over reasons none of us remembered. Erin went to take a shower.

Riley plopped next to me on the bed. "How are you really?"

"Erin doesn't know?"

"That's yours to tell. Not a soul has heard a thing from me." She put her arm around me. "I worry about you. You're the strongest person I know, Mila."

I laughed and studied her face. "You can't mean that. You've always been the strongest person. That's why I've admired you forever."

"No, I'm really not. I couldn't have survived half the stuff you have. But that also worries me more. I mean, with Erin, we always know how she is feeling. She dramatically tells us, and we know. You don't, Mila. I have to wonder what you're feeling and that worries me, because how can anyone be okay after what happened?"

I opened my mouth to say I was fine and shut it. "I'm not okay, but I have hope someday I will be."

"Have you talked to anyone?"

"Yes, not intentionally, but my academic counselor is also a licensed mental health professional. She starts these conversations that I think are only that, then it turns into analyzing my trauma and feelings."

Riley smirked. "I love that! Disguised therapy is perfect for the queen of fine. Can you promise me something?"

"Another promise. You ask a lot of me."

"I have to because otherwise, you won't take care of yourself, but you never break a promise. It's my way to make sure my best friend is alright."

My head whipped to meet her gaze. "You see me as your best friend again?"

"You've always been my best friend. I got stupid for a while and lost sight of what was important. Seeing you at the gas station. Seeing you that way...." She released a shaky breath. "It woke me up."

"Thank you for taking care of Erin. I know you have. Watching over us is something you've always done, and that was unfair because who watched over you?"

Her eyebrows knitted. "You did, Mila. You always did. That night my dad shot Lady because she was trying to kill the cows. You talked your mom into driving you to my house, and you held me all night. That time I broke my arm at school. You showed up in my hospital room with a basket of everything you thought I needed. Every time I've needed you, you were there. I was always the one who failed you."

"No, you didn't."

She pressed her lips and shook her head. "Mila, it's true. You've always loved everyone with your whole heart. What I said at the pool hall was wrong. I chose a stupid man over you, and it was the dumbest thing I've ever done. I thought he was everything, but it was always you and Erin. You forgive me so easily because your heart is that big. But I have a question. How could you forgive me for everything, but you can't forgive Ezra?"

My head jerked to the side. "I told you what he did."

"Yeah, he was an eighteen-year-old guy, Mila. It's pretty normal for marriage to scare him and for him to kiss a girl when he thought he lost you forever. I'm not saying you don't have a right to be hurt. He broke your heart, and I get it if you never want a relationship with him. But I wonder why Mila, who forgives almost everyone instantly, hasn't forgiven the guy who is fantastic at taking care of her."

I thought for several seconds. "Because if I forgive him, I'll want him back. That's not something that can ever happen."

"Why not?"

"There's no way he'd really want me now if he knew."

Riley pulled me closer. "How well do you know Ezra?"

I rested my head on her shoulder. "It's too big, Riley. You know it is."

"He came and saw me at Subway."

"When?"

"About a month ago, he wanted to know if I knew how you were."

"What did you say?"

Erin burst into the room. "You guys are bonding without me!" She jumped on the other side of me. "What are you talking about?"

"Ezra," Riley said.

"Oh, he's a sad puppy without you."

I held my hand up. "Wait. How do you both know this? Isn't he long gone in the army?"

Erin sat straight up and clapped her hands. "No! He didn't go, but I don't know why."

"Seriously? He told me he couldn't marry me because he was going to get deployed, and he didn't even go in." Part of me wanted to march down to his house to confront him about it. "You know what? It doesn't matter."

Erin and Riley sent each other a look.

I glanced back and forth at their faces. "What?"

"Nothing!" they said.

I narrowed my eyes but let it go when they both threw their arms around me in one of our lung-squishing group hugs.

I stopped in to see my birds at the Thompson's. Mrs. Thompson had told me to stop by around 5:00, and I pulled up five minutes early.

She let me into her house, which smelled of fresh bread and cinnamon. "Mila! It's good to see you back here. I wish the girls were here. I'm sure they'd love to see you."

"Yes, that would have been great. How are they doing?"

She grabbed a pitcher from her fridge. "Iced tea, honey?"

"Yes, I'd love some."

She handed me the glass. "Ruby just graduated early and has started a courtship with Alec Swanson. Hannah and Jennifer should be back from college next week for Christmas. We're very proud. They're getting their teaching degrees. Kyra got married in November."

I nearly choked on my tea, and my heart slammed against my chest. *Please! No! Please, No!* My brain had gone into overdrive when I realized that maybe that was why Ezra hadn't joined the military. He'd married Kyra, and she'd squashed his dreams.

"Are you okay, Mila?" She leaned in to get a closer look at me.

I blinked out of the horrible images flashing through my unkind brain. "Fine. Who's the lucky guy?"

She pointed over at the wall. "That's their wedding picture. His name is Jerry Anderson. Do you know him?"

"No."

After tea, she took me to see my babies. I thanked her for caring for them and drove back to Riley's. The entire car ride, it nagged at me why Ezra hadn't gone into the army after he'd seemed so sure.

I was staring at the glowing stars on Riley's ceiling when she walked in from work.

She flipped on her light. "Why are you wide awake and staring at my ceiling?"

"I like constellations."

"We didn't even make them right when we were nine. What's up?"

I pointed to the plastic stars. "Those."

She rolled her eyes. "Mila, what's bothering you?"

I told her about tea with Mrs. Thompson. "When she told me Kyra was married, I immediately thought it was to Ezra. I panicked. Why did I panic?"

"Because you're in love with him, Mila."

"There's no doubt I will love him for the rest of my life. But I'm not in love with him. Not anymore."

"What if I told you he married someone else?"

I shot forward. "What?" My eyes welled with a deep sadness. "Who is it?"

She laughed. "No one, but you made that very clear you aren't in love with him." She rolled her eyes for the second time and changed out of her work clothes. "I was hoping you could do me a favor tomorrow?"

"Okay. What is it?"

"I need you to go to the garden department at Big R and bring me home a pretty plant."

"What kind of plant?"

She pointed to her window. "One that will sit on the sill."

My eyes shifted at her odd request. "We could go together."

"No, I have to work, and they will be closed by the time I get off. I really need a tiny plant to sit in my window by tomorrow."

"Okay. I can do that. Do you have a color preference?"

"Nope. I trust you."

Big R was a farming store with gardening items in the back left corner of the store. I walked past the feed bags, which had a hay-like scent. Grills lined up along the outside wall, and gardening tools hung above them. The plant section had a lot of choices, but it was tough finding one I thought wouldn't fall off her windowsill.

After my fifth time around the entire area, I realized there didn't seem to be any plants small enough. A greenhouse on the other side of town might have had them.

"Do you need some help?"

I froze at the voice and then stupidly turned around as though my eyes needed to confirm Ezra. His widened, and he let out a little gasp. He had on a black apron and name tag. His hair had its chaotic controlled look.

"Mila?" He didn't seem to blink.

I ran, most likely looking like a shoplifter to the cameras. Riley had set me up.

"Mila, wait!"

My tears started because I missed him saying my name, but my legs kept going until I reached my car.

"Mila, please. Wait!" Ezra jogged up to me as I got my car door opened.

I took a deep breath and shoved the tears away before turning around. "Hey."

"Hey."

We stared at each other, and I wanted to ask him so many questions. His familiar hazel eyes pulled me in.

"You're back," he said.

"Not for long. I'm going up to Denver in three days."

"We could go grab a bite. Catch up."

My chest clenched at everything I had to say, and I got into my car. "It was good seeing you, Ezra."

His face fell. "You too, Mila."

I started to shut my door but grabbed a paper from the compartment between the two seats. After writing on it, I handed it to him. "My new phone number."

He looked at it and smiled. "Merry Christmas, Mila."

"Merry Christmas, Ezra."

I drove away, and he went back into the store.

Riley put her keys in the bowl by her bedroom door. "Hey! You want to do a movie marathon?" She lifted a sack. "I brought your favorites."

I pointed to her windowsill, where a small cactus sat in a red pot. "Your tiny plant. Got it from the greenhouse."

"You didn't go to Big R? I really wanted it from Big R."

"Well, I did go to Big R, and a certain guy works there. Did you know?"

Her eyes shifted about. "I had no idea Ezra worked in the gardening department at Big R."

"I didn't say who the guy was."

She jumped on the bed and wiggled a bag. "I brought your favorite sandwich. You can have it for details on how bumping into Ezra went."

I told her what had happened. "Though I'm not sure why I gave him my phone number."

"It's a start, but I wish you were on an amazing date with him."

"Our lives aren't a magical Hallmark movie."

"They could be. You and that boy could have been the perfect romance novel."

I opened my sandwich, flattening the layers of paper. "Real life is messier than something wrapped up with a little bow. Ezra and I aren't going to run to each other and be magically reunited in a dramatic kissing scene. Too much has changed."

"The day you wake up and realize you deserve happiness, let me know. I'm waiting for it."

I didn't entirely know why I'd given Ezra my phone number. Months ago, I'd promised myself I'd never to speak to him again, but as I sat on Riley's bed, I realized maybe the number was possibility. It left the option for Ezra and me to make it back to something, even if it was just friends.

Chapter

Thirty-Four: Drunk

♥

Christmas happened in Denver, and I went to a family reunion while I was there. It happened every New Year's Eve on my mom's side. College started about a week later, and I returned to my routine. I'd signed up for creative writing class with Louis even though we were told it wouldn't count the second time or third for him. Dr. Stanley basically let us come to class for free.

I'd started to welcome sessions with Dr. Newcomb and went to her office twice a week. She thought I'd made a lot of breakthroughs, and I felt on a healing path. Some things would never fully heal. They would stay scars that could reopen into wounds at any point, but I now had a lot of tools to cope and find my way back from setbacks. Winter turned into Spring, and I found myself content.

Ezra hadn't called or texted me, and I figured maybe he'd realized the same as me, that too much had changed. Since seeing him, the present in my trunk had bothered me, but I kept ignoring it. Louis helped me carry a few boxes of craft items to my car. I helped at Wednesday night kid's Bible club to fulfill my ministry requirement, and I was cutting out construction paper flower pieces for the kids to glue together.

"That's a shiny present. It's for me, right?" Louis winked.

"No, not that I don't love you, but it's actually for me."

"Why is it sitting in your trunk, collecting car dust?"

"It's complicated."

He shrugged. "Not really. You just remove the paper. Do you want me to demonstrate?"

"I'll get to it eventually."

"Aren't you even the slightest bit curious? I don't know how you can handle the suspense."

"My anxiety is very good at making me patient at not finding certain things out."

"An unopened present is such a waste." He stared at it like he wanted to grab it and run.

I drove back to my apartment. My parents still hadn't upgraded to a two-bedroom. Anytime I asked, they'd make excuses about why it hadn't happened yet. I'd given up asking. As I went to grab the craft boxes, the present caught my eye again, and I placed it in one of the boxes to carry up.

I started on the craft project but kept glancing at the present. It did seem like a waste. The last thing Ezra had given me had gone unappreciated and putting it that way filled me with overwhelming sadness because he deserved better than that. Our last couple of months together had been rough, but everything before that - all the times he was there for me - should have counted for more.

I carefully removed the shiny red paper from a shoe box, and inside was a VHS tape. It had my name written on the label. We still had a DVD/VHS combo player, and I popped it in. Ezra, with his guitar, appeared on the screen.

"Hey, Beautiful." He closed his eyes and took a deep breath. "I'm nervous. That's silly because this is prerecorded. I can delete and tape over it."

I laughed and tried to calm my bouncy emotions.

He strummed his guitar for a bit before singing "Crazy for That Girl" with his eyes closed tight. When he got to the end, he looked at the camera. "You know I had you play that song all the time, hoping you would realize that was my song for you. Even when it wasn't entirely true, because nothing big had happened to us. Then Val died, and that song entirely became ours. You held me the day the sky fell. And what was I thinking when the world didn't end? I was thinking I wanted to spend the rest of my life with Mila Sadler because life is way too short not to live with the way she makes every bit of me love breathing.

"Now I've gone and lost you. Screwed up more and kissed Kyra. And I don't think you'll ever forgive me. I'd never blame you for that. But I'm sitting here wishing I knew what I know now back when we were sixteen. Back at the moment, I realized I was in love with you. I'm sure it was way before that. Maybe even at the point, I helped you save that frog from the basement. And you smiled at me. You could take me out with your smile, and it made me want to do things to make you smile at me like that.

"But it was when I'd done a crazy thing and signed up to watch preschoolers with you. You talked to that crying little boy, and I watched you. What you said, and the way you moved. It was all beautiful, and I realized right then that Mila Sadler was the girl I'd love for the rest of my life. No matter how far life would take us from each other, I would love you until my heart stopped. That's how deeply in love I am with you. If I could go back, I would have told you. That night I would have said, Mila, I love you. Not as your best friend, though I want to stay that, but as someone who wants to wake you up in the morning with kisses, carry you to bed when you're tired, and climb a hundred mountains with you.

"I love you like someone who wants to spend the rest of my life making sure Mila knows how worthy, beautiful, and loved she is." His eyes widened, and tears rolled down his cheeks. "I love you, Mila. Find Happiness and embrace it." The Screen turned to static.

The video destroyed me in the best possible way, and I curled into a tiny ball on the living room floor. Tears and sobs consumed me. When I calmed enough to form words, I pulled out my phone and dialed Ezra's number.

The robotic voice picked up. "I'm sorry. This number has been disconnected. If you feel you have reached this recording in error, please hang up and try again later." The line went dead.

I ran to my car and popped Mila's mix into the player for the first time in months. As I listened to it, I soaked in every word in all the songs as love letters Ezra had written me at a time he didn't know how to find his voice.

The semester came to a close, and I had decided on something. I called my parents to the tiny living room that had doubled as my room. "I'm not going back to FBBC next year."

My dad narrowed his eyes and shook his head. "Not this again, Mila!"

My mother rubbed her forehead. "You have to go back! If you take a break from college, you'll never go back. People do this all the time, and they never go back."

I nodded and didn't feel the twinge of anxiety I used to when talking to them. "That's my intention. To never go back. Bible college isn't for me. It never was, and I'm pretty confident you both knew that. You made me a promise, Mom. You said if I went for one year, I could do whatever I wanted after that. You thought I'd be sold going here. Instead, it showed me I knew myself all along."

"You don't really have a choice. We're not going to let you stay here if you aren't going to Bible college," my dad said.

I pulled out a key. "That's fine. I got my own place."

My dad got angry, and my mom cried. I got up and left them to it. I wasn't sure what I would do, but I'd gotten a small apartment across town to think about it and got a job at Petco as the small animal expert. It included the birds, and I was in heaven. I wrote short stories but never tried a novel. Maybe someday I'd write one and fulfill that bucket list item.

I woke up to my phone ringing, and dread built that it was two in the morning. Late-night phone calls always meant terrible things. It couldn't have been a church member giving my dad bad news, but it still made me want to vomit into the trash can next to my bed.

I didn't know the number but answered because no one would not do that with a late-night phone call. "Hello."

"Mila?"

"Yes?"

"It's Ezra."

I shot forward in bed and turned on my lamp, like that would help me see him through the phone. "Ezra?"

"Yeah, I want you to know I'm sorry. So sorry for not being a good friend to you and Val." Each word came out slurred.

"Are you drunk?"

"Yeah, it's what I do now when I think about you. My dad kicked me out because it happened too much. I mean, I think about you every day."

"You get drunk every day?" I got out of bed and put my robe on.

"No, only the days it becomes too much. It's more and more lately."

"Ezra."

"I didn't call you. I didn't call you when you gave me your number because I thought Mila looks great. Why ruin that? But I'm calling you now because I don't know what else to do."

"Where are you?" I rubbed my eyes to wake myself up more.

"Denver. You know that hotel we went to the conference at? I'm sitting there, thinking about how you held my hand for the first time because the movie scared you. The one where the Christians were killed by the antichrist in the only horror movie our parents ever wanted us to watch. Gore was okay if it scared someone into following Jesus."

"Why are you in Denver?"

"My dad kicked me out for drinking. Be not drunk with wine in excess. You know that verse, Mila?"

"Yeah, I do" Worry for him grew. I'd only heard him that distraught a few times before. "What are you going to do now?"

"I'm sorry, Mila! For everything."

"Ezra, I forgave you a long time ago, and I'm sorry, too. You need to know I have never hated you. Not for a second. Not even when you kissed Kyra. I'm sorry I said that to you. I love you, Ezra. I always have. From the moment you helped me save that frog."

"Same, Mila, same. I've been searching for you. Always searching. I slept with other women, and I'm not proud of that. You'll probably never forgive me for that, but you need to know it. I'm ashamed. I kept looking for something to fill this emptiness. To give me connection and for someone to see me. It was always empty because I was looking for what I had with you. I couldn't find it. How is it possible, Mila, that all we've done is kiss, and looking into your eyes feels more intimate than all these other things I've done with the other women? How is the way you feel against me the most connected I've ever felt in my life? I've gone and blown it, and I'm sorry because, in all my searching, it was always you. I was looking for you." He hung up.

I sat on the end of my bed and realized I was at a line in my life. I'd had a few before. The day I met Ezra, the first time we climbed on a roof and stared at the mountain, the day we climbed the mountain, our first kiss, Val's death, the night he was supposed to marry me, the day he kissed Kyra, the night Riley had picked me up from a gas station, Ezra chasing me through the Big R parking lot, and now this moment. They were all lines where my life deviated into something it had never been.

This time, I had a choice of the way I wanted my life to go. I could go back to bed and continue my life the way it was. Or I could run to a hotel where I first held a boy's hand.

I got dressed, grabbed my keys, and drove toward Colorado.

Chapter Thirty-Five: Back to Us

♥

I drove through the night and into the afternoon. When I got close, I got a hotel and freshened up, doing my makeup and curling my hair. I'd ditched my bangs about three months ago and wondered what Ezra would think. Lastly, I changed into a blue dress because the color always made my matching eyes pop.

His hoarse voice answered on the third ring. "Mila?" Even in his exhaustion, the way he said my name made my stomach flutter.

"Ezra, I'm in Denver. Are you still in the hotel parking lot?"

"Security made me move. I'm at Flat Irons."

"I'll be right there." I drove to the mall, remembering the way because it was the mall I went to every time I visited my grandparents. When I got there, I asked him for his location, and he told me the east side and gave me a few store names. "Okay. Honk your horn so I can find you."

A loud and long honk poured from the back parking lot, and I zoomed my car until I saw the rusty truck I'd ridden in many times. He jumped out, and I ran for him. We collided and held each other for a long time.

He pulled back and held my face. "Look at you. Dang, Mila!" He had a few days' worth of accumulated stubble over his square jaw, and his hair flopped in about eight different directions. It flashed memories of the nights he would stay over, and we'd wake up on the couch together. The familiarity alone was undoing me.

"Is that a good dang?"

"Definitely. This dream I've wished for a million times is standing in front of me."

My breath caught at his words. "What are you doing out here?"

He released me and leaned against his truck. His sadness became transparent as he stared off toward the mountains. "I'm not sure. Going to Iowa."

"You were coming to see me?"

"Yeah, but I got scared you wouldn't want to see me, so I went to the hotel to remember you. Started drinking and called you."

I threw my thumb behind me and looked back. "I got a hotel if you want to get cleaned up. We can talk."

He laughed while running his fingers through his hair. "Cleanup would be good. Sorry, you have to smell me."

"I don't mind." He still smelled like him. Alcohol was mixed in, but I could still make out the scent that comforted me through many rough days.

He followed me back to the hotel and showered first thing. I sat on the bed, flipping through channels. Nothing appealed to me, so I shut it off, realizing nerves ruled my actions.

He exited the bathroom in black jeans that hung on his hips. His hair dripped with water, and he ran his towel through it. He'd shaved and looked fully like the Ezra of my memory again. My heart tumbled something into my stomach that edged tears from my eyes.

He set the towel down and studied me. "Are you okay?"

"Yes, and no."

"Oh. This is a lot. I know. You didn't have to come all this way."

"I wanted to."

The left side of his mouth grinned. "Yeah?"

"Yeah."

He climbed on the bed beside me but kept several feet between us. "I should go get my own room."

"You could or you couldn't. It's up to you."

"You're okay with me staying in your room?"

I shrugged. "I've never felt safer than with you."

"You need to feel safe?"

"Yeah, it's a nice thing. Plus, we need to talk. If that's anything like old times, it'll take a while."

He lifted his sleeve to show me a tattoo of a mountain bluebird.

I took in every line, curve, and shade of the well-done tattoo. "Val?"

"And you. Val was definitely a thought with it, but when I see it, I think of you."

"That must be a lot of thinking about me."

His finger brushed back his hair from his eyes. "You have no idea."

"What are you going to do now?"

"I'm not sure. My plan was to drive to you and go from there."

"No army?"

He sighed and leaned back on a couple of pillows he'd stacked together. "After I lost you... After I screwed up. I spiraled."

"I'm sorry, Ezra."

He held up his hand. "It was all my fault, Mila. I did it to myself. To you." He shook his head when I opened my mouth. "It's true. You're probably going to argue, but it's true. I withdrew from everything. My dad threatened to kick me out then, but I got the job at the Big R. gardening department because it seemed relaxing, and it kept me sane until I saw something that reminded me of you. That was a problem because everything did. I went to Zapata a lot and thought about the cabin we were supposed to have and why I didn't marry you in Vegas. You were right there. Beautiful.

"Beautiful isn't a strong enough word for what you were that night. What you still are. But that was the problem, wasn't it? It scared me how someone like you could want to marry me. The only thing that made sense was you were marrying me because I was the safe option. The person who would protect you from your parents' dreams for you. Someday, you'd wake up and realize you could have done that all on your own."

A potent sharpness struck my chest at his terribly wonderful words. "You have no idea how I see you. That's the problem for us both. I didn't see the way you saw me, either. When you wouldn't marry me, I assumed you didn't love me. Not that you didn't love me at all, but that you weren't in love with me."

His face paled a little, and he gasped subtly. "How could you not see that every time our eyes met, I fell all over again? I used to snap pictures of you with the cameras I kept in my pocket sometimes."

"I know. Even of me eating."

"I was capturing as many times as I could of when I realized how much I love you. You always had this brightness about you. Erin always told me it was your aura. Bright, white, and enormous, she always said, like she could see it too. It came alive like it danced around you when you saw something beautiful; I think everything was that to you. It fascinated me."

"My aura fascinated you?"

"You did. The energy you shared when you embraced a moment like no one else I have ever met, and I fell in love with that and the girl who made it happen."

I laced my fingers with his. "I fell in love with kindness. The gentle way your larger hands held mine through difficulty. Whether that be a narrow mountain trail or burying our best friend. I loved how you always said my name like a lyric and sang to me with your guitar. Your profile as it stared at the stars, and your lips parted slightly as you took in the sky like it was a miracle each time. How you flew on your skateboard like you had this cohesion with physics that few ever found. You knew how to fly, but the Earth kept pulling you back to try it again.

"I love the way your scent pulls me to you, and I want to wrap myself in it because it feels like my greatest dream. You were always my greatest dream, Ezra. I wanted to marry you, not to fight my parents, but because you are everything good that matters. You were the everything I wanted for the rest of my life." I wiped his tear with my thumb. "You're so amazing. It's always been easy to believe you couldn't love me back."

He laughed with his eyes still watery. "We're quite the pair, aren't we?"

"The best pair." I got under the covers, scooting closer to him.

He held me. I felt whole, flooded with the peaceful way his arms always made me feel, and we slept.

I woke up to the smell of coffee, blueberry muffins, and butter. He'd gotten breakfast from the hotel and brought it up. We sat on the bed with our legs tucked under us like we used to on the Sonic tables. We ate and talked.

I finished a bite of muffin and wiped my mouth. "I have two months left on my apartment lease. Would it be weird if you came and stayed with me, and we took things from there? If you don't want to, I get it."

"You want me to come to stay with you for two months? I wouldn't be intruding? I could get my own place."

"Why?"

He laughed. "Because your apartment belongs to you."

"It could belong to you, too. I have a spare room. You could use it, or we could do this every night."

His smile went lopsided. "I wouldn't mind it."

"Then, if you have nothing better to do, stay with me. It'll give you time to figure things out, and me, too."

"We're doing this?"

"I think so."

We finished breakfast and turned on a movie. I called down to the lobby and paid for another night. We'd leave in the morning but wanted a day in bed, doing nothing but existing. It was a language we both spoke well.

He got his guitar from his truck and sang me "From Where You Are" by Lifehouse. He kept his eyes locked with mine as it poured from his soul, and it added to the perfect morning.

It took me most of the morning to work up the courage to tell him what I had to next. It was something I held close and didn't have to tell him, but I knew if I was to free my mind entirely from doubt, it was something I wanted to tell him.

He shut the TV off and studied my face. "Are you having doubts about me going with you?"

"No, but you may when I tell you something."

He sat up in the way he always gave me his full attention, as though letting me know nothing could tear him away from my thoughts. "I doubt it but try me."

"It's difficult."

"You don't have to tell me anything, Mila. Especially if it hurts you."

"I'm scared to tell you."

"Then let me show you, you don't have to be."

I closed my eyes and told him all about Mark and the after. My eyes didn't open until the entire story was out, and when they did, he was crying too. "If it's too much, I understand." I grabbed a tissue on the nightstand and blew my nose.

"Is it okay if I hold you?"

I nodded and let his arms soothe the pain and fear. He said nothing for a long time, and doubt played friends with my anxiety. He brushed my hair from my eyes. "This is all your speed, Mila. You tell me what you need. What is okay for me to do and say, and what's not? This is all your speed."

My lip quivered, and I took a few seconds to recover it. "You don't see me as tainted now?"

"What I see is the woman I'm desperately in love with, and I want her to know nothing will ever change that."

I relaxed against his chest, absorbing his heartbeat into memory. I loved him, and I would for the rest of my life. He meant home, and it was time to fight for us.

Epilogue: Every Mountain

E zra returned with me to Iowa, and we spent two months there. It was simple and wonderful. He didn't stay in my guest bed or on the couch. At the same time, we kept our relationship to talking and cuddling. He took some temp jobs, and I gave my notice at Petco. When my lease came up, I had little to move because the furnishings came with the apartment.

Ezra used his savings and bought an RV to check mountains off our list. We put up a bulletin board and had two maps. One had every mountain we could reach with our RV. Each mountain had been highlighted in a different color and corresponded to a page in a notebook where we put in notes about each one that we'd learned from research. It would guide us through them with places to stay or park rules.

We took our time and got up each morning with no agenda but reaching the next mountain, but along the way, if something stole our attention, we leaned into it and embraced the life that breathed in every moment. He chased me in a hundred rivers and lakes, and I always let him catch me.

The stars we grew up loving shone from a thousand different angles as we made our way across the United States and sometimes into Canada. We danced in the rain and kissed in forty states.

We circled back around to Colorado eventually and up to Zapata. Ghosts danced around us in the waterfall, the wildflowers, and the snowy peaks. Out of all the mountains we'd seen, Mount Blanca owned everything we were. We were remnants in its soil that would remain until the Earth crumbled to dust.

He led me through another mountain—our second favorite one. Steam rose from the water, and I slipped down to my underwear. He did the same.

He dived in. "Race you!"

"Cheater!" I rushed after him and caught up, shooting past.

He grabbed my foot and pulled me to him. His lips magnetized to mine, and we kissed, leaving me dizzy. He rested me on the ledge he had a few years back, but this time he didn't stop. All doubts were removed from us as we finally gave into everything we were meant to be.

He rested his forehead against mine. "I love you, wife."

"I love you, husband."

We stayed in the hot springs, enjoying our wedding night.

The boy who climbed mountains with me had grown into a man, and he was mine. Conflict had remained a rare thing for Ezra and me. We drifted through life together with a peace I found with no one else. I'd always said that when Ezra and I found each other in stillness, it remained. It was the outside world that brought storms to tear us apart. It wasn't that Ezra and I couldn't have lived a different life without each other. It was that we didn't want to, so we didn't.